A RELUCTANT ENTERPRISE

Praise for Gun Brooke's Fiction

Fierce Overture

"Gun Brooke creates memorable characters, and Noelle and Helena are no exception. Each woman is "more than meets the eye" as each exhibits depth, fears, and longings. And the sexual tension between them is real, hot, and raw."—*Just About Write*

Coffee Sonata

"In *Coffee Sonata*, the lives of these four women become intertwined. In forming friendships and love, closets and disabilities are discussed, along with differences in age and backgrounds. Love and friendship are areas filled with complexity and nuances. Brooke takes her time to savor the complexities while her main characters savor their excellent cups of coffee. If you enjoy a good love story, a great setting, and wonderful characters, look for Coffee Sonata at your favorite gay and lesbian bookstore."—*Family & Friends Magazine*

Sheridan's Fate

"Sheridan's fire and Lark's warm embers are enough to make this book sizzle. Brooke, however, has gone beyond the wonderful emotional explorations of these characters to tell the story of those who, for various reasons, become differently-abled. Whether it is a bullet, an illness, or a problem at birth, many women and men find themselves in Sheridan's situation. Her courage and Lark's gentleness and determination send this romance into a 'must read.'"—*Just About Write*

Course of Action

"Brooke's words capture the intensity of their growing relationship. Her prose throughout the book is breathtaking and heart-stopping. Where have you been hiding, Gun Brooke? I, for one, would like to see more romances from this author."—*Independent Gay Writer*

September Canvas

"In this character-driven story, trust is earned and secrets are uncovered. Deanna and Faythe are fully fleshed out and prove to the reader each has much depth, talent, wit and problem-solving abilities. *September Canvas* is a good read with a thoroughly satisfying conclusion."—*Just About Write*

The Supreme Constellations Series

"*Protector of the Realm* has it all; sabotage, corruption, erotic love and exhilarating space fights. Gun Brooke's second novel is forceful with a winning combination of solid characters and a brilliant plot. The book exemplifies her growth as inventive storyteller and is sure to garner multiple awards in the coming year."—*Just About Write*

"Brooke is an amazing author, and has written in other genres. Never have I read a book where I started at the top of the page and don't know what will happen two paragraphs later. She keeps the excitement going, and the pages turning."—*MegaScene*

Visit us at www.boldstrokesbooks.com

By the Author

A RELUCTANT ENTERPRISE

by

Gun Brooke

2016

A RELUCTANT ENTERPRISE

ISBN 13: 978-1-62639-500-8

This Trade Paperback Original Is Published By
Bold Strokes Books, Inc.
P.O. Box 249
Valley Falls, NY 12185

First Edition: June 2016

Credits
Editor: Shelley Thrasher
Production Design: Susan Ramundo
Cover Design By Sheri (graphicartist2020@hotmail.com)
Cover Art By Gun Brooke

Acknowledgments

Thank you to Len Barot (Radclyffe) for sticking by your resident Swede. I'm so happy to be part of the BSB family.

No writing experience is the same without Dr. Shelley Thrasher, my editor, whom I adore. You are priceless and a very good friend. I love working with you. Sheri, the graphic artist—we've worked on tons of covers together and for me that is a huge part of the fun. Sandy, you deserve your own shout out as you are the best!

Thank you to the rest of the BSB crew—Sandy, Connie, Stacia, Cindy, Lori, and those of you I don't know the name of, you are all tremendously important to the finished product and you may not be readily visible to the reader, but they'd know if you weren't around. Thank you for being such pros.

To my first readers—my dream team—Maggie, Laura, Sam, and Eden. You're such troopers going through my stories with your respective eagle eyes. You each bring your own flavor with your comments. *hug*

Thank you naturally to my readers. Those of you who read and buy my books, some of you even buy all of them, and to those who like my fan fiction, I owe you so much. Your lovely comments, emails, and tweets, mean the world to me. I love corresponding with you.

On a personal note—some people are helpful by their mere existence. My immediate family, Elon, Malin, Henrik, Pentti, grandchildren, Ove and Monica, how could I write if you guys weren't there to cheer me on and express pride in me? Other friends, such as the ladies in my book circle, and my online friends around the world, including the people I care about in Rhode Island, all add on to the safety net I rely on.

Dedication

To Elon
It's always been you

To Maggie
Nine years of friendship isn't nearly enough—
just so you know!
bigga huggar

To my friend Jack
Stay afloat. Spot more subtext. That's all!

Prologue

Aeron read through the text on her computer screen yet again. This novel was the closest she'd come to expressing what was in her soul. The fear, the determination to carry on despite profound loneliness, and—now this. Grief and ultimately losing the chance to find out the truth about herself. Her latest character embodied her emotions.

If she didn't use a pen name, A.D. Solo, which in itself was rather ironic, people would learn far too much about her, both from the metaphors and her protagonist's feelings.

Unable to reread what she had written even once more, she decided to send the excerpt to her publisher as it was.

> *Two guardsmen stood in her path. Knowing her duty, she gripped her poison-laced dagger and raised it to her neck. "Let me pass or I will forfeit my life."*
>
> *"A woman. No wonder we've been so unsuccessful." The man to the right laughed scornfully. "Devious little creatures. I say we let her do the deed for us."*
>
> *"Are you insane?" The other man roared. "Don't you know only her breath can break the seal on the scroll? Her* living *breath, I might add."*
>
> *"Damn. I guess we capture her then."*
>
> *"I will use the dagger. It will kill me in less time than it takes you to dismount." Oddly this part of her duties*

didn't scare Dajala. She was born into a family of all men, as her mother died while giving birth to her. Her father and brothers thought nothing of her, and the loneliness had made her think of ending her life several times. Now she pressed the dagger against her skin and readied herself for the excruciating pain.

"Not so fast," an alto female voice said in her ear and twisted the dagger away from her neck. "I have a better idea." She tore the dagger from Dajala's hand and tossed it toward the man who had just belittled women. It cut his cheek and he fell off his horse instantly. The other man growled and dug his heels into his horse's sides. Before the horse gained momentum, the woman behind Dajala fired a small arrow from her miniature crossbow.

"See?" she said, chuckling mirthlessly. "You should never be so quick to volunteer to die, Dajala of Helogius. Life has too much to offer."

Excerpt from Beyond the Sorceress's Grave, *by A.D. Solo.*

CHAPTER ONE

Manhattan—Present Day

The dark-purple clouds that hovered over most of Manhattan were especially dark over the Trinity Cemetery. Sylvie Thorn had prepared herself emotionally during the entire car ride on the way here; she refused to show how much she loathed funerals. In a black skirt suit, she shivered as the wet wind rushed along her stocking-clad legs. She prayed the priest would take pity on the crowd and be brief, as she began walking toward the covered seating area on either side of the coffin.

"Sylvie. It's good to see you. I'm sorry it's under such tragic circumstances." Her friend and mentor Helena Forsythe kissed Sylvie on the cheek. "Noelle and I just got here and saw your car pull up."

Sylvie gripped her umbrella harder. "Yes, it's a sad day. Maeve was only forty-five." Sylvie pressed her black clutch closer to her body. The summer rain was colder than she'd expected, making her shiver. Glancing around her, she nodded politely at the passing people. Also dressed in black, the movers and shakers of New York old money exited their cars. Most arrived in chauffeured vehicles and were met by men and women in uniform handing them large, black umbrellas. Sylvie had one, and Helena and Noelle shared one.

"I'm glad you're here. My staff arranged the funeral, but Maeve's, um, *friends*, or perhaps the right word is entourage, took care of the reception at her house." Sylvie began walking toward the part of the cemetery where Maeve DeForest would be laid to rest after the ceremony.

"Did you find out why she wanted you to arrange the funeral?" Helena murmured discreetly in Sylvie's ear. "I knew she was your silent partner, but I didn't realize you were that close."

"I got to know her well these last few years. As my silent partner, she enabled me to conduct my affairs regarding Classic Swedish Inc. with complete autonomy." Sylvie's throat constricted. "I suppose I initially judged her by what I read in the gossip columns, like most people do. We hardly moved in the same social circles, as I'm a relative newcomer in Manhattan. Not that I'd be inclined to barhop the way she loved to. That said, there was more to Maeve than people realized, which I'm sure you know."

"There was. I'm just worried one of those younger people she used to hang with has had too much to say about the reception." Noelle crinkled her nose. "I shudder at the idea of them having turned it into one of her infamous theme events."

"Let's hope not," Helena said darkly.

They reached the seats around the blindingly white casket boasting a large arrangement of white roses on the lid. The turnout was impressive, especially when you considered the weather. Sylvie scanned the crowd and recognized business people, politicians, socialites, celebrities, and some she couldn't pinpoint.

Just as everyone began to sit down, she spotted someone making her way through the people on the other side of the casket. Umbrellas swayed as the person murmured something inaudible, perhaps excusing herself for nudging people aside. Eventually a woman stood across from Sylvie. Her soaking-wet hair of undeterminable color hung just past her shoulders. A young man asked her to join him beneath his umbrella, but she merely shook her head.

"Who's that?" Noelle murmured.

"No idea. Although…no, it can't be." Helena's eyes narrowed as she studied the young woman. "There were rumors, but surely that was just the tabloids?"

Sylvie couldn't take her eyes off the pale, slightly freckled face of the woman before her. Rain had soaked her charcoal trench coat.

Then she raised her gaze and met Sylvie's eyes. Dark green, they scanned her slowly, as if the woman considered it her right to pass judgment on Sylvie's reasons for being there.

Once again, Sylvie asked herself why she'd agreed to arrange Maeve's funeral. Not only that, but she had been summoned to participate in the reading of Maeve's will the next day. Yes, she had a vested interest in how Maeve's wealth was distributed, as Maeve's estate owned unquoted shares in Sylvie's chain of spas located throughout the US. Their joined business endeavor was her ticket to freedom once she managed to buy out the heirs of Maeve's estate.

Yet another cold fist gripped her stomach and twisted it painfully. So much could go wrong. As if all this wasn't enough. Maeve's accident. The uncertain financial state of their mutual affairs...Sylvie's grip on the umbrella slipped and she squeezed the handle harder.

Damn. She truly hated funerals.

❖

Gothenburg, Sweden—1983

"Daniel. She's too young, don't you think? And so sensitive." *Mommy stood over by the half-open window, blowing cigarette smoke away from the room. Daddy hated that Mommy smoked. He called it a filthy habit with that hard voice that meant Mommy was in trouble. But Mommy wasn't afraid of Daddy. Not the way Sylvie was. When Daddy looked at Sylvie with his blue eyes all shiny and cold, like her marbles, she felt the need to rush to the bathroom. On several occasions, she had almost peed in her pants, which would have been terrible. She was a big girl now, eight years old, and big girls didn't have accidents.*

Daddy often reminded her she was a Thorn. This meant being important and better than other people. Sylvie knew from her school this wasn't true. The other kids didn't think she was better. They didn't think she was good at anything. Everyone could already read and write some, and Sylvie couldn't even spell her own name.

She and Mommy had practiced so many times, but the letters only looked funny and backward when Sylvie tried. Once, Daddy had come home while they sat in the kitchen with her crayons. When he saw her wobbly letters, he snorted and shook his head.

"Sometimes, Camilla, I think you must've made this kid all on your own. I could read and write when I was four."

"Oh, good for you," Mommy said and looked angrily at Daddy. "All kids are different. Some learn later and some are early like you. It's nothing to boast or be ashamed about."

"Don't even try. If she could've written at four, you'd be the first to brag." Daddy had stomped off, and Mommy put the crayons away and said it was time to eat. They hadn't practiced very much since then.

"Nonsense, Camilla," Daddy said now and placed his hands on Sylvie's shoulders. Big and heavy, they sat there like anchors pulling her down. He wanted Sylvie to come along to the funeral with him and Mommy. That's what it was called when they buried dead people. "She's eight years old. At that age children know about life and death. That church group you have her attend makes sure of that, don't they?"

When they left the house, Mommy and Daddy both wore black, and Pernilla, Sylvie's nanny, had dressed her in the new dark-blue and white sailor dress. White knee socks and Sylvie's much-coveted black, shiny buckle shoes completed her outfit. Mommy tried to tell Daddy one more time she thought Sylvie was too young for funerals, but as usual, when Daddy used that stern, impatient voice, even Mommy obeyed Daddy. Everyone in their house did, and everyone at Daddy's office too. Mommy said Daddy was the boss.

Mommy took Sylvie by the hand and they walked out to the car. Mr. Carlsson held the backseat door open for them, and Sylvie hurried to scoot over to the right side of the seat. She didn't want to sit next to Daddy, as he was in such a bad mood. Mommy said it was because his Uncle Stefan had just died. "You must forgive Daddy," Mommy had said the previous evening as she tucked Sylvie in. "Uncle Stefan was like a father to him. Remember I told you your grandfather died in Hungary during World War II? Daddy was only three years old then. Your grandmother was so upset and sad. She let Uncle Stefan take care of Daddy until she felt better. Now when Uncle Stefan is dead, it's the same for Daddy as if he lost his father."

"Again." Sylvie had sort of understood. It was strange how someone could lose a father twice, but even if Daddy often scared her, she knew she would be sad if he died. Of this she was certain. When Daddy was in his best mood, he was so funny and took her into his library, where they looked at maps. He could tell her long stories about travels to foreign countries, and Sylvie knew she was a little bit like Daddy after all since she wanted to fly around the world or go by boat. Or train.

Sylvie glanced at Daddy. He wasn't happy right now. In fact, his face was so dark that it looked like he could never, ever be happy again. What if their pretend travels with the maps in the library were over? What if Daddy would be sad and angry forever? Mommy had told her Daddy would feel better soon, but the way her father spoke and looked at her, Sylvie wasn't so sure. Placing her hands beneath her legs, she willed them to stop shaking by sitting on them.

Afterward she barely remembered the long, wordy ceremony in the church, but she would never forget the sight of the casket being lowered into the ground. Daddy stood very close to the big hole, holding Sylvie's hand so hard it hurt. For a moment, she thought he might throw her in after the big, wooden box where Uncle Stefan was resting. How could he be dead if he was resting? Was he alive in there? Had they checked to make sure?

"Stop fidgeting," Daddy hissed. "What's the matter with you, child?"

"Sorry, Daddy," Sylvie whispered and looked behind them for her mother. She couldn't see her. "Where's Mommy?" she asked, desperate enough to overcome some of the shyness.

"Hush. And didn't I tell you to stand still?" Daddy squeezed her hand even harder.

Now Sylvie wanted to get as far away from the hole with the big box as possible. She tugged at Daddy's hand and he hissed at her again. This time he yanked her toward him so hard, she came dangerously close to the hole in the ground.

And this time, she proved to her father she wasn't a big girl after all as hot pee ran down her legs, ruining her socks and her beloved black, shiny shoes.

❖

Manhattan—Present Day

Aeron DeForest sighed inwardly.

How strange. Such sad, tragic circumstances and she couldn't feel a thing. A cold, wet blanket lay between her and the emotions she should be experiencing. She should cry, for sure, or at least feel cold with shock. Instead she was numb, and as the priest spoke about the stranger that had been her mother, she let her gaze fall upon the people across from her on the other side of her mother's casket.

Aeron recognized some of the people from when she was little. Mainly some of the staff at the condominium where she had lived with her mother most of her first eight years, and from the house in the Hamptons. Then she saw some of Maeve's old friends, women who had aged, some gracefully, but most combatting time with nose jobs, facelifts, and collagen.

Her eyes fell upon a woman most of the world would recognize. Noelle Laurent, soul-pop princess turned singer-song writer and married to the woman next to her, Helena Forsythe, business tycoon. Out and proud, the two women had been a hot commodity for the press, paparazzi, and bloggers for a couple of years.

Next to the celebrities, a woman with chocolate-brown hair kept back in a twist stood regarding her with interest and—confusion? Who was that? Aeron hadn't seen her before, not as a child and not before leaving Manhattan years ago. She would have remembered the piercing dark-blue eyes and the way this woman seemed to take in the world with her chin defiantly raised. Was she really one of Maeve's friends? She didn't seem the party-socialite type. In fact, she regarded the people on either side of Aeron with disdain.

Having been back to New York for only a few days, Aeron wasn't staying at Maeve's condo, but at an unassuming hotel in

Midtown. She'd heard from Maeve's attorney, who would also serve as executor when it came to her mother's will, that the house was never empty. Friends came and went, as Maeve had been generous with handing out keys and alarm codes. It was amazing someone hadn't murdered her in her bed.

Instead Maeve had died from driving into a tourist bus under the influence of cocaine and some designer drug. Nobody else was injured, but Maeve had suffered trauma to the chest and head, as she had not worn her seat belt. Apparently she had been alone in the car.

The priest nodded to Aeron, who dutifully placed her white rose on the casket. She didn't wait around. The rain had soaked straight through her clothes and was running along her spine in chilly rivulets. Making her way along the casket, she didn't speak to anyone but left the large crowd to grieve—for real or to fake it, she didn't care. When she reached the chauffeured town car she'd arrived in, the driver wasn't there. No doubt he surmised she would stay for the duration of the ceremony. Not a chance. Aeron began to walk and pulled her cell phone from her coat pocket. She texted the driver that he could take off and consider himself done. She would simply walk to the closest subway entrance and return to her hotel that way.

Tomorrow Mr. Hayes of Shaw, Hayes, & Walters would go through the will, and then Aeron would bid her childhood, such as it had been, farewell forever and go back to being A.D. Solo and writing her horror novels in her cabin in the Adirondacks.

Shuddering, she folded her arms around her. Aeron hadn't known her mother very well, as she had kept her distance ever since Maeve sent her to a private girls' boarding school in Vermont and, later, upstate New York when she was eight. She spent all of the semesters there and Christmas and New Year's mostly with Maeve's household staff. Paulina, the cook and housekeeper, had been a buoy in the stormy sea that was life around Maeve.

Something warmed Aeron's cheeks despite the chilly rain. It took her a while to realize it was her tears. Huh. Imagine that. Tears for Maeve after all.

CHAPTER TWO

Manhattan—1996

"Is the child shy or is something, you know, wrong *with her? She's been standing there for a while now." The short woman sitting next to Maeve on the couch wrinkled her nose and motioned toward Aeron.*

"What do you mean?" Maeve turned and frowned with impatience, but her glossy red lips still smiled. "Aeron? Why aren't you in the kitchen with Paulina?"

"Paulina says lunch is ready," Aeron said and curtsied as Paulina had taught her. She was wearing one of her favorite dresses with pink roses on the skirt.

"Oh, please, what was that? Do you think this is some old movie?" Maeve shooed at Aeron to leave before turning to her guests. "Come on. Last year I finally found a decent cook who also doesn't mind babysitting Aeron."

Maeve and the short woman strode past Aeron, who now had her back pressed to the wall. She wasn't sure if Maeve wanted her to go back to Paulina before they left the room or after.

A dark-haired woman suddenly appeared at the patio door and said, "Well, I, for one, thought you did a good job."

Aeron jumped and began moving along the wall toward the kitchen. The dark-haired woman stepped closer, and now Aeron saw she was wearing a blue dress. Aeron had never met her before. The woman knelt before Aeron and extended her hand. "My name's Hannah. I'm a friend of your mother. Why don't you show me where we're having lunch?"

"In the dining room," Aeron whispered and pointed.

"Excellent. How old are you?"

"Eight." Her voice grew a little stronger now, as she had seen Hannah's kind eyes and began to relax at how gently she held Aeron's hand. Not strong and jerky like Maeve when she pulled Aeron along behind her. Maeve was always late and in a hurry. When Aeron couldn't keep up, Maeve tugged really hard at her.

"Eight? You're getting to be a big girl. Let's go have some lunch." Hannah simply began walking in that direction, still holding Aeron's hand. "Are you in second grade?"

"Yes. After the summer I'll be in third." Aeron's stomach ached at the thought.

Hannah squeezed her hand. "You don't look too happy about that."

"I like the school I go to now."

"Then what's the problem?" Hannah looked like she really wanted to know. Like she cared.

"I'm going to another school far away. In Vermont."

"Vermont? But—yes, that is far." Hannah's eyes darkened and she squeezed Aeron's hand. "I see."

They entered the dining room, and Maeve looked up from where she sat at the head of the large, rectangular table. "Oh, please, Hannah. She's not eating with us."

"Of course she is," Hannah said and pulled out two chairs. "Here you go, honey." She simply lifted Aeron up on the chair and nodded at Paulina, who came into the room carrying a tray. "We'll need a plate for Aeron too, please."

Looking uncertain at Hannah's request, Paulina paled and glanced at Maeve. "Madam?"

Maeve shrugged. "Oh, why not? Hannah clearly has her heart set on playing the nanny."

"I'm sure Aeron is so well behaved she doesn't need any nanny." Hannah placed a napkin on Aeron's lap and then ruffled her hair. "I'm right, aren't I?"

Aeron nodded and tried on a smile. In her heart she knew she would have to pay a price for Hannah's kindness, as Maeve was the boss of the house. She told Aeron this often. She hardly ever referred to herself as Aeron's mommy, but instead always claimed she was in charge. The boss. Right now, she allowed Aeron to sit at the table as if she mattered, and perhaps, if Aeron was lucky, Maeve's mood wouldn't fall once the short woman and Hannah had gone home. Perhaps she would forget about it and not send Aeron to bed without her dinner.

When this happened, Paulina sometimes risked giving her something after Maeve left the house in the evening. On those rare occasions that Maeve stayed in, Paulina didn't dare getting caught, and Aeron had to go to bed hungry. Perhaps she should sneak some bread rolls into her pockets just in case?

"She looks like such a scared little bird," the short woman said and leaned with her elbows on the table. Her smile seemed strange to Aeron. It showed a lot of teeth and made her think of an animal.

Aeron didn't dare look very long at the short woman. She had once overheard Maeve telling another friend she only kept this friend around because her sarcasm made her laugh. Aeron wasn't sure what sarcasms were, but if they had anything to do with the short woman, she didn't like them.

Sitting next to Hannah was very different. This friend of her mother's was nice and warm. Aeron was almost always right when her feelings told her things about another person. Like that girl, Greta, at the playground. She was so popular and always had at least ten other kids around her. When Aeron joined them at the swings, Greta immediately started whispering with the others, and soon they all moved to the slide or the trampoline.

It didn't take Aeron long to realize how much the other kids idolized and feared Greta. If someone objected to her ordering them around, she soon managed to turn the rest of her group of kids against them. They rarely talked back to her more than once.

Aeron would never be accepted into Greta's gang. She liked some of the kids hanging around with Greta, but for some reason, she was invisible to them when Greta was at the playground. And she wasn't imagining all this. Aeron was used to being invisible.

"Are you really sending this child away to boarding school at the age of eight?" Hannah spoke lightly, but Maeve's eyes narrowed and Aeron cringed.

"I can tell someone's been telling tales." She sent Aeron a sideways glance. "Actually, it's a specialized school for children with Aeron's needs. I'm rarely home and she needs more stimulation than poor Paulina has time for. This school, it's in the countryside in Vermont, not far from Stowe. A charming family setting. They will help bring Aeron out of her shell. She can't rule my empire one day if she doesn't dare open her mouth."

Aeron sank back against the chair and lowered her head. Now they all knew something was wrong with her. Maeve had a long list she let Paulina take to the doctor when it was time for Aeron's checkups. This list grew longer with each visit, and yet, every time Dr. Burke shook his head and scribbled something on his notepad. This made Maeve so very angry, and she sometimes yelled at Paulina for not doing her job. Sometimes Paulina cried, and Aeron once heard her say she would quit if it wasn't for Aeron. She thought Maeve would fire Paulina for that, but instead she gave her the rest of the day off.

"Still. She's eight. She needs her mother." Hannah put her arm around Aeron's shoulders and squeezed lightly.

Maeve's eyes darkened and her voice trembled. "I don't want to talk about it."

Hannah didn't continue but was very nice to Aeron the rest of the visit. Once they left, Maeve took Aeron and put her on her lap. "You do know I'm sending you to this school because it's what's best for you, pumpkin?" Maeve only called her pumpkin when she was in her best mood.

"Yes, Maeve." Aeron dared to rest her head against Maeve's chest.

"Hey, when we're alone, you can call me Mommy. I've told you that."

It was hard for Aeron to remember this, and for the most part, she used her mother's first name. "Mommy," she whispered now, and the slow-burning glow of longing in her chest expanded. "Mommy."

"There you go." Maeve held her close and actually hummed a song Aeron recognized from MTV. Her perfume, so familiar and what Maeve called her sig-na-ture scent, surrounded Aeron, and she closed her eyes and let her mother hold her. This didn't happen a lot, and who knew when Maeve would feel like cuddling her again.

Chapter Three

Manhattan—Present Day

Aeron walked into her mother's lawyer's office. It held a somber ambiance: all mahogany, dark-red carpets, crystal, and a faint trace of expensive cigars. It spoke of a long history of representing wealthy, influential clients. As for the five people present, including her, she wasn't certain what she had expected, but not the dark-haired woman she'd observed at the funeral. Dressed in a dove-gray skirt suit and with her dark hair in a loose twist, she looked the part of a Manhattan businesswoman. Next to her, a young man sat taking notes as she murmured something inaudible to him.

Behind them a woman in her sixties looked at Aeron with tears in her eyes. Aeron blinked. It had been too long. "Paulina?" She ignored everyone else and rounded the two in front of Maeve's housekeeper and cook. "I'm so glad to see you."

"Aeron." Paulina rose and hugged her. "I'm so sorry for your loss, sweetheart. I saw you at the funeral, but you left before I had a chance to give you my condolences. I didn't attend the reception."

"Neither did I." Aeron felt herself travel twenty-some years back in time. At one point, Paulina's hugs and affection had been the one constant in her life. "Do you have time for coffee after this?"

"I do. We'll talk more later." Paulina patted her cheek and retook her seat.

As Aeron returned to her chair, she saw the dark-haired woman study her with guarded curiosity.

"As we're all here," Mr. Hayes said after clearing his throat, "let's get started. Ms. DeForest's last will and testament is as simple as it is unorthodox. She recorded her will in 2009 to be played in the office in the event of her death."

Flinching, Aeron stared at the tall, lanky man as he raised his hand holding a remote. To her left, a large flat-screen TV flickered and a young-looking Maeve smiled broadly at them.

"Hello there! If you see this at dear Lucas's office, it means I've somehow managed to get myself dead. I hope I was at least ninety-three, but if not, hmm, well, bummer." Her voice, so chirpy and facetious, cut deep into Aeron's chest.

"Oh, God," Aeron said and inhaled deeply. "I'm not sure—"

"Especially my little Aeron, I hope you're married to the man of your dreams with children and even grandchildren around your feet. I haven't seen you in a few months. Or, it might actually been a year since you didn't come home at Christmas, naughty girl." Maeve shook her head, her blond, perfectly separated and styled curls bouncing around her stunning face. *"I can't imagine I'd leave this earth before you're grown up and have a family of your own... that's simply unseemly, if you ask me."* Her eyes seemed to darken, and she adjusted her gold statement necklace with unsteady fingers. She was clearly uncomfortable and struggled to remain her usual extravagant self.

"Please..." Aeron tried to find her voice to ask "dear Lucas" to stop the recording, but her vocal chords failed her.

"Paulina, if you're here, my pillar of strength. You kept me fed and my homes in perfect condition for all these years. You were there for Aeron. I hope you still are. If I'm an old lady and you've passed on, your inheritance will go to your heirs." Maeve paused and shifted and straightened her back. *"Sylvie Thorn. I hope we've been business partners for many years when you see this. If our agreement has changed during the years, Lucas knows how to proceed. If we're still on course with Classic Swedish Inc. and all our plans, then this part of the will still stands. So—here goes."*

Maeve put on pink reading glasses and winked at the camera. *"Aren't these cute? I'm sure in the future, a long, long time from now, nobody wears these, but in 2009, reading glasses are still a must-have. So, all right, let's get to it.*

First, as it is the easiest part, Paulina Nieves. You will inherit my New York condo on the Upper East Side. You will also receive a pension consisting of twice your salary at my demise, and the same for your husband Arthur, for both your natural lives. The upkeep and fees associated with owning the condo will be paid for the same duration." Maeve put down the first paper and began reading from the next. *"Aeron, my beloved daughter."* Maeve looked up into the camera. Her eyes shone from tears refusing to dislodge. *"Don't freak out now. You inherit the rest. What doesn't go to Paulina, or her heirs, should she no longer be with us, goes to you. I do have conditions. You have to keep my charities going. All twenty-eight of them, or more, if I've added some at the time of my death, which I hope I have. You must also keep any business agreement I made with Sylvie Thorn, unless she and I have already parted ways financially. I gave her my word I'd see this investment through. Before I go into the details of the part of my will that concerns both of you, I want to say something. Perhaps if I was an old bat before I kicked the bucket, I've already told you, at least I hope so.*

I was a crappy mother, and I can only hope I've managed to rectify this as I planned. If not, please don't give up on me. Examine my last will and testament, my girl. Carefully go through old documents. Don't throw it all away unread because of old hurts. Please."

Maeve smiled with trembling lips, and it was clear to Aeron her mother really was teary-eyed. *"And now, Sylvie, and I hope you're here. If you're not, Lucas will stop the DVD now."* Maeve sat still, as if she actually expected Lucas Hayes to come and turn the DVD off.

"Sylvie, you are one of many who approached me over the years with the idea of becoming a silent partner and investor. In fact, I initially chose to partner with you because you were my very first Swedish acquaintance and I had this insane idea you might be able to introduce me to ABBA." Maeve chuckled and wiped at her

eyelashes. *"Silly, I know. Then I got to know you, and even if you don't need my input when it comes to business, you are always willing to hear me out. After all, I'm our best customer and know from that end how the business works."* Maeve looked intently at them and then cleared her throat again. *"Sylvie, here's the thing. I want you to work with Aeron like you did with me. Take her under your wing and mentor her. I keep telling her she has so much going for her, but she doesn't listen to me, and who can blame her? Teach her about the cutthroat nature of business. Once you've done that and Aeron knows enough to make an informed decision, the investment I made in Classic Swedish Inc. will be turned into a gift from me to you. It's not enough for everything you taught me, but at least you need not worry about not having absolute majority.*

This way Aeron can learn enough to decide if she wants to manage the DeForest fortune or allow the board of directors and trustees to keep their power of attorney. If Aeron turns you down, I can only surmise my daughter has finally decided to reject me once and for all. Then, the entire estate—after Paulina has received her share—will go to the Belmont Foundation in Rhode Island. As you are the two most important people in my life, it's my genuine hope that you find a way to work together. Most of all, though, I hope I died at the ripe old age of 103. See you later. Much later!" She blew the camera a lavish kiss.

Mr. Hayes turned off the DVD player and flat-screen. Aeron tried to gather her thoughts, turning her head in Sylvie's direction. Sylvie's assistant scribbled on his notepad as if his life hung in the balance, while her mother's business partner calmly sat with her hands folded on her lap, her eyes locked on Aeron in what had to be a silent challenge.

Mr. Hayes cleared his voice. "That's Maeve DeForest's last will and testament in short. A more detailed print version exists, but she outlined it well on the video. Among Ms. Aeron DeForest, Ms. Sylvie Thorn, and Mrs. Paulina Nieves, you have inherited all of the DeForest estate at different levels, which boils down to roughly worth 25 billion dollars. Mrs. Nieves does not have to worry about any stipulations, but Ms. DeForest and Ms. Thorn and her company Classic Swedish Inc. do."

Aeron couldn't breathe. She was stuck in a weird nightmare and couldn't move the air in and out of her lungs. She hadn't had an anxiety attack in a while, but this was how it felt: throat-constricting and sweat-producing, like her hands and feet were immersed in ice. She had to get out of here. No matter what anyone else in the room said, she couldn't stay. Standing up fast enough to knock over her chair, she hurried through the elegant office.

"Ms. DeForest!" Lucas Hayes called out. "I have a lot more information—"

"I don't care. I don't want any of it. Give it away. Give every cent to that foundation."

Chapter Four

Tears streaming down her cheeks, Aeron darted along the corridor to the outer office. There, the elevator doors were about to close and she slipped inside, grateful the car was empty. She pressed her back against the wall after pushing the button for the lobby. Her heart boomed, and she had to make herself breathe deep and slow.

As she stepped outside, the sun shone brightly. New Yorkers hurried up and down the wide sidewalks, and cars crawled on the congested street. Nobody paid her any attention, which was a good thing. She began to walk, and after a few blocks, she saw one of the few old-fashioned coffee houses left in Manhattan and stepped inside. Only when she sat down with her latte did she remember she was supposed to have coffee with Paulina.

"Fuck," Aeron muttered under her breath. She didn't have Paulina's phone number. She hoped Paulina would think to ask Mr. Hayes for it and call her. Now Aeron felt utterly foolish for running, but after seeing Maeve, looking so alive and, in the strangest way, so familiar yet alien, she'd freaked out. She'd had to run or have a full-blown panic attack right there in front of everybody. Even if she knew how to cope with her anxiety better these days, at times the panic would wash over her and make her feel as if she were actually drowning.

❖

Vermont—1997

"This will be your room, Aeron. You'll share with another girl your age. Her name is Melissa, and she's at the library right now with her group." The tall, thin woman, Mrs. Marie Crenshaw, motioned toward the bed to the left. *"I understand Aeron's belongings are sitting in the lobby still. We'll help you carry them up later and get settled, pumpkin."*

Pumpkin? Aeron blinked. That was what Maeve called her when she was in an extra-good mood. What an odd thing for a teacher to call a student. Her teacher in Manhattan had called them strictly by their first name, no nicknames whatsoever. She had even complained about Aeron's unusual name once and asked if she had another first name that sounded more normal. As Aeron was called only that, she had to disappoint that teacher.

"We look forward to having you as our special guest for dinner, Mrs. DeForest—"

"Oh, I'm not staying." Maeve was all smiles and big hand gestures. *"I have an appointment back in New York later this evening, and I should get going right away."*

"But parents are encouraged to participate in installing their child, especially when they're this young. Several days in some cases, actually. It helps the children to transition and reassures them." Still sounding kind and not mad at Maeve at all, Mrs. Crenshaw tilted her head.

"Aeron, you will find, is a very easy child to be around. She rarely cries and carries on, and she's very good at playing by herself."

A small voice inside Aeron's head wanted to object. She did cry. Just not when anyone saw her. She did play by herself, but only because she had no friends.

"I'm fine, Mae—Mom." Aeron knew she sounded like a polite robot. *"You should go to your meeting. I look forward to meeting Melissa and the others and to starting school here."* In fact, Aeron dreaded it. She would hate it if the other children were far ahead in their studies. And the opposite was just as bad. Enough kids

had called her a four-eyed nerd at her last school for doing her homework. And having glasses.

"Are you sure, pumpkin?" Mrs. Crenshaw put a gentle hand on her shoulder.

"I'm sure." Did the lie look convincing?

"Very well." Clearly not pleased with Maeve taking off, Mrs. Crenshaw stayed with them while they said good-bye.

Maeve kept smiling broadly, and every now and then she bit her lower lip, only to break out in another dazzling smile as she let go. "Have fun with all your new friends here. I'm sure you'll do me proud and learn tons of new stuff. I'll see you around...eh... Halloween."

It was early August and Halloween was almost three months away. It felt like forever. Without being able to stop herself, Aeron's chin started trembling as Maeve rose.

"M-Mom? You're coming back, right?" This was usually a surefire way to annoy her mother, but the words popped out on their own.

"But of course!" Maeve threw herself on her knees and pulled Aeron in for a long hug. Too stunned to reciprocate, Aeron's heart pounded hard at the unexpected embrace, but mostly at how her mother trembled against her. "I have to do what's best for you, and trust me, Aeron, that's not me right now. You'll have a real home here during the semesters, and you can tell me all about it during the holidays." She stood, and now her smile wasn't as dazzling, but more tense and her eyes shiny. Turning around quickly, Maeve nodded at Mrs. Crenshaw and walked out the door of Maeve's new room.

"Maeve..." Forgetting she was supposed to say "Mom," Aeron stood alone in the center of the cozy room. Built-in bookshelves of dark wood, a bed with lots of pillows, a mauve rug stretching from her part of the room over to Melissa's, two desks, and two walk-in closets.

"Listen, pumpkin," Mrs. Crenshaw said, and cupped Aeron's chin. "I think your mom left because she was too upset about not having you with her and she didn't want you to know."

"Why?" Feeling instinctively that questions were not only allowed here, but encouraged, Aeron leaned in to the kind touch.

"I don't know. When your mom said you rarely cry, I think she thought of herself. Neither of you shows your tears to anyone, I reckon. But you know what? If you need to have a good cry for any reason, you come to me or any of the teachers that you feel comfortable with. We can always sort things out, you know."

Aeron gazed up into Mrs. Crenshaw's friendly eyes. She wasn't used to having someone's full attention directed at her for very long at a time. Paulina was always at Maeve's service, and Maeve kept reminding Paulina and Aeron who paid her salary. Maeve's needs always came first.

"What do you say, pumpkin? Should we try to find Mr. Crenshaw and have him help us bring your luggage up?" Mrs. Crenshaw grinned. "His first name is Horatio, but I call him Horsey. Don't tell him I told you, all right?"

Aeron had to giggle, and the secret joke took a tiny bit of the sadness and anger away. She held on to Mrs. Crenshaw's hand as they walked down the staircase. This house did look like a real home. Much more than Maeve's condo that was full of things she wasn't allowed to touch. Here, it appeared you could sit on the couch with your feet up, like in the movies, and perhaps even drink hot cocoa by the television. It was strange that despite so many things being right with this place, she still missed Maeve so much it hurt.

❖

Manhattan—Present Time

Aeron's cell phone rang, and she transported back from the past and saw it was the lawyer's office.

She answered, hoping it was Paulina. "Hello?"

"Aeron, sweetheart. Are you all right?" Paulina's voice was so concerned and warm that Aeron had to blink against her tears. "Aeron?"

"I'm here. Yes. I'm okay. I'm sorry for leaving you behind like that. I just...I just couldn't..."

"I know. You don't have to apologize. Are you close by? Do you still want to have coffee?"

Aeron told Paulina where she was and that she'd wait for her. "They have pies and sandwiches too. We can have lunch if you want."

"Sounds terrific, Aeron. I'll be there in a little while. Here's Ms. Thorn for you."

What? Aeron grew rigid and clutched the phone.

"Ms. DeForest? Sylvie Thorn here." Her voice was stern, and she spoke fast, with a faint accent Aeron couldn't place. "As I'm sure you understand after hearing your mother's will, we need to meet up and talk."

"I don't see why." Cringing at how rude she sounded, Aeron covered her eyes with her free hand. "The Belmont Foundation can have Maeve's money. I don't want it."

"I think that's your grief talking." Sylvie Thorn's voice was low but not without compassion. "I didn't know Maeve had a daughter, but other sides of her I knew quite well. Please give me a chance to explain why you need to not make this type of decision while in this frame of mind."

"And how could you possibly know which frame of mind I'm in?" Aeron spat. "You don't know me." She huffed to herself at Sylvie Thorn's obvious attempt to get the money Maeve had promised her if she fulfilled the terms of the will.

"No, but I would imagine losing your mother, no matter what your relationship was like, is difficult. All I ask is that you meet with me and hear me out. If you still are completely against your mother's wishes, I...I won't bother you again."

"I've already made my decision. Forget it." The words actually pained her as she let them escape. Aeron wasn't sure why she suddenly was so guilt-ridden, but she was.

The silence at the other end stretched out. "I'm truly sorry you feel this way. I knew Maeve in a different light from how most people perceived her. It would've been nice to get to know the daughter she kept such a secret. But, as you've made your decision, all I can do is wish you well for the future. Good-bye."

After a brief silence and then some noise, Paulina spoke again. "Aeron. I'll be with you in just a little while. Ms. Thorn is dropping me off at the coffee shop."

"I'll be here." Aeron tucked her cell phone into her pocket. Something in Sylvie Thorn's voice had disturbed her, but she wasn't sure how. Had she meant she wasn't one of Maeve's party-till-you-drop entourage? Aeron didn't think that was even possible. When had her mother had time for any friends of substance? She'd lived her life at rocket speed, enjoying one new club after another. She regarded drugs as her prerogative and used them as if no laws applied to her.

It had taken Aeron until she was in her late teens before she realized how deeply addicted her mother was to cocaine, different designer drugs, and alcohol, mainly champagne. She had no idea if Maeve ever did any heavier drugs. When she finally found out about them, she was eighteen at the time, she understood the mysterious mood swings that had plagued Maeve and affected her. She had then withdrawn and given up her futile struggle to have Maeve validate her. What a blow to realize Maeve would never become the mother she needed and dreamed about. Moreover, Aeron would never know why Maeve lived her life this way.

Aeron had finished her second latte when Paulina came into the coffee house. She strode up to Aeron's corner table and pulled her up from the chair and hugged her. "My poor girl. This was a hard day for you. I'm so sorry."

"She's really gone." Aeron's words echoed, empty. "I'll never know her now. I'll never know what I did wrong or why she did drugs or…Paulina…" She slumped down in the chair again. "I just want to go back home to the Adirondacks. I don't want any more lawyer meetings or to deal with Maeve's estate. I truly don't."

"I know, but to some degree you have to. You have to sign a plethora of documents and decide which things of your mothers you want to keep. She kept your room intact, so there's the matter of your own belongings as well."

Aeron's jaw sagged. "What?"

Paulina tilted her head as she held on to Aeron's hand. "You didn't know."

"No. I was pretty sure she might have put everything in storage and turned my room into a gym or bar or whatever." The idea of her room being as she left it made her dizzy. Aeron sobbed and clasped her free hand over her mouth. "Do you mean I have to go back there?"

"It's been way too long, my girl. Five years since you saw her. Eight years since you left the condo for good."

"Feels a lot longer." It did. Going away to college had meant almost severing her contact with Maeve, unless she counted a couple of Christmases and Thanksgivings when she'd more or less vanished in the massive crowd in the condo when Maeve had decided to "have a few friends over."

"How about we go over some things together tomorrow?" Paulina patted her hand.

"Do you want the furniture? I mean, if it's similar to what I remember, it's nice."

"But it's yours, sweetheart." Paulina blushed. "Most of it is as you remember. She had a few rooms redesigned, but the living areas are as they've always been."

"So, if you like any of it, please keep it." Aeron couldn't imagine any of the luxurious couches, tables, or lamps in her rustic cabin.

"All right. Let me know if you change your mind. It's all right if you do."

"I won't." Aeron sighed. "God, where are my manners. What can I get you? Coffee? A slice of pie?"

"Stay here. I'll go up to the counter and order us some salads." Paulina rose, and Aeron gazed dimly after the woman who'd been more of a mother to her than Maeve had ever managed. Paulina had taught her the basics in early childhood: how to tie her shoes, brush her hair, eat at the table properly, and so on. Maeve had probably implied that these menial tasks were beneath her—or that she simply didn't have time. Paulina, who was actually only the cook/ housekeeper, had stepped up to the plate, and Aeron had no idea what her life would have been like if Paulina hadn't loved her like one of her own daughters.

"Here we go." Paulina broke through Aeron's reminiscing as she sat back down with two large glasses of iced tea. "Now, why don't you want to talk to Ms. Thorn? She seems to have her head screwed on right, if you don't mind me saying so. Not like some other people your mother attracted. Some of them used her, and others just loved to party and found her a kindred spirit."

"And you're saying Sylvie Thorn was never at her parties?" Aeron found that hard to believe.

"Maybe once or twice when Maeve hosted regular dinner parties. I remember Ms. Thorn leaving early at one point when some of Maeve's party friends crashed the dinner and everything became really loud. I brought her coat and she asked me who those people were. I, of course, couldn't be disloyal to Maeve, so I just said, 'Ms. DeForest's friends.' She shook her head and said 'some friends.' She was right, of course."

"What was their relationship?" Curious against her will, Aeron sipped her iced tea.

"You heard her on the tape. They were business partners. I don't know the details, but Ms. Thorn asked Maeve to invest in her company that runs a chain of spas in several cities all over the US. I can't remember the name of it, but you've probably heard of it. Tons of celebrities have found their way there, some of them through Maeve."

"Ah. So she needed an investor as well as a name to drop. A gold digger?" Aeron wrinkled her nose, and Paulina gave her a disapproving glance.

"No. Ms. Thorn's from a prominent family in Sweden that apparently has a lot of old money. She runs the US branch of Thorn Industries here. From what Maeve said, the spas are Ms. Thorn's own company, not involved with the family business."

"I see." Well, that was a lie. Aeron couldn't figure out why her mother had suddenly shown an interest in business. Had she always done that and never told Aeron about it? Aeron had always assumed Maeve was a social butterfly who never worked but let the board of directors in charge of the DeForest fortune run it as they saw fit, as long as she had the money to do as she pleased. Was that a major misconception?

"How much did Maeve invest in this spa chain?" Reluctantly curious, Aeron plucked at her straw. A waitress showed up with their salads, and they ate some before Paulina answered.

"You're going to have to ask her yourself. I don't know. Judging from how she looked at the lawyer's office, I'd guess enough to cause problems if the two of you can't see eye-to-eye."

This was unexpected. "But didn't you just say this woman is super wealthy?" Aeron chewed on some baby spinach dipped in Italian vinaigrette.

"Yes, but as I also said, the best way to find out the details is to actually meet with her." Paulina gave her a long glance. "That way you might be able to find out how she saw your mother, as I'm sure her concept differs from how I saw her and how her friends perceived her as well. Not to mention, the image you have of her. What do you have to lose?"

"My sanity for being in Manhattan longer than absolutely necessary." Grimacing, Aeron put her fork down and wiped her mouth, her appetite waning. "Maeve is gone, and no information, old or new, can change that. I gave up on the dream of having a loving, doting mother a long time ago. She had all the chances in the world to get to know me and show she cared. Twenty-six years, to be exact." Blinking at treacherous tears, Aeron folded her arms over her chest.

Paulina took a long sip through her straw. "Are you sure about that, sweetheart? You kept away from her once you left for college. You used money from the trust fund set up for you by *Maeve* and bought your little cabin, and how many times did you visit here after that? Three times? Four?"

Aghast at Paulina criticizing her, Paulina who was always on her side, Aeron drew a trembling breath. "She never came to the cabin."

"Because you told her to never set foot there. You made it clear that was your space, and I think she was trying to respect that wish in her own way." Paulina spoke in a sorrowful tone, which made the hair at the nape of Aeron's neck stand up.

"I needed space. And time." Offended now, Aeron gazed around for the waitress. She wanted to pay for the food and simply get out of the coffee shop.

"Listen, Aeron. I'm not blaming you for being alienated by your mother. You're right. Maeve missed a lot of chances when it came to your childhood and adolescence. When she realized it looked like it might be too late to rectify her past actions, it nearly broke her. At times I thought she was trying to commit a slow suicide via alcohol and drugs. When Ms. Thorn showed up asking for partnership regarding the spas, I'd say she was in the nick of time."

Slowly unfolding her arms, Aeron gaped. "Are you telling me Sylvie Thorn saved Maeve from self-destructing?"

"It's as good a theory as any. Maeve found a purpose, and I know when she came home from having 'talked nothing but business,' as she put it, she looked determined and serious in a way I've never seen before. She even talked about moving permanently to her house in the Hamptons."

Aeron had visited that house only a few times while on break from college. Her mother had renovated the beautiful two-story, 6000-square-feet house she inherited from her parents, and Aeron liked it, as it had a private beach and an Olympic-size pool.

Maeve had even offered her the run of the pool house, which was just as luxurious as the main building. Despite knowing better, Aeron had begun to lower her guard, and she and Maeve had enjoyed a more relaxed time than ever together the first week. Then the weekend came around and so did the main part of Maeve's entourage. Aeron stayed as far away from the crowd as she could and spent her last days there at the beach, where few of her mother's guests ventured. God forbid any of those women got a grain of sand in their perfectly coiffed beach-wavy hairdos.

"Why would she move to the Hamptons permanently?" Aeron shook her head. "The place is pretty dead in the winter."

"She'd made other friends out there. Some of them are also friends with Ms. Thorn, who I think had a good influence on your mother."

Her head spinning, Aeron knew she'd never felt this confused before now. She'd gone through many emotions regarding her relationship with her mother, but this feeling of having a hole open up under the very chair she sat on…She just didn't get it. Who was this Maeve that Paulina described? Where had these characteristics of sincerity come from? Why had her mother never approached Aeron this way if this was actually true? Aeron reeled her rampaging mind in. Paulina would never lie to her. She was a constant in the many variables in this mystery. Sylvie Thorn was a dark horse of whom Aeron knew practically nothing.

"I'm going to have to bite the bullet, aren't I?" Aeron said, moaning at the mere thought of being pulled into her mother's web even after her death.

"If by that you mean approaching Ms. Thorn and apologizing for speaking too soon, then yes. I believe so." Paulina wiped her mouth and put her napkin on the table. Her formerly black hair, now with a becoming white highlight at the hairline above her left eyebrow, danced against her shoulders as she shook her head. "I have a feeling you won't regret getting to know other parts of your mother's life. As children we think we know everything about our parents, but that's never the case. Talk to Ms. Thorn. Perhaps you'll enjoy getting to know her as well."

This last part made Aeron flinch. "Nah. I don't see us having anything to talk about." What would a horror novelist using the pen name A.D. Solo from the Adirondacks have in common with a Swedish business tycoon in Manhattan?

Paulina grinned broadly now. "Oh, you just never know."

CHAPTER FIVE

Sylvie sank into her favorite recliner by the panoramic window overlooking some lower buildings and, farther away, Central Park. She didn't regret not getting the penthouse condominium, which she considered something of a cliché. The twelfth floor was high enough to help her feel secure and low enough to feel connected to the streets around her.

She loved Manhattan. Ever since she'd moved to New York fifteen years ago and started learning the ropes at Thorn Industries Daughter Company from the bottom up, she'd inhaled the city and made it a part of her. Back in Sweden, Gothenburg had always been home, but now she only visited during stockholder meetings and other major events. Her parents always went completely overboard with such events, as if they thought they were hosting the Nobel Prize banquet. Sylvie snorted at the thought as she undid her hair from the austere twist. Her family's wealth went all the way back to the days of King Gustav Wasa, as her father used to say. Her ancestors had already laid the foundation for the Thorn fortune in the 1600s by trading along the East India route. Sweden had been a superpower then, and the Thorn family had profited both by the spoils of war as well as the war effort itself.

"Lovely family, the Thorns," Sylvie muttered and reached for her glass of Madeira. She sipped carefully, letting the well-rounded, sweet taste roll along her tongue. "Profiting on other people's loss and misfortune." She loved being in New York partially because this branch of Thorn Industries had nothing to do with weaponry or strategic software. Here, she worked with real estate, building office complexes and malls, and developing residential areas. She devoted her time to that and the charity program Thorn and a few other companies had set up to provide housing for homeless people and supply food and necessities for shelters. Sylvie found this part of Thorn Industries US-based undertakings the most rewarding. And after she'd worked herself to a pulp taking care of all that, she'd focused entirely on her guilty pleasure and ticket to validation and, ultimately, freedom—Classic Swedish Inc.

The chain of luxurious spas now consisted of eighteen day spas scattered over the US, plus one in Toronto. Maeve DeForest's unexpected death had been disastrous in more ways than one. Sylvie had relied on her silent partner not only for financial backing, but also for her connections. As different as they had been, Sylvie would miss the flamboyant Maeve, who had a perpetual smile on her face and whose eyes often glittered with mischief. What would she do now? Her other sponsor had turned out to be a mole planted by her father to check up on her activities. If he bought Maeve's unquoted shares in Classic Swedish Inc., Sylvie would lose control over her own company and wouldn't be able to accomplish what she'd set out to do. Daniel would have won again.

She'd long wanted to show her father once and for all that she could manage without the Thorn fortune or his constant interference. Perhaps she was being immature, but she yearned for independence. After all these years of dancing to Daniel Thorn's pipe, she wanted to be able to stride into his office and shove her resignation into his face.

Of course, she'd been offered promising positions over the years and could have worked for someone else, but she didn't want that. Her father would have snickered and called her hired help if she'd chosen that route. To him, those who didn't create their own path or run the show were spineless followers. Working for a company, even as its CEO or president, would be in his eyes a huge step downward. Did her father's employees know of his opinions? Perhaps he paid his closest associates so well they didn't care.

Sylvie didn't regard the people she worked with like that. She took pride in being a modern, humane boss, making a conscious effort to not become a carbon copy of her father. This said, she wanted to one day rub it in his face how she'd used her own money and found investors who believed in her business sense and ideas enough to trust her with their money in exchange for equity. Then she'd resign from the US branch of Thorn Industries and finally escape from under Daniel's shadow.

"But right now I have to find a new investor." Sylvie spoke to the empty glass in her hand. "And not only that. I have to figure out how to guilt the long-lost daughter of Maeve DeForest into selling those unquoted shares to me and not my father's front man." If Aeron for some unfathomable reason decided to forfeit her inheritance, all bets were off. Who knew what future trustees would do when it came to Classic Swedish Inc.?

Aeron DeForest, yes. Sylvie thought back to when she and Thomas, her personal assistant, sat waiting for the DeForest heiress to arrive to the lawyer's office. Sylvie had been stunned at how different the drenched young woman from the cemetery looked when she finally appeared. Rich, slightly wavy hair, in a unique dark-blond shade with golden highlights framed her face and reached just below her shoulders. She wore a long, light-blue shirt over black leggings, ankle boots, and a short, brown leather jacket. A small denim backpack hung over her shoulder. Her face described a perfect oval with a band of freckles adorning her narrow, slightly bent nose, and she regarded them all with level, sea-green eyes through wire-framed glasses.

When what felt like Maeve's ghost had read the main points of her will, Sylvie had studied Aeron furtively and noticed how she became increasingly pale. It wasn't a major shock when the young woman couldn't take any more of the things thrown at her. In fact, had it been Sylvie's father reading the same type of will to her after his death, Sylvie would probably have thrown up. "And there I go, fretting about dear old dad again," Sylvie muttered, rubbing her neck.

Feeling silly for talking out loud to herself, Sylvie rose and carried her glass to the dishwasher. Always the neat freak, as her best friend at Berglund's boarding school used to call her, Sylvie wiped off the kitchen counters and made sure even the sink was shiny. Meticulously turning off the lights in all the rooms except the hallway, where a night-light shone the way to the front door in case of emergency, Sylvie walked toward the master suite.

This was her favorite part of her condo. Here, she had refused to let anyone from the design team have their way. Blue, cream, white, and gray made this into a calm space. She didn't even have a television in here, something most people found weird. Cheating a little bit by bringing her laptop with her, Sylvie sometimes read her emails before bed, but not always. On those days when her head spun with details of her insanely busy days, she just wanted the Zen moment of crawling into bed after a hot bath and turning off the lights. She rarely drew the blinds, as she found the flickering light from Manhattan reflecting off taller buildings in the distance soothing.

Now she put her cell phone to charge in the hallway before going into her bedroom. Just as she passed the threshold, the phone rang. She frowned. Had her mother misjudged the time difference again? It didn't seem to matter how many years Sylvie had lived in New York, Camilla called at all hours, always surprised that she had the time wrong again. A quick glance at the display of her smart phone showed it wasn't her mother. In fact, it was an unknown number. No one but a very select few had her private cell-phone number. Something must have happened. She answered and tried to calm her racing heart by sheer willpower.

"Sylvie Thorn speaking."

"Oh. Hi. This is Aeron DeForest. I apologize for calling so late." The woman at the other end sounded jittery.

Sylvie caught herself before she actually took the phone from her ear and glanced at it like they did in the movies. "Ms. DeForest. Don't worry about it. I'm still up. What can I do for you?"

"I was rude to you today and I want to apologize." Aeron inhaled audibly.

"Apology accepted, but honestly, it could have waited until tomorrow." What was this about? Sylvie walked into her bedroom and set the cell phone down on speaker mode. Unzipping her skirt, she slid it over her hips and hung it on a chair.

"Yes, but no."

"Excuse me?" Having started to unbutton her silk shirt, Sylvie stopped and turned toward the phone.

"I mean, yes, a mere apology could have waited until tomorrow, but the rest of what I have to say can't." The words gushed from the speaker.

"Go on." Sylvie resumed undressing.

"I wasn't feeling well at the lawyer's office and totally rushed everything. I just wanted to get out of there. When Paulina called and put you on, I was still freaking out about watching my dead mother talk to me, and what I said was a stupid, knee-jerk reaction."

Sylvie sat down on the side of her bed slowly. "I see." But she really didn't. "And now?"

"We need to talk. I'm prepared to negotiate some terms with you if you're still interested."

Letting a few seconds go by, Sylvie kept from shouting the obvious answer, but only barely. "Yes, of course. Are you free sometime tomorrow?"

"All day, more or less. Paulina insists that I go with her to my mother's—well, Paulina's really—condo and pick out things I want to keep." Aeron sounded as if this was a terrible idea. "We need to meet in the presence of Mr. Hayes, so why don't you make an appointment that fits your schedule and call me later?"

"All right." Sylvie hesitated, afraid to jinx this new turn of events. "May I ask why you changed your mind?"

"You may. Tomorrow. It's kind of hard to explain and it's late."

"Very well." Sylvie hoped Aeron's terms wouldn't be horrendously expensive or strange.

"See you tomorrow. Good night."

"Good night." Disconnecting from her end, Sylvie took off the last of her clothes and walked into the bathroom. Drawing a bath, she lit her favorite vanilla candle and let that be the only source of light. She stepped into the warm, bordering on hot, water, and her aching shoulders and back finally relaxed. The last few days' tension hadn't exactly helped her strained muscles. This had always been a problem for her. Already in middle school she'd been all tied into a knot when she had to take a test. She grew so rigid that her peers had called her the queen because of her ramrod-straight posture and regal way of walking. They had no idea her stiffened muscles were to blame. As a shy and introverted person, she was considered fair game by the press, due to her family's notoriety, which was stressful in itself. She'd felt pressured into becoming as successful and respected as her father, even if her mother insisted that others feared Daniel rather than revered him.

Now, Sylvie moaned in bliss and dared enjoy a tiny glimpse of hope. Perhaps everything she'd fought so hard for wasn't slipping through her fingers after all. Tomorrow she'd find out what terms Aeron would offer for keeping the partnership going like before. Sylvie would put her staff at Classic Swedish Inc. to work. They'd already prepared a folder of information for Aeron, but now they had a few hours to polish the content some more. Apart from that, Sylvie needed to call Helena Forsythe. Helena had known Maeve for a long time, though not closely. Surely she must have heard of Aeron's existence?

Willing her mind to calm down, Sylvie leaned back against the edge of the tub. She focused on the candle's calm flame and forced the last conscious thoughts from her brain. This was all about relaxation and recharging. Everything else could wait.

Aeron sat in the dark hotel room, curled up on the bed with one of the spare blankets around her shoulders. Was she making a huge mistake after all? Even if she got her way, she would still have to prolong her stay in New York for weeks. Perhaps more. She wanted to go home to her cabin more than anything. She longed for the rustling of the trees, the sun glittering in the lake, and the lack of city sounds. Most of all the latter. Here in the Big Apple—the bustling city most people seemed to love and enjoy—she found no peace and quiet. Yes, she could spend time in Central Park, but so did many other New Yorkers, not to mention tourists.

At home, she sat outside under her favorite tree with her laptop and wrote her hair-raising horror stories filled with suspense and terror. Her latest trilogy, *The Sorceress Chronicles*, her first supernatural horror storyline, had proved to be harder to write than she thought, but also so very gratifying. The calmer her life was, the more she wanted to boost the horror. Perhaps something was wrong with her after all. Maeve had certainly held that opinion for many years.

Would she be able to write in New York if she had to spend several weeks or, God forbid, months here? She was so used to her calm existence in the Adirondacks, where her closest neighbors enjoyed the peaceful refuge as much as she did. Aeron checked the time. She could ponder all this after she knew for sure how her meeting with Sylvie would pan out.

Sylvie Thorn wasn't a stereotypical Swedish woman, unless you assumed her icy demeanor was a national Swedish trait. Her chocolate hair and pale complexion emphasized her piercing, dark-blue eyes. Only Sylvie's curvy, full lips softened her somber features. She seemed tall, but it had to be an optical illusion since she couldn't be more than a couple of inches taller than Aeron's average five feet and five inches. Her elegance appeared to come effortlessly, and certainly her assuredness added to her authoritative persona.

How the hell could she have anything in common with Maeve? Aeron's mother could be elegant when it suited her, but she was hardly this composed and serious. Instead, Maeve had been the epitome of a woman seeking the fountain of perpetual youth.

Chapter Six

Manhattan—1999

"If anyone asks, you're my kid sister, okay?" Maeve was busy applying yet another layer of mascara. "Can you remember it this time?" She glanced at Aeron in the mirror. "I really like Mark, and it's not the right time to fill him in on all the details."

Aeron stood so straight her back hurt. This wasn't the first time her mother had wanted her to be someone else. Despite it being Christmas Eve and Aeron home from boarding school, Maeve had made plans with another Mr. Right. At least tonight Aeron could be a sister instead of a distant cousin. "But if Mark likes you it shouldn't matter." Flinching at the darkening thunder in Maeve's eyes, Aeron knew this hadn't been a smart thing to say.

"You're eleven years old, Aeron," Maeve said between tense lips. "You're too young to understand anything about guys, let alone hand out advice."

"I'm sorry." Studying her shoes for a moment, Aeron gathered courage to meet her mother's gaze. "It's just...you're so beautiful that it shouldn't matter." "It" referred to her birth and awkward presence in Maeve's life.

Maeve's expression changed completely. "Aw, you little pearl. My looks won't last for all eternity, even if I'm working on it. I can't be twenty-eight forever."

Aeron knew they were skidding along a topic that could set off Maeve's mood swings at any given moment. Her mother was the youngest mom among the parents of the kids in Aeron's class. Aeron's friend, Graeme Brody, always made it his business to feed Aeron the latest news. Usually, it was about other classmates or even celebrities, but the topic that kept coming up was Aeron's mother and how she affected the other parents.

Sometimes, Maeve sent Paulina to the parent-teacher meetings in Vermont, but mostly she went, almost looking ready to pick a fight. Maeve often complained about people criticizing her for having a child so early in life. "Those sanctimonious idiots," she'd hiss. "They're not concerned about Aeron. They probably assume I drove my parents to an early grave."

Aeron wondered if Maeve actually felt hurt and camouflaged her pain as drama and anger. Or did her mother truly enjoy riling the other parents that much? Maeve used certain phrases when others confronted her for being an unfit mother. It was as if she rehearsed in front of her enormous vanity mirror for any eventuality.

At one point, before she went off to boarding school, Aeron had overheard her first principal, Mrs. Davis, tell her mother that Maeve's lack of parenting skills had caused Aeron's introversion and extreme shyness. Aeron had been barely eight at the time and didn't know what introvert and extreme meant, but she would never forget how Maeve had yelled, even growled, at Mrs. Davis. Words had poured from her lips. "You clearly don't live in the modern world." Maeve had spat every letter, and even out of sight Aeron could envision her mother's expression. Pale, but with bright-red cheeks and her lips pulled back from her teeth like Paco, their neighbor's dog. "Your views are like that of a dinosaur—ancient. And just like with them, your views will eventually become extinct."

Maeve had stormed out of the office that time, furious enough to startle even the otherwise so frightening secretary who had listened to the exchange, her mouth half open. Now she snapped her lips closed as Maeve halted in front of Aeron.

"Why don't we go for ice cream?" Maeve asked, her voice suddenly soft, like she had flicked a switch.

"Ice cream?" Smiling carefully, Aeron wasn't sure if this was a trick or something Maeve said just because Mrs. Davis and her secretary could hear.

"Yes. All you can eat. We can have it instead of dinner, what do you think?" She didn't look at Aeron when she spoke, but glanced back at the principal with a triumphant expression.

"Ice cream for dinner?" Aeron gaped, much like the secretary earlier.

"Yes. You like strawberry, don't you?" Maeve pulled her down the corridor, walking so fast Aeron could just hang on and hold on to her school bag.

Aeron actually liked chocolate ice cream the best, but any ice cream for dinner was amazing. No doubt, Mrs. Davis and her secretary frowned upon Maeve's idea, but Maeve never cared about such things.

Shifting back to her memories of her eleven-year-old self, Aeron recalled how Maeve had stood in front of her large mirror. "Mark works on Wall Street. He's practically as loaded as I am, which means he's truly interested and isn't after my money."

"That's good," Aeron said weakly. She was unsure how the topic of money could have anything to do with really liking someone. If you disliked someone, all the money in the US couldn't make you like them. Not to mention love. Aeron didn't know a lot about love, but if you liked someone and then multiplied the liking by ten million, then it was love.

"Do you like him a lot?" Aeron dared to ask, proud that her voice carried.

"I do. I like him a lot." Maeve got up from the vanity and pulled off her robe. She was always like this, uninhibited and free-spirited. Having watched her mother walk around the condo in all kinds of undress ever since Aeron could remember, she paid hardly any attention to the flimsy undergarments. "I may even grow to love him one day."

"What is that like?" Aeron asked the question before she thought better of it.

"What is what like?" Maeve spoke absentmindedly as she held up two dresses on hangers and scrutinized them.

"Loving someone." Aeron instantly regretted asking, but part of her desperately wanted to know.

"Oh, love." Maeve plopped down on the bed and looked dreamy-eyed. *"I suppose that depends. But the best kind is when you forget to breathe whenever you see the person you love. You want to be with him all the time, and you never want anything, or anyone, to come between you. You know you would never be happy again, ever, if that happened."* She tilted her head and looked inquisitively at Aeron. *"Why do you ask? Any potential boyfriend I should know about?"* Maeve giggled. *"Let's hope it's not that geek Graeme Brody. He's not boyfriend material."*

That didn't make sense at all. Why wouldn't Graeme be boyfriend material? He was smart and nice, and he cared about the environment. *"Is Mark boyfriend material?"* Hiding her hands behind her back, Aeron rocked back and forth on her heels.

"You bet he is."

"Why?" Aeron knew she was pushing it, but the words broke free.

"Because he's damn sexy." Giggling again, Maeve covered her mouth with her left hand. *"If Paulina heard me she'd force me to apologize. He thinks the same thing of me, I believe. He might be the one."*

"Did you ever love someone like that? Like you never wanted to be apart?" Aeron thought she better get more questions in before Maeve resorted back to mild annoyance, which normally was the case when Aeron asked too much.

Maeve put the hangers down, her movements slow. Her eyes grew big and she sighed so deeply, Aeron feared her mother might cry in front of her. She had never witnessed her mother in tears and was pretty sure she'd freak out if Maeve actually started sobbing.

"Yes. Yes, I did." Maeve pulled her robe back on again and tied a firm knot. She now moved fast and jerkily. *"Your father."*

Aeron sat down on the vanity chair so fast her teeth nearly caught the tip of her tongue as they slammed shut. *"My—my father?"*

"You must have realized you have one?" Smirking unhappily, Maeve sat on the foot of the bed. "And yes, despite what anyone might think or say, your father was the love of my life. We weren't meant to be, that's true, but that doesn't matter. I loved him."

"You never talk about him." Aeron made sure she didn't sound accusing.

"Same reason. Too much love. Too painful." Maeve stood abruptly, indicating this talk of love and Aeron's father was over. "I'm going to wear the blue dress. Once you zip me up, you can go pick out a blue outfit from your closet. And I mean blue. Not aqua, not something bordering on purple."

Aeron burned to ask more questions about her father. Every time she brought the topic up with Paulina, the housekeeper only shook her head. "I can't tell you, Aeron," she'd say. "I didn't know him. I don't think anyone did, apart from your mother. You have to ask her."

Aeron didn't dare. Not until today, when Maeve had opened up. So now she knew two new things: Maeve knew who Aeron's father was and loved him most of all. From what Maeve had just sounded like, Aeron figured her mother loved this man more than she did her. She should be upset about that. It wasn't a nice feeling to come in second, after all. But Aeron didn't look at it that way. She'd always doubted her mother's love for her, with good reason. Now her mother talked about this amazing love she'd felt, and if she did love Aeron's father like that...surely Maeve allowed some of that love to spill over on Aeron?

She expertly zipped up her mother's dress, even if her fingers trembled. Walking back to her room, she passed a large hallway mirror and stopped to scrutinize her face. Oval and pale, with freckles on her nose and glasses that filled half of it, her face sure didn't look like her beautiful mother's. Maybe she looked like him. Her father.

As she hurried back to her mother, Aeron knew she would hate sitting at the dinner table tonight more than she usually did on her school breaks. Normally, she found it stressful and feared she might say something wrong. This evening, she realized she didn't want

Maeve to smile and carry on with some guy. She wanted to hear more about the mysterious man Maeve still loved.

"There you are. I heard Paulina get the door." Maeve reached for Aeron's right hand and squeezed it. "Remember? You're my little sister."

It was so strange. When Maeve had told her this earlier, Aeron hadn't thought anything of it. It was just her mother's way of thinking. Now, after finding out that Maeve had loved—still loved— Aeron's father, posing as her mother's little sister broke her heart.

❖

Manhattan—Present Time

Sylvie greeted Aeron and made sure her wariness of the situation didn't show. A lifetime of perfecting her mask let her smile easily at Maeve's daughter. "I'm so glad you agreed to see me, Aeron. Thank you."

Aeron pulled off her sunglasses and returned the handshake firmly, but not the smile. "As it turns out, I have quite a few questions I need answers to, and you seem like my best bet."

"I'll be happy to assist in any way I can." Wondering if she sounded too servile, Sylvie kept the polite smile going. "I find we can truly help each other if we only find a way to communicate."

Aeron took a seat at the conference table after greeting Lucas Hayes. Again, she'd arrived last, but not late. "As I see it, we need to hear my mother's will in greater detail before we draw up any agreements worth the name."

Taken aback at the cool tone in Aeron's voice, Sylvie merely nodded. "Of course."

"Well, now. I'm glad the two of you decided to at least hear the details," Lucas Hayes said after sitting down with a tablet and a folder in front of him. "Maeve's will is fairly uncomplicated and to the point. She wanted me to handle everything personally at this stage. No nosy assistants, as she put it." He smiled tightly. "She was adamant that I use as little of what she called legal mumbo-jumbo as possible. Clear rules and conditions, but nothing fancy, I believe she also said. As I mentioned yesterday, Maeve thought I was a foolish mother hen of a lawyer who kept pestering her to update her will. She was young and living her life as she saw fit, and she didn't want to think about something as unpalatable as her own demise. Eventually I managed to reach her by bringing up your future, Aeron. I never got to meet you—"

"That's not unusual. Not very many people did after I started school," Aeron said and snorted unhappily, but then made an apologetic gesture with her hands. "Sorry. Please go on."

Sylvie filed Aeron's comment away for future use. Maeve had kept the fact she had a daughter from her as well. Sylvie had never been allowed to either know about, let alone meet, Aeron, which mystified her. Why would a modern young woman, *very* young at that, have to conceal the birth of a baby? Yes, Sylvie regarded the US as quite reactionary in certain areas of the country and in some urban circles, but Aeron had been born in the late eighties—not during the previous turn of the century.

"I saw pictures of you as a young child when your mother took you on a cruise, I believe." Lucas smiled amicably. "When Maeve finally started thinking about her assets and her life situation as a single mother, it didn't take her long to figure out what she wanted. Now. I turned all essential points into a list of bullet points for you. These are the terms we have to work with." He handed a printed document to each Aeron and Sylvie.

Sylvie glanced quickly at hers. She hated being without Thomas, her personal assistant, but the meeting was too important to jeopardize anything by showing up with someone to take notes. Now she squinted at the letters, and the lines began to blur and move in an all-too-familiar pattern. She managed to make out a few words, enough to understand the essence of a few of the points. When she managed to decipher yet another sentence, she thought her eyes would pop out of their sockets. Was this what Maeve had in mind for her and Aeron? Really?

"As you see, the first item is relatively simple. The two of you need to be on good speaking terms. According to Maeve," he said, and smiled a little too broadly, "neither of you can truly learn from each other unless you, er... 'cut the bullshit.'"

"Sounds like Maeve all right." Sylvie glanced furtively at Aeron, who looked unaffected by her mother's wording. What did Maeve mean by "each other"? What was she supposed to learn from Aeron? She sure wouldn't cut it when it came to English literature or science unless they came as audio books.

"The second point stipulates how she wants you, Ms. Thorn, to—"

"Please, call me Sylvie." Raising her hand in a deflecting manner, Sylvie motioned for him to continue.

"Thank you. Anyway. She wants you and Aeron to work together at least three days a week."

"What?" Aeron raised her voice. "Three days? You're kidding. I've got a deadline to keep, and I also need to return to the Adirondacks."

"It gets worse," Sylvie said just below her breath. "Go on, Lucas." She used his name with the ease that came with moving among the rich and powerful in Manhattan on a daily basis.

"Of course. Aeron, your mother stipulates that you take the opportunity to have Sylvie guide you through the DeForest stock and investment portfolio. As of now, several different financial advisors monitor and handle your wealth, and a highly regarded board of directors supervises them. With Sylvie's assistance, Maeve wanted you to know what they're doing and learn about where the DeForest fortune stems from and how it's being used. You may have certain ideas regarding how you want the money placed, and Maeve wanted you to know how that can be done. Sylvie has the know-how."

"This might turn out to be somewhat of a challenge." Sylvie knew she wasn't helping her own agenda by sounding so perplexed and critical, but honestly, to understand the intricacies of the stock market and the machinations of it without a degree similar to her own was impossible. What had Maeve been thinking? "You're an English major, right?"

"I am. I double-majored in English and history." Her eyes darkening to an olive green, Aeron sat straight in her chair. The only thing betraying her anger was how her knuckles whitened more by the second as she held on to the documents. "I can assure you, I can be taught." She clearly dismissed Sylvie and turned to Lucas Hayes again. "Does Maeve stipulate anything else? My time is as valuable as yours."

Sylvie was reluctantly impressed that the young woman managed to keep her cool more than she, business major and then some, did.

"No. If you read farther down, your mother wants you to know enough to make an informed decision of how involved you want to be—or not."

This sounded like a smart move, something most wouldn't expect of Maeve. Sylvie hadn't witnessed the frivolous side of her business partner, only read about it in the gossip columns. According to those sources, Maeve had gone through some of the clichéd situations common to young celebrities. Drunk in public, booked once for driving under the influence, and involved in the destruction of a hotel room, which wasn't her fault, but she was there. Maeve had probably been the very first to have a so-called crotch-shot taken by the ever-present paparazzi. In between that, she'd hosted charities, which she claimed was just another reason to throw parties, but they had also brought in a lot of money for worthy causes.

"Listen," Sylvie said, determined to reel Aeron in before she decided this proposal simply wasn't worth it. "I'm sure you don't want to lose your cushy trust fund. All we have to do is work together. I fully believe we can accomplish these goals." Sylvie regarded Aeron cautiously. "As you say, you're a double major, which suggests a keen mind. I'm nothing if not clear and precise. You will also get to know my assistant, who keeps all the information on hand."

"Why the hell do you want this so much? I mean, apart from Maeve being your silent partner and you being friends or whatever." Aeron leaned forward on her elbows. The ceiling light glimmered in her wire-frame glasses and ignited the highlights in her hair.

Sylvie considered how much she wanted to reveal. "With your mother on board and according to the power of attorney she signed for me to have complete autonomy, I had the majority of the unquoted shares and ran Classic Swedish Inc. as I saw fit. Now with her unquoted shares in your hands, our agreement when it comes to the power of attorney is nullified. You're free to exercise the power of having those shares and even vote against me together with the other person who owns the rest of the shares. The two of you would have a majority. I knew I risked having Maeve and the other person outvote me, but as Maeve signed a power of attorney immediately, I felt safe. I planned to buy her out within another couple of years."

"It sounds like you really need my cooperation. So, she wants me to learn about the DeForest holdings. I wonder if she wanted the business world to entice me enough to perhaps change lanes." Aeron raised a very deliberate eyebrow. "I don't see that happening."

"Perhaps not, but as I see it, Maeve wanted you to be able to make an informed decision." Sylvie held up both her hands, palms forward.

"That may be. Anyway. So you have to show me the ropes to earn my votes, so to speak."

"That's about it," Lucas Hayes said, smiling tightly now. "What your mother had in mind—"

"Only Maeve knows what went on in that jumbled brain of hers." Aeron huffed as she knew firsthand how untrustworthy Maeve's spur-of-the-moment decisions could be. "This is yet another of her multitude of ways to bring me back into the fold. During the last five years it was her favorite pastime."

"Hey, no matter what, she was still your mother," Sylvie said without realizing what words were going to pass her lips.

"Yes, we share a gene pool. She gave birth to me, not that she ever wanted to, I'm sure. The moments she acted like a mother were so few and far between, they're irrelevant." Flustered, Aeron pressed her palms against the table as if attempting to get up. "And now you tell me I need to respect her memory? That's rich, considering how conveniently she forgot my existence whenever it suited her."

"I'm sorry." Sylvie couldn't bear to see the pain contorting Aeron's finely drawn features. Her green eyes held such shadows, yet she radiated a defiance that demanded respect.

"Don't be sorry. Let's do this. Screw Maeve's terms. I have questions and you might just sit on the answers. If you want to keep the power over your precious spa chain, you'll answer me as much as you can. We can do this while we fulfill Maeve's terms. I'll vote with you when need be, as long as we're sticking to the agreement." Wiping away a solitary tear at the outer corner of her right eye, her movements angry and rigid, Aeron projected an attitude that challenged Sylvie to respond.

"All right," she said, sounding a lot surer than she felt. She didn't know this woman. She could be entirely impossible to deal with. What if she didn't like the answers to whatever questions she had in mind? Would she suddenly decide to vote against Sylvie when it came to Classic Swedish Inc.?

"We need to draw up an agreement for this exchange so I'll know you'll stick to your promise. There's a lot at stake for me as well." Sylvie groaned inwardly at the truth in her last statement. Everything would come to fruition this year, and she would venture out on her own, independent of her father and the entire Thorn dynasty. She couldn't fail.

"Very well." Lucas Hayes spoke fast, like he was anxious to wrap up this discussion and continue with the intricacies of the will. He rubbed his temple with his thumb and straightened his legal pad. "I've written down your respective terms, and if you can fulfill Maeve's wishes in the process, I don't see any problems. There is a time limit, though."

"A time limit?" Sylvie looked from Lucas Hayes to Aeron.

"Yes. You have to show results within six months." Lucas Hayes smiled encouragingly.

Aeron snorted. "And then what? A corporate pop quiz?"

"Of sorts. Maeve suggested a written essay of your experience learning about the world of business. She thought it fitting."

"And who judges this essay?" Her eyes now narrow slits, Aeron scrutinized Lucas Hayes.

"Maeve gave me two names to contact. Let's see." He glanced down at another document, but Sylvie guessed he knew the names perfectly well yet needed to stall to get a few seconds' reprieve when it came to the laser focus of Aeron's eyes. "Helena Forsythe and Eleanor Ashcroft."

"Wonderful." Aeron groaned. "All right. Fine."

Sylvie felt bad for Aeron. Obviously, jumping through hoops designed by her mother didn't sit well. In fact, Sylvie knew she'd feel manipulated and even humiliated, as she had many times when her father pulled the strings. But if she showed any sympathy for Aeron regarding the conditions of the will, she most likely wouldn't appreciate it. After running the US branch of Thorn Industries, she'd learned to read people. The way Aeron's delicate skin tensed in fine lines around her eyes and how she kept adjusting her glasses with unsteady fingers showed how much pressure she was under.

"And you, Ms. Thorn...I apologize. Sylvie. Do you have any stipulations other than having your original agreement with Maeve honored?" Lucas Hayes lifted his glance from his legal pad.

Sylvie was about to say no, she was content, when she reeled herself in. This was her one chance to register any demands and use Aeron's presence to her advantage. "Yes," she answered firmly. "I'm flying home to Sweden for some meetings, and this would be a golden moment for Aeron to see some big sharks in action." She didn't add that the biggest of them all was Daniel Thorn. Her father made sure he ran the show no matter who else was present.

"Go to Sweden?" Aeron momentarily lost her look of cool aloofness. Instead she appeared genuinely taken aback.

"Yes. It's a month from now."

"Oh, God. I'll never be ready to meet my deadline." Muttering, Aeron adjusted her glasses once more. "But sure. Why not? I haven't been to Europe since the cruise Lucas mentioned. I suppose I can manage."

"What deadline?" Sylvie had no idea what Aeron was talking about, and Lucas Hayes seemed just as nonplussed. It hadn't dawned on Sylvie that Aeron might have a job.

"Oh, for heaven's sake." Aeron shook her head at Sylvie. "Regardless of my cushy trust fund, I do work. But I don't suppose you or anyone else would believe that. Well, go figure."

"I'm sorry for being presumptuous." Sylvie was angry at herself for losing her edge and jumping to conclusions, no matter how logical they'd seemed earlier. In fact, this was like looking into a mirror of sorts. Sylvie had also set out to make something of herself, albeit for different reasons, but still...Maeve had been eccentric and irresponsible, but not deliberately cruel and disdainful like Sylvie's father could be. "May I ask what you do for a living that entails a deadline?" She could feel her own quotation marks around the word hanging between them.

"I have a deadline with my publisher." Aeron spoke in a meticulous, mock-pedagogical tone as if she spoke to a preschooler.

"Publisher?" Of all things Aeron could have said, this was the most unexpected.

"I'm a horror novelist," Aeron said casually, as if this were something entirely ordinary.

"Excuse me?" Sylvie tried to grasp the concept.

"I write horror stories."

Oh, God. How the hell would this give-and-take agreement work out? Sylvie considered herself well-read and accomplished in many topics, but this genre was so outside her comfort zone, it was ridiculous. She pulled herself together. "I'm impressed. It's normally quite hard to surprise me."

The tiniest of smiles played at the corners of Aeron's full pink lips. "Always something."

Sylvie had always presumed that horror novelists were young men, or even older ones, but hardly a young, privileged woman like Aeron. Then again, a privileged woman, Mary Shelley, had written *Frankenstein* a long time ago, so clearly her prejudice was talking. "Well, from what it seems, neither of us knows very much about each other. Why don't we wrap it up for today? Or do you want to throw yourself into it?"

"Really? Wow. I thought I'd have to make an appointment to see the CEO of Thorn Industries US." Aeron tilted her head, a smirk playing on her lips.

"As a matter of fact, I canceled today's meetings and appointments. If you want to get started, I'm game."

The smirk vanished. "I'm planning to meet Paulina at Maeve's condo. She insists I take some of my childhood things back home with me. If you want, you can tag along. Might be good to talk a bit outside of these offices." Aeron winced and looked through her lashes at Lucas Hayes. "No offense."

"None taken. I'll have the paperwork ready for you to sign tomorrow. If you have any idea where you will be, I'll swing by before I'm off to DC." The lawyer looked fatigued and also relieved, for which Sylvie couldn't blame him. Handling Maeve's unorthodox will must feel like sitting on her childhood's crazy pony that seemed hell-bent on sending her headlong into the hedge around the paddock.

"Sounds good." Sylvie stood and so did Aeron. A gentle scent of lilacs and vanilla emanated from the woman she'd spend a lot of time with during the upcoming months. Sylvie's lungs caved in and she found it near-impossible to inhale new oxygen. She hadn't had this type of reaction to another woman in ages—and now, Maeve's daughter? Not likely. She stole another glance at the woman dressed in a wide, flowing skirt and leather jacket. Sylvie would never consider wearing such a combination, but it suited Aeron perfectly. A mix between rural and urban. Surprisingly attractive.

"You ready? I thought I might just get it over with." Aeron pulled her shoulders up and shuddered. "Paulina can be very persuasive."

Sylvie nodded curtly. "I'm all set. You will contact us when you have the paperwork ready, Lucas?"

The lawyer quickly stood. Perhaps he'd feared bloodshed or something equally violent. Sylvie smiled inwardly.

"I'll send digital copies for you to sign via your computers." Lucas Hayes shook their hands and escorted them to the elevators. "Have a nice day, ladies." He waited until the door opened and then strode off.

"Was it just me, or did he almost run to get away from us?" Aeron pressed her fingertips to her lips, but she couldn't hide the smile.

"I think you're right." Sylvie relaxed. "Guess that's why we get the paperwork as digi-documents."

Aeron nodded and stood silent as they rode the elevator to the first floor. As they stepped out on the sidewalk, she turned to Sylvie after putting on her sunglasses. "You can change your mind if you want to."

"What?" Sylvie flinched.

"Hang on. Don't freak out. I meant about going to the condo. If you'd rather not." Aeron kicked the toe of her shoe into the ground behind her. Was she that nervous?

"I don't mind joining you. That way, you can start with your questions right away, and perhaps being around Maeve's things will make you come up with new ones. You never know what you'll find."

"Okay. Thanks." Aeron hailed a cab, and as they climbed into the backseat, Aeron's enticing scent once again overwhelmed Sylvie's senses. *God help me.*

CHAPTER SEVEN

The condo was eerily quiet. Aeron stepped inside, almost on her toes, and half expected her mother to greet her with a "Now look what the cat finally dragged in." She would move with her typical saunter: feline and seductive no matter whom she was talking to. Instead, the silence filled every part of Aeron and once again confirmed that her larger-than-life mother was truly gone. It was hard to breathe, and her steps echoed against the hardwood floor in the hallway.

"This is bizarre," Aeron muttered. "I knew it was a bad idea." A movement to the side made her jump. Paulina came from the kitchen, wiping her hands on a dishtowel.

"Aeron. And Ms. Thorn. What a nice surprise. Did everything go well at the lawyer's office?"

"For the most part," Aeron said, glancing at Sylvie. "Maeve's conditions were rather specific, and as much as I want to wash my hands of it all, I...I just couldn't."

"I'm certain Maeve somewhere, somehow, is aware of this."

"Who knows?" Aeron barely managed the brief response, and she didn't want to go into detail. However, the interested and caring expression on Paulina's face made it impossible to remain cold and distant. This approach had worked fine with Maeve, as she usually chatted about this and that and barely made sure she had Aeron's attention. Usually she relayed some juicy gossip about celebrities or people Aeron had never heard of. Tuning out her mother's bright, animated voice, Aeron would get lost in thought about some story she yearned to write.

Now she looked around at the condo that used to be her home. It seemed like an empty shell without Maeve at its center, keeping it alive. Maeve, who had liked white, gold, and marble. Some rooms had accent colors in light blue, pink, or pastel green. It was like a little girl's cotton-candy dream home, and for a moment, Aeron wondered if the color choices indicated how Maeve never quite grew up. Only Aeron's room had stood out. A navy-colored accent wall, light-gray wallpaper on the other three, and a bedspread with the pattern of a starry sky.

Maeve had surely turned her room into a guestroom, or even a gym. Glancing back at Sylvie, she shrugged uneasily. "This room used to be mine." She turned the doorknob and half closed her eyes at what she might see.

"What do you mean, used to be?" Sylvie peered over Aeron's shoulder. "Looks like a teen room to me."

Snapping her eyes open, Aeron stared at her room. It really *was* hers. As far as her darting gaze could tell, Maeve had kept it just as it was all these years.

"Your mother had this dream you'd come home one day and be surprised," Paulina said from behind.

"Maeve was right. I am...surprised." Shocked even, she stepped inside and studied her room, so much as she remembered it but also different. Realizing the room hadn't changed, but she had, Aeron slumped down on the foot of the bed. The books in her built-in shelves were still filled with all her favorite novels from early childhood to late teens. She needed to ship those. She hadn't thought they were still here, but since they were, she couldn't imagine getting rid of them.

"No wonder you majored in English," Sylvie said. "May I look?"

"Sure," Aeron said, absentminded. She continued to her desk by the window. Maeve had suggested a girly looking one, white with glass knobs and gold ornamental décor. Instead, Aeron had managed, together with Paulina, to persuade Maeve to buy her a large, practical desk. Maeve had insisted she hire someone to paint it white, something Aeron had agreed with as long as there was no gold or glass.

Instead, when it came to glass, her collection of orbs sat in a glass cabinet on the left wall. Eighteen of them, carefully selected at markets and thrift stores, reflected the light from the window.

"She had me dust them twice a week even if they sit in a cabinet." Paulina smiled reverently and stroked Aeron's arm.

"Really? Well, you must've kept everything clean and tidy over the years because it looks like I'm still living here, which is surreal as hell." Trembling inside, Aeron didn't know where to look to calm herself. She'd spent so much time here, mostly alone, as she hadn't wanted to subject what few friends she had to Maeve's eccentricities. If one of her friends had mentioned one word at home about her mother, she wouldn't have been allowed to spend time with Aeron anymore.

"Pippi Longstocking!" Sylvie's unusually excited voice was a welcome reprieve.

"Yes. I have all of them." Aeron walked over to the bookshelves, where Sylvie stood caressing the spine of the first Pippi Longstocking book. "I used to dream I was Annika. Not Pippi. That was reaching for the stars, but her best friend suited me well. Then I'd have a brother, Tommy, and I wouldn't—" She almost said "be so alone" but stopped herself in time.

"I wanted to be Pippi." Sylvie kept reading the spines of the books. "I wanted to be strong, capable, and fearless."

"And judging from your position in the business world, you must have succeeded." Aeron spoke casually, but the deepening frown between Sylvie's perfectly arched eyebrows made her realize she'd hit a nerve.

"One would think so, yes." Sylvie took a step back, and her stilted words showed how uneasy she'd become.

"Which objects do you want me to ship to the Adirondacks?" Paulina asked.

Grateful again for the interruption, Aeron thought fast. "The orbs. The books. Everything in the desk drawers. I guess the desk has to go into storage for now, but that's it."

"But what about the closet and all the clothes?" Paulina looked up from her notepad.

"Charity. Furniture, too, if you don't want it. If you want to give anything here to your kids and grandkids, go right ahead."

"Are you sure?" Paulina looked hesitant. "I don't want you to regret it later—"

"I won't."

"You need to go through your mother's desk and the safe. I have the key and the code. Mr. Hayes has already inventoried the safe for the sake of the will, but he said you needed to look at these things yourself."

"Can I wait and sort through them when I'm back home?" Oh, please, she couldn't go through all that now. The mere thought of having to immerse herself in Maeve's private things...As much as she wanted to find out about the real Maeve, who her mother genuinely was, she was now close to nauseous.

"If you weren't staying at a hotel—" Paulina looked around them for a moment. "You should stay here, take your time and sort through everything. If you rush through the documents, you may miss something important."

"No. Paulina, you know why I can't stay here. Besides, you need to start putting your own mark here to make it your own." Aeron didn't want to say as much, but in her mind, this was like Maeve's tomb and perhaps a memorial of sorts to her weird childhood. Her mother's ghost seemed to float through the rooms. At this thought, Aeron had to pinch herself to avoid a full-blown panic attack. This wasn't the time or the place for that. "I'll be staying at the hotel for the next few months or so. I'll have everything shipped there."

"I have several spare rooms," Sylvie said.

Astonished, Aeron turned to stare at her. Sylvie stood resting one hand on the back of what used to be her favorite place in her room, second to the bookshelves, her navy-blue armchair. She looked composed and in command as usual, but something new in her eyes, something that set off tingles in the back of her neck under her hair, made Aeron pause.

"You mean I should store all the paperwork and so on at your place?"

"It's large. I never use the room at the end of the hallway anyway. If you can stand a few boxes and knickknacks, you're welcome to it." Sylvie's posture didn't change, but her hand curled into a loose fist. Aeron was curious if Sylvie expected her to decline or if she was wary Aeron might accept.

"I'm not sure that's a good idea." Aeron spoke slowly, wanting her words to sink in. "I'd be in your hair often until I finished going through everything. Then consider the fact that we'll be together to fulfill the terms of the will...God, Sylvie, you'll be totally fed up with me, and that might jeopardize everything for both of us."

"The contents of the safe and the desk might stir questions and thoughts I can help you with, or at least help find the answers elsewhere if needed. I don't think we'd be anywhere near each other's hair. You'll be in the back room with your things, and I'll be working in my study like I normally do."

Sylvie sounded so self-assured and logical, it was damn near impossible to argue with her, but Aeron knew she herself had a point also. "I'm still worried I might alienate you and make you back out."

Paulina shook her head. "Aeron. That's a good suggestion. As I understand it, you both have a stake in keeping a collaboration going."

"We do. Remember you're traveling with me to Sweden later on. If you have all the papers sorted, at least roughly, you can look at it as a vacation or a study trip." Sylvie's smile was tenser. Was she worried this hurdle would break their fragile commitment before they actually signed the deal?

"This is awkward as hell, but all right, since you insist. We'll decide on designated hours when it's okay for me to come over."

"Sounds all right to me," Sylvie said, looking relieved in a way that didn't make sense, unless she truly was close to panic that Aeron might cause her to lose control over her company.

"Excellent," Paulina said and wiggled her notepad. "Give me your address and I'll handle everything."

"What...no." Aeron knew she was repeating herself, but this was just wrong. "You're no longer employed by my mother—"

"Actually, I am. Until the last of this month. Please, let me to do this for you." She placed a gentle hand on Aeron's arm.

How could she ever deny the woman who'd been like a true mother to her? Of course she couldn't. "Okay. Thank you, Paulina." She squeezed Paulina's hand.

Sylvie gave Paulina her information and then called her building supervisor to let the movers in with the boxes in her backroom.

Aeron walked through the other rooms, glancing from one object to another. She added most of the finer pieces, heirlooms that she mostly remembered for never being allowed to touch them. Maeve would shriek at her if she came too close, but Paulina had taught her a way to watch them with her hands behind her back. As far as she remembered, Maeve must have stopped worrying so much about them eventually. Aeron couldn't remember how old she'd been back then, but perhaps five or six.

"Why don't you open the safe?" Paulina caught up with her and handed her a sealed envelope. "Here's the code, and I don't believe you'll find more than you can carry."

"All right." Accepting the key, Aeron left Sylvie and Paulina in her room and walked slowly into her mother's study. She'd rarely been in here. Maeve used this room only for the minimum of paperwork she took part in.

A large mirror, hanging on the wall into which the safe was built, swung outward without a sound. Aeron's fingers trembled as she ripped open the envelope. Reading the numbers on the card, she had a vague sense that they were familiar. As she began twisting the wheel on the safe, it dawned on her. It was the time and date of her birth, but in reverse.

She pulled the handle, and the safe door opened just as quietly as the hinged mirror had. A few thick envelopes on the top shelf turned out to contain hundred-dollar bills. Aeron blinked. All that cash. Didn't Maeve use a credit card like everyone else? Or did she keep this in case of emergency only? How strange. She didn't count it now but knew she would later, just to try to figure out what kind of sum her mother would consider enough for an emergency.

The second shelf held at least ten different cases of jewelry. Sighing, Aeron knew she wouldn't take any of them with her. Not only were they not her taste, but she rarely wore any jewelry except for her beloved watch. Diamonds, rubies, and emeralds crowded the velvet boxes. It was odd. Even if she would never put them on, they fascinated her.

❖

Manhattan—1996

"Look, Aeron," Maeve said and held up a red, sparkly necklace. "The son of a Saudi-Arabian sheik gave me this. He said it complemented my eyes. Here. Let's see it on you."

Aeron stood willingly next to her mother's desk and allowed her to place the necklace around her neck. The stones chilled her skin and Aeron didn't like the feel of the necklace, but she remained still and basked in the warm smile on Maeve's face.

"You look like a little princess," Maeve said. "But you need more. Look at these matching earrings that clip on." She attached them to Aeron's earlobes and snapped them shut. They hurt and Aeron wanted to tear them off, but she didn't dare. Her mother was playing with her, and that hardly ever happened. She clenched her jaw to endure the pinching sensation in her ears. "But you have to smile, like a real princess. They all smile. All the time."

Aeron did her best. She stretched her lips but couldn't keep the tears from forming in the corners of her eyes. Panicked now, she tried to blink, fought all she could to force them back, but blinking only made them spill over and run down her cheeks.

"You're crying?" Maeve's glittering smile vanished. "You're wearing princess jewelry worth eighty thousand dollars and you're crying?" She leaned back and folded her arms across her chest.

"I love them, Maeve. I really do. B-but they hurt."

"What do you mean, hurt?" Looking only slightly less angry now, Maeve ran her eyes over the rubies. "For heaven's sake. Your ears are like tomatoes." She unclipped the earrings and winced as she looked at Aeron's ears. "Are you allergic?"

Allergic? Afraid her not knowing would make her mother even more annoyed, Aeron only shrugged.

"I'll have Paulina bring it up with Dr. Burke on your next visit. Perhaps this time he'll do a proper workup and not just brush my worries away." She took Aeron by the shoulders and shook her lightly. "I worry about you all the time, you know."

"Yes." Aeron did know this. Maeve told her this often, especially after Aeron made her angry somehow.

"You're smart. I've told your teacher this, and that god-awful principal too. I've told them you're smart. You're too shy. That's your biggest problem, and you better grow out of it fast or people will walk right over you. I learned that the hard way."

Confused, Aeron only nodded. What did Maeve mean about people walking right over her? Would they push her to the ground like some kids liked to do on the school playground? She debated asking Maeve if that's what she meant but thought better of it and saved the question for Paulina. Paulina never made Aeron feel nervous or that she needed to think about every word in advance.

"Good thing you're off to school in Vermont soon. There you'll be just one rich kid among other ones. I'm told this will build your character and bring you out of your shell." Maeve unclasped the ruby necklace and replaced it in the velvet box with the earrings. "This means we need to be apart a lot, but you can't be around me all the time. It's not good for your independence."

Aeron wanted to call out to her mother to stop speaking like this, with such frightening words and not to use words like "independence" that she didn't quite understand. Did it have something to do with the Fourth of July? She had no idea.

"When will I go to Vermont, Maeve?" Aeron dared to ask in her most girly, polite voice. She needed the information but didn't want to get Maeve all angry again.

"When you start third grade. In a year."

"Oh."

"Aren't you pleased that I'm looking out for your future? If we get you into the list of schools I've looked up, you're a shoo-in at any of the Ivy League universities. Anyone who told me I'd just end up screwing up my kid by being a young mom can eat their heart out."

Feeling her eyes go big at the last part, Aeron hoped this was yet another one of what Paulina called "Maeve's sayings" and that nobody would actually be forced to eat their own heart. She had no idea what Ivy League meant other than it was important and had to do with school. Shoo-in. Curious at that particular word, she dared to ask her mother again.

"That just means you're sure to get in and be successful."
Maeve stood and patted Aeron's head. "Run along to Paulina now. For some reason, she thinks you need to learn to set the table, though I don't understand why. I'll put the jewelry away for when you're older. We'll toughen those little earlobes up before you know it."

Afraid Maeve would want to start right away after all, Aeron scurried toward the door.

"Aeron? Aren't you forgetting something?" Maeve's voice made her stop and turn, her heart thundering. Her mother pointed at her cheek. "Don't I deserve a kiss for playing princess?"

Relieved, Aeron hurried back and pecked Maeve neatly on the cheek. "No sloppy kisses. We're not dogs" was one of Maeve's sayings.

To her surprise, Maeve pulled her in for a hug. "You were so pretty in those rubies. I'll give them to you when I'm old. By then you will be used to wearing all kinds of jewelry."

Inhaling Maeve's scent, Aeron pressed her forehead gently against her mother's neck and nodded.

"Now, run along and set the silly table. Tell Paulina I'm dining out after all. Marcel is picking me up in an hour."

Disappointed that Maeve wouldn't see how well she could set the table with Paulina's help, Aeron was still thrilled about the hug. Usually she had to settle for quick fingers through her hair or perhaps equally quick strokes by the back of them across her cheek.

Aeron turned to look at her mother from the hallway. Maeve was leaning back into her large leather desk chair and held the velvety box close to her chest for a long time with a dreamy expression. As happy as she was for the hug, it stung that Maeve would hug the precious ruby necklace and the hurtful earrings for so much longer.

❖

Manhattan—Present Day

"Aeron? Do you have any questions for me as far—oh my. They're stunning." Sylvie gazed down at the open jewelry boxes spread out before Aeron on the desk. As she turned her eyes back to Aeron's face, she realized she'd interrupted a not-so-good situation. "I'm sorry. I didn't mean to intrude. I'll go back out to Paulina."

"No. Stay." Aeron's voice was deeper than usual and husky in a way that made Sylvie wonder if she'd been crying. Her face didn't show any traces of tears, but she was pale and her eyes had definitely glazed over. "You like them? The rubies?"

"Of course. They're stunning. I actually saw Maeve wear them."

"Oh, yeah? I never did. Not that I can remember." Aeron examined the contents of the box again. "Funny. I remember the earrings being clip-ons."

"Now there's a coincidence." Sylvie kept her voice even as Aeron looked close to tears still. "She told me that too. She changed them because apparently the clip-ons hurt her earlobes."

Aeron jerked her head up, and for a moment Sylvie thought she might burst into tears for real. Instead, Aeron began to laugh. She held on to the box and laughed and laughed. Once she was able to control herself, she refocused on Sylvie. Something devilish danced in her eyes. "You like them? You can have them. Any of these." She gestured toward the boxes.

"What?" Sylvie could hardly believe her ears, but then deduced that Aeron was being facetious. "Thank you for the offer," she said with mock sincerity. "I rarely wear any jewelry. Mostly watches." She raised her sleeve.

Aeron gaped. "You're kidding."

"What?" Sylvie said again, realizing too late she was repeating herself.

"We have the exact same watch. A black Zenith Zero-G." Aeron held up her arm, making her sleeve fall back. "See?"

The coincidence was remarkable, Sylvie had to give Aeron that, but that wasn't why she couldn't stop looking at the woman surrounded by jewelry worth a fortune. Aeron's eyes glittered at the welcome break in all the somberness of late. Aeron's laughter was the most adorable, contagious sound Sylvie had heard in a long time—if ever. And what worried her most was how alluring Aeron looked where she sat looking up at Sylvie, completely guileless, at least for the moment.

Sobering quickly, Sylvie reminded herself she was in this for her independence and to secure the investment Maeve had made. Aeron in turn had her own agenda, based in what seemed to be a highly dysfunctional relationship with her mother. Sylvie knew they had more in common than cool watches. In her opinion, Maeve's eccentricities were nothing compared to her father Daniel's ideas about how to raise a child. Then again, she hadn't grown up in this condo, so perhaps she was wrong.

"I'm not joking," Aeron said, breaking Sylvie's train of thought. "If there's any jewelry you'd like, feel free."

"I assume you know some of their worth?" Sylvie glanced at the sparkling stones, the muted rose gold, and the intricate filigree white gold. All of it was enough to pull anyone in, no matter if you actually wore such pieces or not.

"I do. At least I'll never forget that this," Aeron pointed at the ruby set, "was worth eighty thousand when I was seven years old." She closed the boxes. "Paulina?"

"I'm here." Paulina stepped inside. "Oh my."

"That's what I said," Sylvie murmured, which elicited a raised eyebrow from Aeron, another thing far too charming about Maeve's daughter.

"Paulina. I intend to auction Maeve's jewelry. All of it. The money will go to the Belmont Foundation. Somehow Maeve found out about it, and since I'm greedy enough to not let the entire estate go to them, I can at least sell a few things that neither of us wants and give them the proceeds." She tilted her head. "Unless you'd like to have any of her necklaces, Paulina?"

It was close to comical to watch Paulina's expression. "Oh, absolutely not." Shock mixed with horror at the idea slid across her face.

Sylvie liked Maeve's former housekeeper and cook more and more. She seemed like a woman with a good head on her shoulders who really cared for Aeron. If some of the indicators proved correct, Maeve had left a lot to be desired as a mother, and Sylvie surmised that Paulina had picked up as much slack as she could. Now she'd reside here, unless she chose to sell, which would be totally in her right. Either way, she wouldn't have to worry about the upkeep or the maintenance. She'd no doubt earned this and more by having to deal with all sides of Maeve on a daily basis.

"All right. I'll leave them here for now, Paulina. I'll call Sotheby's and have them appraised and so on, later." Aeron put the boxes back in the safe and pulled out a thick envelope from the bottom shelf. "And what's this?" she murmured. She opened the envelope and peered inside. Frowning, she examined the first document, kept in a transparent plastic folder.

"Oh, fuck." Aeron grew pale and squeezed the edges of the document through the plastic. "I hadn't even thought about this."

"What is it, Aeron?" Paulina walked over to the now-slumped figure in the leather desk chair. She didn't try to read the document but looked worriedly at Aeron.

"My birth certificate. Look. She told me the truth all along. She said I'd never find out who he was."

Paulina took the document and read quickly. "Oh, honey." She handed the document back.

"What's wrong? Can I help?" Sylvie felt useless in the face of such resignation.

"Not unless you're psychic. She listed my father as unknown on my birth certificate. On several occasions, she told me he was the love of her life. Then she'd be either drunk or high, or both, and she'd say I was half an orphan, that I'd never know this wonderful man's name because she'd omitted it on my birth certificate. I suppose I thought she was just being vengeful and that when I became an adult, I'd be able to find out. When I grew older, I'd moved on and didn't care anymore one way or the other. Kind of." Aeron regarded Sylvie with empty eyes. "I'll never know how you could put any sort of faith in that woman."

"I'm not psychic, not even by a long shot, but she did talk about a man she referred to as the love of her life to me as well. She let slip his first name and her nickname for him on more than one occasion. That should be at least something to go on."

Aeron sat up straight so fast, she nearly clocked Paulina on the chin. "Shit. Sorry, Paulina." Placing both hands on the desk, Aeron made Sylvie feel positively nailed to the wall. "For real? Are you certain she wasn't fooling you?"

"Yes. I'm quite real, thank you. No, I can't be certain, but what motive could she have for lying to me?"

"Oh, I can think of a few." But now the fire was back in Aeron's green eyes. "And?"

"She called him either by a nickname, Captain Aero, or simply Joshua." Sylvie wished she could have told Aeron more. She hadn't paid much attention to anything but the business up to a point. Only when she'd realized that Maeve was trying to learn and was asking both her and Helena Forsythe about business did Sylvie became aware of the person behind the socialite and party princess. When she'd let Maeve in, she also felt she was about to gain a really loyal friend. Perhaps if Maeve had lived, she'd have told Sylvie about Aeron and what caused her to live such a dangerous, destructive life in between bouts of true regret and remorse.

"Sylvie? Captain Aero. Aeron. That can't be a total coincidence, can it?" Aeron's voice was small as she sat there with her knees pulled up to meet her chin. The skirt flowed around her, and she'd removed her leather jacket. Her hair, slightly wavy and curling around her temples, made her look even more vulnerable.

"No," Sylvie said softly and sat on the edge of the large desk. "I don't think it's a coincidence at all.

Chapter Eight

Y ou're kidding!" Noelle sounded so stunned, Sylvie had to smile as she set her cell phone on speaker mode. She could envision the young woman tossing her blond-and-black hair back over her shoulder and frenetically waving Helena over. "I'm stunned. Absolutely stunned."

Sylvie was cooking for once, a skill she'd learned later in life, which made it a true pleasure. "She's moving in with you?" Noelle's voice nearly squeaked the last word.

Nearly choking on a piece of raw broccoli, Sylvie coughed to clear her throat. "No. No! Listen to what I'm saying. Aeron DeForest is storing her mother's paperwork here in my back room. She'll come over and have a place to read in peace and quiet. She can't keep such documents in her hotel room. Maeve's unexpected death is still a hot topic in the tabloid press. Sooner or later they'll figure out about Aeron—I'm honestly not sure why they haven't already—and then all hell will break loose for her. I wonder if she realizes this."

"As a person who's been through my fair share of misleading headlines, I don't think she does. Maeve kept her well-hidden. Helena knew of a child but had honestly forgotten about it, as Maeve never said a word. And according to Helena, there were rumors about an illegitimate younger sister, or even a poor cousin, or whatever story Maeve used to spin." Noelle sighed.

"That's yet another thing I don't get. Having a child out of wedlock, even if you come from ancient money and your parents are close to Manhattan royalty, wasn't that big a deal in 1989, was it? Not in Sweden anyway." Sylvie placed the pieces of broccoli in the boiling water. The thought of a Swedish potato-broccoli gratin made her mouth water.

"Ah, but that's where you're wrong." Helena's well-modulated voice came over the speaker. "Anna-Belle and Graham DeForest ran a tight ship. Maeve was a bit of a wild child, as you can imagine, and her parents came down hard on any sign she might disobey their strict set of rules. As I recall, and as rumor has it, Maeve fell in love at a very young age, and Aeron was the result. I can't even imagine her parents' reaction."

Sylvie began chopping vegetables for a salad. Her mind spun around the vision of Aeron sitting among the extravagant jewelry in Maeve's study, looking as if she'd returned to her childhood for a moment. "What happened to her parents? I mean, really?"

"They were killed in a plane crash when their private jet ran into an electrical storm on its way back from Rio." Her voice somber, Helena spoke gently. "I believe it was in 1992. Maeve was twenty-one years old and the sole heir to the DeForest empire."

Sylvie stopped chopping. That would make Maeve a twenty-one-year-old single mother of a three-year-old at the time. Orphaned, an heiress, she'd surely had to pay some sort of price for having a child with a secret lover at her age. That could screw with anyone's mind, and it didn't take a genius to figure out it'd ultimately ended up hurting Aeron.

"What are you doing? Tap dancing?" Noelle probably felt it was time to change the subject and lighten the mood.

"Sorry. I'm making a salad."

"You're *cooking*?" Noelle gave a contagious chuckle.

"I am. I like to keep up with my Swedish heritage, you know."

"Aha," Noelle said. "Don't tell me. Meatballs."

"Not at all." She told them what she was making.

"Hold on. We're coming over." Helena joined them again. "Sounds really good."

"And here I thought you were all about sushi and Asian food and so on." Sylvie tossed the salad and placed the bowl in the fridge. "This is pretty big on carbs, you know."

"I'm told every inch of me is adorable and lovable—ouch. Why are you nudging me?" Now Noelle was laughing out loud. "Helena just went the loveliest shade of pink."

"I bet." Sylvie tried to picture her stylish, in-control friend blush. Only Noelle could cause the stern business tycoon to react like that. "You should be ashamed of yourself." She grinned to herself.

"Oh, I am. My lack of decorum devastates me." Noelle sighed dramatically, and then Sylvie heard the sound of a kiss. "See? Very contrite."

"God, woman. And why am I marrying you again?" Helena asked, sounding a bit strained.

"Again? Oh, you mean, why at all? You adore me. You *love* me. We've already been through this."

"Hey, you two. I'm hanging up if you're going to get all lovey-dovey on me." Sylvie was only half joking. She loved these two women, who indeed were her closest friends in the US, but their love was radiant whether on the phone or if you were in the same room. Noelle was a stunning, biracial young woman, and Helena was of the same stock Maeve and Aeron came from—old, white money. For Helena and Noelle to find love and come out as they did amazed Sylvie. She wasn't envious, not in a begrudging kind of way, but she couldn't help feel a sting in her abdomen every time she saw the two of them together. They only had to be in the same room for everyone to realize they were soulmates to the core.

"Aw, don't do that," Noelle said, sounding both apologetic and amused. "We'll behave."

"What do you mean 'we'?" Helena snorted.

"Yeah, yeah. Now back to Sylvie and her tenant," Noelle said.

"She's not moving in." Sylvie groaned. "But," she said, "she will be here quite a bit while she goes through Maeve's papers. Combined with us being forced together by the will, I'm...concerned." Not sure how she could, or if she even should, explain what she meant,

Sylvie left the rest unsaid. If she let on how Aeron had managed to seep in through a forgotten crack in her armor, Helena and Noelle would ask follow-up questions and try to strategize. Especially Noelle, who undeniably wanted the entire world to be as happy as she was with Helena. Such plans and intrigues could only lead to heartache and unimaginable trouble.

"You're worried she'd crowd you or go back on her word?" Noelle sounded sympathetic.

"She can't do the latter once she signs the mutual agreement," Helena said. "But crowd you, yes. I can see where that might screw with your Swedish desire to have your space."

"You make me sound like some old recluse." It was Sylvie's time to snort, but Helena wasn't wrong. She did have a deep desire for solitude that her former lovers had never understood. They'd figured once they were seeing each other, they ought to try for the super-glue approach. One woman in particular had, uninvited, brought a suitcase with clothes, toiletries, medication, and, to Sylvie's horror, framed photographs of her immediate family. She only made it past the door because of Sylvie's complete shock, but soon found herself out in the corridor—suitcase, framed photos, and all. After her, Sylvie vowed to not date for a long time.

Considering she hadn't actively sought any woman out, not even a one-night stand, in more than two years, Sylvie wondered if she was becoming a hermit. In the early days of her friendship with Helena and, later, Noelle, they'd dropped subtle hints about many lovely women they both knew who might be a good fit for her. Sylvie had gone on a few blind dates, but as one of them had turned out to be the I'm-moving-in lady, she'd asked them to put a brake on their efforts. In retrospect it was interesting to notice that her friends must have considered her rather gloomy, as their proffered friends were mostly upbeat, and Moving-In had been downright chirpy.

"We can always pop over and defuse any potential situation if we're in town." Noelle's jewelry, which she always wore in abundance, rattled as she took the phone. "Once I've cut the last two tracks on my next album, we plan to visit Carolyn and Annelie. We haven't seen them for five months. It'll be great."

"In California?" Sylvie's mood sank below zero. She knew of Caroline Black, as the woman was one of America's most famous screen actors. When she had married Annelie Peterson, it had given the beautiful blonde instant fame as well. If Helena and Noelle weren't planning to be in New York while she was at the mercy of the agreement with Aeron, things would be much harder.

"No, are you kidding? California in the summer?" Noelle said. "It's even worse than New York that time of year. They've invited us to their cabin in the Adirondacks. We were there last winter during a storm, remember? It'll be great to see it all green and lush."

"Adirondacks? You've got to be kidding." Sylvie had begun to select a red wine but now stopped in front of her wine cooler.

"What do you mean?" Helena asked.

"Aeron DeForest lives in the Adirondacks."

"Oh, shit." Noelle gasped. "That's such a coincidence. Or...a sign!"

"Not again," Sylvie said with something between a moan and a whimper. "A sign."

"Yes!" Sounding enthusiastic rather than deterred, Noelle continued. "What an amazing opportunity. You can come with us, and the two of you can stay at Aeron's place and we with Carolyn and Annelie, and—"

"Hold it, hold it." Sylvie had pulled a bottle of Coppo Barbera from the cooler but now shoved it back in. She needed a real drink. "I'm not going to crash your friend's cabin, nor am I going to invite myself to Aeron's home. Please, Noelle. No more scheming. I know you mean well—"

"But—"

"Darling. Remember last time you tried to convince Sylvie to go out with your studio manager's sister?" Helena asked gently. "You were so certain then, and that's when Sylvie came close to issuing a friendly restraining order."

"Shit. I know. I know. I'm sorry. Again."

Sylvie couldn't bear for Noelle to sound so contrite, even if she was relieved her friend was backing off. "Don't apologize. You couldn't know she was as needy as she was crazy."

Noelle guffawed. "But surely Aeron's not needy and crazy?" she asked, her voice almost pleading.

"Noelle." Sylvie had reached the living room and poured herself a finger of brandy.

"Right. Right." Clearly giving up, Noelle chatted amicably about her latest record and about their honeymoon details. As the gratin was ready, they hung up after arranging to have lunch together in a few days.

Carrying her food out on the balcony that faced the back of the building, she felt a certain chill in the air. She switched on the gas patio heater and hurried in for a cardigan and her cell phone. As the CEO of Thorn Industries, she had to be available in case of an emergency. Her subordinates knew exactly what qualified as such, as she'd taught herself, and then them, the art of delegating.

She'd decided to air the wine after all and now poured herself half a glass to go with her vegetarian meal. She once in a while had fish, but never red meat or poultry. As a young girl she'd come to hate meat of any type. Her mother and her two brothers, Sylvie's uncles who lived in northern Sweden, loved hunting just about anything all over the country. Their freezers were always stocked with moose, deer, duck, and hare, which didn't sit right with the fourteen-year-old Sylvie.

Taking a stand against killing for sport, rather than out of necessity, Sylvie had refused to listen to her mother's arguments. In retrospect, it had been her first true rebellious experience. It was also the first time she'd experienced what happened when she openly went against her father.

❖

"I don't understand why you're so upset, Sylvie. It's not like we leave the game to rot in the woods. We do eat the meat. You know that," Camilla Thorn said with exasperation as she put on her bright-orange vest and hat. The rest of her hunting outfit was camouflage patterned, which didn't make much sense to Sylvie. Unless the deer were color-blind, why bother with camouflage

when you wore safety-colored garments so your own hunting party wouldn't shoot you?

"Some of it you eat, yes." Sylvie wanted to stomp her foot from sheer frustration. "You don't get it, Mother. It's not like we have to. We're not some impoverished, starving family whose only means of survival is to shoot a hare or a duck every now and then."

"This type of meat is no different than what we buy at the store. Steaks and pork chops have all been living beings as well, you know." Camilla resorted to that tone of pompous disdain when she wanted the argument to be over and done with.

This time, Sylvie was even angrier. She watched as her mother dressed in the gear she wore when she was going hunting with her brothers. Normally Sylvie loved staying at their family retreat in the countryside northeast of Östersund, on the shore of a vast lake. Not this year though, when Camilla and Sylvie's uncles, Leif and Jan, kept bringing home more and more game. At first, Sylvie didn't intend to say anything, as she knew this was her mother's favorite thing to do up north. Only when they wanted her to help prepare one of the deer did she let them know she'd had enough. "I'll never help with that," Sylvie growled, shoving her hands into the pockets of her denim jacket.

"How's she going to get her hunting license if she refuses to clean the game afterward?" Leif asked, sounding more incredulous than angry.

"I don't want a hunting license." Rocking back and forth on her soles, Sylvie didn't back down.

"Why not? We're doing a community service by keeping the numbers down." Camilla looked genuinely surprised. "I know you've never shown much interest, but I was sure you'd grow into this." She made it sound like a hunting license was something inevitable and that Sylvie needed it, just as she should develop the proper shape to fit one of the ridiculous-looking ball gowns her mother insisted on buying her.

"And having great fun killing animals in the process." Sylvie's eyes filled with tears. The thought of the deer hanging from one of the beams in the barn haunted her.

"But the country has too many deer and moose. Someone has to hunt, or the animals will starve when there isn't enough food to go around." Camilla tried her arguments with an increasingly louder voice. "And this isn't much different than buying a pork chop from the supermarket." She tended to repeat herself when she was trying to make a point.

"Yes, it is. You enjoy the hunt. It's the whole idea. You find your prey, you outsmart it, set your dogs on it, and then you get the thrill you're after and then you—you—"

"What the hell is all the yelling about?" Daniel Thorn entered the living room. "What's going on? You're screaming so loud the neighbors will hear."

"Just a difference of opinion, darling," Camilla said quickly, sending Sylvie a warning glance. "You know, mother-daughter issues." Her laughter sounded forced, and Sylvie could tell her father wasn't buying it. She straightened her back, as she had around her father for many years, and refused to let him intimidate her.

Camilla sighed with mock impatience. "Well, what do you know, Daniel? We have a little vegetarian on our hands. Guess we better tell cook to stock up on carrots and broccoli."

"What? Whatever for?" Daniel frowned, looking genuinely puzzled. "A vegetarian? Sylvie?" The storm clouds gathered in her father's eyes. "You're kidding, right?"

"No. I hate hunting. I hate how you all hang the dead deer upside down in the barn, and I hate how you send all the animals we breed to slaughter to feed us. Most of all I hate that you assume I want to be a part of it all. That will never happen. Never." Her fists so tight now it hurt her knuckles, Sylvie watched with a weird kind of fascination how her father's complexion turned a dark, bluish red. Was he ill? Did she cause this?

"Darling," Camilla said and hurried to Daniel's side.

Sylvie's Uncle Jan had stayed out of the argument until now, when he seemed to think Sylvie might need reinforcement and moved to stand by her side. "Come on, Dan. You know kids. They get the craziest ideas. Vegetarian? One week on broccoli alone will change her mind, and she'll be begging for a chicken leg or even a piece of the damn deer." He chuckled and put her large hand on Sylvie's shoulder. "Right, kid?"

Sylvie knew it would be smart to play along with her uncle's way of defusing her father. She had to say it was probable, but she couldn't. Her father looked at her with inexplicable anger, bordering on contempt. It just didn't make sense. Why would he be so furious because she wanted to become a vegetarian?

"No. I'm a vegetarian from now on. Several of my friends at school are. I'll join every single activist group and fight for—"

"You will not!" Daniel roared, making everyone jump. "You will not join any illegal organization and tarnish my good name."

Ah. So that was why. Feeling stupid for not realizing it sooner, Sylvie refused to stand down. "I'm free to choose whatever friends I want and belong to any organization I please. Besides, vegetarianism isn't illegal!" Her fury matched his, and she trembled with each labored breath.

"Those idiots releasing caged minks into the wild are criminals," Daniel spat. "No daughter of mine will ever be caught anywhere near the same postal code as those fools. Can you imagine what the press will make of it?" He directed this last sentence at Camilla, who merely gestured helplessly.

"Daniel. She's just going through a phase." Camilla raised her hands, pleadingly. "This is her youthful sympathy—"

"It's fucking insubordination!" Daniel growled and took a step closer to Sylvie.

Sylvie's uncle wrapped an arm around her and pulled her close. "Dan. Calm down. You're being unreasonable. You can't speak to her like she's one of your employees. I don't think you even address them like this. Sylvie's a kid, and as far as I know she usually breaks her back to please you."

"Oh, really. I sure as hell don't feel pleased." Daniel relented, but only marginally. The muscles on his neck were thick as ropes and his eyes narrow slits. "Sylvie, I won't have you disobey me. I can't force-feed you meat, but if I get even an inkling that you're cavorting with these...these terrorists, then I'll be even more angry than I am now. Is that clear?"

She couldn't answer. This furious man, spitting his consonants as if the very language was foul tasting, vaguely resembled her father. Daniel was normally strict and could also be disdainful and brazen, but this man frightened her to no end.

"Is—that—clear?" Moving in on Sylvie, Daniel yanked her close. "Answer me."

"Yes. Yes, Dad."

"Fine then." He stabbed the air toward her mother with his index finger. "Make sure you're on top of this. And, Camilla? You're done hunting." Letting go of Sylvie, Dan began walking across the room.

"Daniel?" Camilla looked startled. "You can't mean—Daniel?"

"Let him go blow off some steam, Millan," Sylvie's oldest uncle, Leif, patted his sister's back. "You know Dan. He'll return in an hour or two and pretend he never said anything wrong at all."

"I've never heard him sound so furious." Camilla rounded on Sylvie. "And all this because you had to play high and mighty over something you know nothing about." She slapped her right palm against her thigh. "Honestly."

"I do know. A lot." Was this how being shell-shocked felt? Sylvie's heart was pounding, but she stood as if rooted in place, cold to the core.

"You don't know the intricacies of your father's business. The board of directors' decision to hand over the reins meant a great deal more stress, and now when he's bought a nationwide meatpacking company, you go and spout your ready-made, romanticized ideas of how cruel we are to kill and eat Bambi. Don't you understand what damage you could do as his only child? If you breathe a word about cruelty to animals, or even being a vegetarian all of a sudden, the press will eat you alive, and your father's business—the same business that clothes you very well and keeps you warm and safe, I might add—might just receive a blow that'll make the board of directors change their mind."

Sylvie's head spun. Images of her father's dark-red hue as his blue eyes bore into her made her nauseous from pure fear, but mostly from a fury not unlike his. How could he be so unfair? She wasn't a slave without a mind of her own. She'd spent so much time trying to make up for her problems in school, but this, this—*he should reward her for standing up for her beliefs, not reproach her. Trust her father to see it his own selfish way. Daniel Thorn thought he could crush whatever didn't benefit him like a bug beneath his loafers. It didn't surprise her that Camilla had joined ranks with him after the fact, but it made her furious.*

"All right," she said, pushing her shoulders back and shrugging off her well-meaning uncle's awkward pats. "I won't join the demonstrations. I will, however, never eat meat again." Her uncles looked at her with a new expression of respect mixed with confusion. She'd never stood her ground before, but now she did. They had no idea of the promises she'd made to herself to prove her father wrong. He'd counted her out years ago when her severe dyslexia made attending school agony. Sylvie was set on finding a way around her learning disability and making Daniel see that she deserved her seat among the Thorn titans.

She refused to fail.

CHAPTER NINE

The doorman in Sylvie's building let Aeron through without even checking the ledger. "Ms. Thorn is expecting you, Ms. DeForest. She's issued a visitor's pass for you and your own key, should she ever be detained or delayed." He handed over an envelope and showed the baffled Aeron where to sign in. "In the future, using the visitor's pass will register your coming and going, and you won't have to physically sign in like today."

"Thank you, sir." Aeron smiled politely and peered into the envelope at a card much like a pass card or hotel key card, along with a pamphlet informing her of all the amenities in the building open to visitors. The gym, pool, and atrium impressed her. The building looked deceptively generic on the outside, but the inside seemed to have been meticulously upgraded. White marble, blue carpets, and rose-gold fixtures gave a fresh and modern appearance without being too stark.

The elevator that took her to Sylvie's floor gave her a feeling of déjà vu from the lawyer's office, which in turn subjected her to yet another bout of strong doubts. So much of this situation made her wary. Being here, about to enter Sylvie's private home and perhaps even spend time there even when Sylvie wasn't around, was almost as nerve-racking as what she might find in Maeve's papers.

Aeron stepped out on the twelfth floor, the carpet here aqua rather than blue, and made her way to Sylvie's door. As she was about to ring the chime, the door opened and Sylvie appeared. She looked different when she was off the clock. Her hair loose in large waves around her shoulders framed her oval face. Wearing hardly any makeup, she looked a bit more approachable in loose-fitted, off-white linen pants and a gray T-shirt than before in her power suits.

"Welcome," Sylvie said and stepped aside. "Make yourself at home."

"Thank you." As Aeron crossed the threshold, she immediately liked what she could see of Sylvie's condo, which was the foyer, living room, and a study. It was modern, but not ultra, and actually looked rather homey.

"Let me take your jacket." Sylvie hung Aeron's leather jacket in a small closet. "Can I get you anything to drink before I give you the grand tour?" Her smile wasn't without warmth but was guarded.

"I'd pretty much kill for a glass of orange juice. Or any juice." It was true. Aeron's mouth had gone dryer in the elevator with each passing floor.

"Sounds good. I'll have one too." Sylvie checked her watch. "I'm due for a teleconference in forty-five minutes and should be tied up with that for an hour or so. I hope. Sometimes these things drag on. After that, I'm all yours if you have any questions."

Sylvie's choice of words made Aeron's already nervous stomach turn yet another somersault. "Thank you. I appreciate it. I mean, all of it." She made some imprecise gesture.

"Come with me and I'll show you the kitchen." Sylvie waved toward the area to the left of the foyer. "You're welcome to take anything you need from there. My housekeeper, her name is Lilly, stocks the pantry, fridge, and freezer every week." She stopped when they reached the kitchen. "God, I sound like a cruise-ship concierge, don't I?"

"Yes, a little. But very informative." Aeron couldn't keep from teasing her. "Thank you again for allowing me to be in your home. Are you sure you're comfortable with my being here alone?"

Pursing her lips, Sylvie seemed to ponder the question. "Are you planning to run off with my stainless-steel cutlery?" She took a carton of juice from the refrigerator.

Snorting, Aeron shook her head. "Now there's an idea."

"Here you go." Sylvie gave Aeron a tall glass of orange juice. "I don't have a very big place so the tour will go quickly." She nodded toward the living room.

Aeron walked after Sylvie through the condo. She'd been certain the CEO of Thorn Industries US would reside in a townhouse, or at least a penthouse. This condo, clearly decorated either by Sylvie herself or through close collaboration between Sylvie and a designer, was a home, not a corporate showroom. Sort of like Maeve's condo. The comparison came out of nowhere. They weren't similar in style, not at all, but this home resembled its owner just as Maeve had put a clear stamp on her home. Which of course had been Aeron's home too until she voluntarily stayed away.

Sylvie's living room had eggshell-colored wallpaper, a blue-and-black intricately patterned Persian rug, and leather furniture. A vast copper coffee table drew her eyes, as did the copper-plated fireplace. Blankets and pillows in muted colors made the otherwise stark, black leather less severe.

As it turned out, Sylvie's condo held an open-plan kitchen that morphed into a breakfast nook and family room. Four rooms with en suite bathrooms served as the master suite, a guest room, a study/library, and a room that didn't have a purpose other than some unassembled gym equipment and a big shelf with binders. The back room. Now it did serve a function, however. Five large boxes and three smaller ones sat on a folding table. A leather desk chair that looked brand-new sat behind the table, which was positioned so she could enjoy the Manhattan view.

Would she ever be able to enjoy this view without yearning for the quiet Adirondacks? She thought of the silence and how only the wind through the trees created background music instead of honking horns, loud voices, and echoes of childhood memories. Glancing furtively at the boxes, she wished herself back so hard, she was fully prepared to be in her rustic cabin kitchen when she opened her eyes.

"Are you all right?" Sylvie spoke carefully. "I know it seems a lot, but I bet you'll feel relieved after you've gone through it all. For what it's worth…" Sylvie pushed her hands into the wide pockets of her pants. "I'm not a stranger to having a, um, challenging relationship with a parent."

Aeron stepped farther into the backroom, lingeringly touching one of the smaller boxes sitting on the folding table. "There's one in every family, I suppose. I mean, one that gives us a lot of headaches."

"That's my experience, yes." Sylvie nodded toward the boxes. "Will this be okay, you think? I didn't have time to get a real desk—"

"Hey. This is great. Thank you. I'll be fine." Aeron meant to deliver the words with bravado, but the small frown between Sylvie's perfectly shaped eyebrows made her unsure if she'd managed it. "You need to get to that teleconference, right?"

"I do. I'll poke my head in afterward to see if you have any questions."

"Thanks."

Sylvie left, and Aeron tried to figure out which box to start with. She broke the seal on each of them and tried to judge from the top paper what order they were in, if any. That's when she spotted a Post-it note on the top binder in each that suggested the order. Of course. She should've trusted Paulina to think of this too. She'd packed the boxes, as they couldn't trust anyone else.

Paulina had mentioned something about the tabloid press sending people under cover to pose as flower or pizza deliverers, or even policemen and firefighters. Aeron didn't envy Paulina and her husband living in her old home. God knew how long the vultures would find their way into the building and knock on the door.

According to the note, one of the smaller boxes was the first one. A brown envelope that looked rather old sat on top of it, and Aeron opened it. At first she thought it was her old school papers, such as report cards and grades, but it turned out to be Maeve's. Her mother had gone to an all-girls private school on the Upper East Side. She pulled out a report card from the sixth grade. Maeve had generally made Bs in most academic subjects, but straight As when it came to English, arts, and physical education.

"Imagine that," Aeron murmured and turned the card over. A teacher had written a fairly long note in the comment box.

Maeve DeForest—1983

Maeve is a strong-willed girl with little or no respect for authority. Her grades are passable, but she requires proper monitoring when it comes to doing her homework. She has had every excuse under the sun this semester why she hasn't completed her assignments. What pains me as her teacher is that she could have straight As if she applied herself. Her test scores are always in the top five percent of her class and, I would even go so far as to say, among all the students her age group.

As for her less-than-stellar record when it comes to behaving responsibly in the classroom, I feel we must schedule a meeting. Maeve should attend, and all three parties need to sign a contract regarding anything we agree on during that meeting. Maeve's future depends on it, and please know I have only her very best interest at heart.

The report card was signed Ms. Charlotte Donner. Aeron leaned back and held the card with trembling hands. So her mother had been some sort of rebellious kid? As she didn't have any memories of her grandparents, she couldn't begin to guess how they might have reacted to Ms. Donner's note.

Aeron pulled one report card after another from the stack. They were all worded similarly. Her mother was gifted but not especially motivated. Some teachers sounded terser than others, and nowhere did she find a report card signed by anyone who appeared to genuinely like Maeve.

The last card was from Maeve's second semester her sophomore year. Now her grades were even more polarized. Still straight As in the subjects she had excelled in during the sixth grade. In the rest of the subjects she received Bs, Cs, and even one D.

Maeve DeForest—1988

First of all, Maeve is a charming girl with a multitude of plans for her future. I have found her especially proficient when it comes to writing fictional stories. Her sense for drama is unparalleled, and I cannot stress enough how she could benefit from joining the school's writers' club. Maeve seems reluctant to join any extracurricular activity, which I hope you and I can help persuade her to do.

As for Maeve's poor results when it comes to conduct and discipline, I think this is the biggest issue standing in her way to success. Both Principal Jones and I have tried to address the problems with Maeve, and with you, her parents, but with little success.

Our school standards are clear. If Maeve receives a third strong warning, we will be forced to expel her, something we would loathe to do. I include this message on her report card only because you and Mr. DeForest do not call us back or reply to our letters.

I am certain if we all work together, we can help steer Maeve onto a path toward a great future.

Mrs. Dorothy Heller

Aeron looked for more report cards but didn't find any. There should be some from her junior and senior years, but if they existed they weren't in the box. Instead Aeron found an envelope with what looked like legal papers. Reading through them, she began to cry.

"Oh, my. Are you all right, Aeron?" Sylvie's concerned voice from the doorway made Aeron flinch.

"Yes. Sure. Of course." She wiped hastily at her damp lashes and cheeks. "I'm fine."

"You're crying. This has got to be hard on you." Sylvie stepped into the back room, and Aeron finally noticed her carrying a stool from the kitchen. "I thought I'd join you, if that's okay. Perhaps I can help somehow?"

Relieved to not be alone with the boxes, Aeron nodded shortly. "Why not?"

Sylvie sat down on the opposite side of the folding table, pulled one leg up, and placed her feet on the rest halfway up the stool's legs. "What upset you so much?"

Aeron swallowed past the tears that constricted her throat and coughed to clear her voice. "Maeve was expelled early in her junior year." She handed Sylvie the document.

"Really?" Sylvie didn't read it but regarded Aeron closely instead. "Tell me what it says."

"She got pregnant. With me. So this high-and-mighty private girls' school obviously thought her condition was contagious or beneath them or something and kicked her out. They had some obscure regulation that any pupil having children out of wedlock had forfeited their spot. It was non-negotiable. I'm thinking she was home-schooled after that, if she was schooled at all."

"That was harsh. I mean, in 1989 it wasn't a big deal to have a kid as a single parent. I know your family moved with the big elephants on the East Coast, hell, probably in all of the US, but still, it wasn't the Dark Ages."

"You'd think so. When you're a DeForest you have a hell of a lot of fuck-off money." Aeron pushed the papers back into the box. "I guess I learned about my mother in a weird way today. I caught a glimpse of how her teachers saw her. She wasn't stupid. She was actually smart when she wanted to be." Feeling confused at how her own vision of her mother had begun to blur, Aeron shoved her fingers into her hair, massaging her scalp.

"I come from a similar background as you, back in Sweden, and I can testify that it can be damn hard. The expectations, especially if you're an only child, are immense. There's talk about the company, the empire, and your obligation from the moment you get out of the cradle."

"Is that why you're here in the US?" Aeron regarded Sylvie curiously. She'd lost some of her lipstick during the video conference, but that only seemed to rejuvenate her looks. Paler now, her lips looked softer and fuller. Her wavy hair caressed her cheeks and neck where it moved when she spoke.

"Partly, I suppose. I have worked for fifteen years to reach the position as CEO of Thorn Industries US. My...my father didn't think I had it in me." It was hard to see if she shrugged with emphasis or if she drew a deep breath.

"Shows what he knows," Aeron said laconically.

"Sure does." Smiling broadly now, Sylvie said, "My parents are driven people, each in their own way, and I suppose I am too. I've worked toward my single most important goal for so many years, I can't slow down now."

"Yet you agree to, no, even suggest, babysitting me." Wrinkling her nose, Aeron studied Sylvie's expression. She expected Sylvie to agree, but instead she gave an open smile and gestured with her hands, palms forward.

"That could well turn out to be my best deal. I really liked the Maeve I got to know over the years, and if I can tell you about her…" Sylvie's cheeks colored faintly. "Did that sound presumptuous?"

Aeron considered the question. "No. No, it doesn't." She couldn't allow this nice and apparently caring side of Sylvie to sway her. Sylvie was in this for the money. She wanted to save her company and shut out whoever tried for a hostile takeover. Dreaming up a scenario that she and Sylvie could become friends when they both had clear, personal agendas was preposterous.

"Anything else of interest in that box?" Sylvie peered over the edge.

"Only some photos, I believe. It was mostly school stuff, so perhaps those are from her high school." Aeron dug them out and began to browse through them. "I don't recogni—wait. This must be Maeve." Staring at the picture of the young, strawberry-blond girl dressed in loose white pants, a white shirt with a mandarin collar, and a blue denim jacket with the biggest shoulder pads known to mankind, Aeron felt her stomach tighten. She turned the photo over and saw the text: *Kelly, Dana, Jack, and me, March 1988.*

Flipping it over again, she examined the faces of the other three. She couldn't remember having seen them while growing up. But perhaps she had. People change when they become adults. Maeve's eyes glittered as she gazed into the lens. She posed, as always, but the laughter evident on her face seemed authentic. "Here. Look." She passed the photo over to Sylvie. "Apart from Maeve, I don't recognize any of the others."

Sylvie studied the photo carefully. "Neither do I. It's unmistakably Maeve in the denim jacket. I can't believe how well she aged. She looked a lot like this."

"She was nipped and tucked a little bit, but not as much as some of her peers." Aeron wondered why that was. Maeve had been as vain as people come, but apart from her teeth, lips, and a few wrinkles around her eyes, her mother had seemed content in her own skin. "She didn't socialize with many of her peers. She hung with people my age or even younger. Booze, cocaine, and even ecstasy, those were the things she claimed kept her as young as her entourage. I stopped trying to convince her about the dangers eventually. Who knows? If I'd persevered, she might have been alive today."

"No. Don't go there." Sylvie placed a hand on top of Aeron's, which made her go rigid. Not very many people touched her, and this kind gesture made her mouth go slack. Still, she didn't withdraw her hand from under Sylvie's, as she somehow knew that would feel worse. Sylvie squeezed her hand for a moment and then removed hers. "This was her life, her choice. I tried to reason with her too, and for weeks at a time, she'd seem to be making an effort. Helena, Noelle, and I began to have hope she meant it."

"Helena Forsythe and Noelle Laurent? I saw them at the funeral."

"Helena and Noelle have a house in the Hamptons across from Maeve's. I suppose that'll be yours too now."

Groaning, Aeron wondered if the room had ventilation issues or if she was about to have a panic attack. "So Maeve let you down, of course." She tried to focus on their topic, but it wasn't easy as vertigo was about to hit any moment.

"Needless to say, we were disappointed several times. Your mother seemed haunted during those times when she had yet another setback."

"Setback? Don't you have to have succeeded for slightly longer than she did for it to be called a setback?" Aeron heard vitriol permeate her voice but couldn't stop. "Maeve was full of good intentions. There wasn't one good intention around she didn't love, or attempt." Aeron flung her hands in the air.

"The thing was, after so many years trying to be like she wanted me to be—to lie to people, preferably guys, about my status, to forgive her every 'setback,' and most of all, to let myself be pulled into her magic—no, I don't deny she had a masterful pull on people, including me." Aeron inhaled and then coughed. It was as if she couldn't breathe properly.

"But eventually even the strongest supporter becomes immune to all the surprises and excuses. She could easily make you adore her when it suited her, only to make sure you knew she could toss you aside at a whim." Aeron was hoarse now, the tears clogging her throat as she refused to let them fall from her eyes.

"Yes, she was all that, but this time, I think she really was trying to change." Sylvie pulled the chair closer to the table and held Aeron's gaze. "I know it sounds contradictory, but she was in the process of turning her life around. She did still go to some parties, and she must've done so the day she crashed."

"With a blood-alcohol level sky-high and testing positive for cocaine. How can you say she tried to get sober? She still drank and did drugs. She still partied." It was strange how cornered Aeron felt as soon as Sylvie tried to be reasonable regarding Maeve. Sylvie hadn't lived her entire childhood with a young woman who had no inkling whatsoever what bringing up a child entailed.

"What's in the pink book?"

Aeron flinched and realized she must have sat lost in thought for a while. She looked from Sylvie's blue eyes to a leather-bound book at the bottom of the pile of photos. She opened it on the first page and froze.

"Oh. Oh, God."

"Aeron?" Sylvie looked alarmed.

"It's a…it's…" Aeron could hardly breathe and wished Sylvie were still holding her hand. "It's a journal. Maeve's journal for 1988 and 1989."

Chapter Ten

Manhattan—Present Day

Aeron curled up on the bed in her barren hotel room and squinted at the pink journal on the nightstand as if it were about to attack. With cold hands, she grasped a mug of hot chai tea, and still she had to pull a blanket firmly around her. She'd asked someone to come look at the air-conditioning unit, but so far, no one had showed up.

Part of Aeron wanted to tear open the journal, but another part wanted to rip it to pieces and flush it down the toilet. Or burn it. Or rip it first and then burn it. She snorted. She'd probably burn down the entire hotel if she tried the fire approach. And who was she kidding? She wanted to read the contents so much it hurt. It was just…she was all alone, and when she tried to phone Annelie, her Adirondack neighbor and very close friend, the call went directly to voice mail.

Annelie would never ignore her without good reason, so either she was in a meeting or out on the lake with her little sister and Carolyn, if she was on a break from taking over Hollywood. Who else could she call? Not Paulina. She was like family, which felt too close. What if Maeve had written anything about Paulina while under the influence of any of her favorite drugs?

Sylvie. Sylvie knew Maeve enough to understand and perhaps well enough to be a sounding board. Would the stern but oddly vulnerable-looking Swedish boss be up for it? So far, only Aeron had gotten anything out of their agreement. Aeron had checked her email earlier and found the document from Lucas Hayes. After reading through it twice, she'd signed it and prayed Sylvie wouldn't get cold feet.

Now, Aeron browsed her contacts on her smartphone and found Sylvie's number. Suddenly hesitant, she hovered with her thumb above the green symbol. Sylvie might be totally fed up with Aeron for one day. She'd spent four hours at Sylvie's condo going through yet another of the smaller boxes, which had been filled only with receipts from expensive Fifth Avenue stores. Apparently, Maeve saved all such documents religiously.

She pressed dial before she chickened out. After four rings, Sylvie answered. "Good evening, Aeron."

That was very formal. Ah. Perhaps Sylvie wasn't alone. "Er. Sorry to call so late. I didn't mean to disturb you." Aeron's cheeks grew warm.

"You didn't. I was getting ready to have a little nightcap. I normally don't drink alone, but after…well, let's just say—"

"That you're a bit fed up with this whole arrangement," Aeron said dryly.

"What? No!" Sylvie sounded stunned. "Don't put words in my mouth. If there's anything I loathe, it's when people assume I don't mean what I say."

Taken aback, Aeron felt sick to her stomach as she blurted out her words. "Sorry. I'll remember that. Anyway, are you sure I'm not keeping you from anything right now?" She might have guests…or a special someone there. That thought didn't help Aeron's sensitive stomach feel any better. What the hell was up with that? What did she care if Sylvie had a thousand torrid affairs?

"I just said I was about to drink alone. If you keep me company over the phone while I have my brandy, I'll listen to whatever question you have and try to help. Sound okay?" Now Sylvie appeared to be amused, which was much better than her annoyance.

"Sounds okay." She might as well get it out. "I've been worried about opening Maeve's diary."

"Ah. I thought as much."

"You did?"

Sylvie paused, and Aeron heard her inhale and take a sip of her drink. "If I found my dead mother's diary and had tons of unanswered questions, I'd be freaking out too."

"Yeah." Those were the right words. Freaking out. Aeron set the cell phone to speaker mode and attached the charger cable. Reaching for the journal, she let it rest against her bent legs as she made herself comfortable against the pillows again. She didn't need the blanket any more. "Okay, here goes."

"Just take your time." Sylvie's slightly husky voice suited her drink. A little smoky, yet silky, it flowed through the phone and gave Aeron enough courage to continue.

She opened the thick, once-glossy cover of her mother's diary. For a moment she thought she could sense Maeve's perfume. Was this her only one, or had she always written? Bracing herself, Aeron started reading out loud.

1988
Manhattan, June 11

So. A diary. What kind of birthday present is that for a girl turning seventeen? I mean, the pink color of the cover alone? My father never did have much sense when it comes to picking out gifts. And as much as I frown upon this diary, the time he gave Mother a two-week stay at a fat-farm still wins first prize. The only thing this diary will be good for is to bitch about the idiots at school. I hate private schools. I detest uniforms. I throw up when I see how some of the faculty members suck up to mother and father just because they're filthy rich.

If I had my way, I'd go to one of the cool public schools where the students dress any which way they want. I'd wear my new jeans, the bright-pink top, and my purple-passion Nike sneakers. But as it is, I go to school wearing a dark-blue skirt, white shirt, and gray cardigan—and a fucking tie. All that I can live with, but the goddamn knee socks drive me insane. One day I tried wearing pantyhose to school, which made the uniform look infinitely better. Of course our principal spotted them at our first break and sent me home to change. I had to take home a note for my parents to sign. I don't think I've ever heard my mother laugh so much. She's rarely on my side, but that day she was.

"What on earth is wrong with wearing pantyhose?" she asked, pouring herself yet another martini. "Half of America wears them."

Father piped up from his armchair. "You can see the girls' legs. They want them covered up so the boys in the private school across the street won't feel tempted."

"To do what?" I was furious. "See a hint of skin and go mad? Are boys really that immature?"

It looked like father was about to answer yes, but mother glared at him.

"Don't be so hard on young boys," mother said and put on her best understanding expression. "Soon enough you'll start chasing them, and we'll have to change our phone number.

I wasn't going to share my biggest secret ever. Not with these shallow people who called themselves my parents. They don't mean any harm, but they're...well, they're more interested in the perks of owning a constantly growing fortune. Spas, vacations, yachting, you name it; they've done it all dozens of time. They have a large estate in the Hamptons, and I suppose that's the perk I can really relate to. I enjoy the parties there, and as long as you carry enough dollars, nobody pays any attention to the fact your ID is fake.

Aeron couldn't take her eyes off the text. This young woman was the same person that would in less than ten months give birth to her. A child, really. Her handwriting was precise, which was a huge difference from the older Maeve's larger-than-life, airy penmanship.

"What do you think? Sound like Maeve?" Sylvie asked quietly.

"Yes and no. I can't remember her sounding this together and even eloquent. Well, you knew her. She sounded more like a teenager than I did, who was one at the time."

"Actually, I think it sounds more like the Maeve I knew than how you describe her," Sylvie said thoughtfully. "Perhaps that's because a few years had passed between your teenage years and her wanting to redirect her life. I got the impression you hadn't talked to Maeve, not face-to-face, for quite a while."

Aeron's chest hurt. "That's right. It had been months since we spoke on the phone and years since I'd seen her. We'd lost each other long before...long before..." She couldn't speak. Tears clogged her throat and immobilized her vocal cords. No matter what she might find out through the diary, or what questions Sylvie could answer... it was too late. There wouldn't be any reconciliation between Maeve and her.

"Hey. Are you all right, Aeron?" Sylvie's voice, soft and calm, interrupted the pain. "Talk to me."

"I don't think I can. Not yet. But I can read some further into the diary, if that's okay."

"Absolutely."

Relieved, Aeron browsed a few pages until a sentence caught her attention as if it were written in fluorescent ink.

Hamptons, June 19

If it didn't sound ridiculous, I'd actually apologize to an inanimate object right now. It turns out that being snarky about writing in a journal was shortsighted of me. Now when my life has changed forever, I need an outlet for all these feelings! And since I can't tell a soul about what's going on, I'm going to have to use this journal and keep vigil over it so it doesn't fall into the wrong hands.

I'm in love. I, who always ridiculed my friends at school when they went gaga for some boy, I've fallen head over heels—which is a stupid expression—and no matter what'll happen, I wouldn't want to miss out on feeling like this.

If I could talk to anyone, I'd know just what they'd say. He's too old. He's not for you.

There. It's out there on paper and my insides are positively squealing.

I met him at one of the coffee shops down by the marina. He was reading his paper, and reaching for his mug, he knocked it over just as I passed him. Thank God it wasn't scorching hot as it splashed all over my naked arms and legs.

He was so alarmed and polite at the same time. We exchanged phone numbers, and he made me promise I'd let him know if I developed blisters. I asked him if he was a doctor, and he said no. I don't dare write his name here, as you never know who might get their hands on my journal. I'll just call him A. I ended up promising to tell A if there were any residual marks from the hot coffee. I already knew I'd be fine, but I also knew I'd call him anyway.

And since I did, we met at one of the less-populated beaches. He brought a ready-bought picnic basket and a blanket. We sat away from what little crowd there was, and I was glad I hadn't told him my age or he might not have shown up and perhaps not offered me champagne. Not that I haven't had champagne before, but like this, alone with A, it was different. Grownup different.

He's tall. I fit just underneath his chin when we stand next to each other. His eyes are green and his hair has the funniest dark-blond color. I don't know what it is about his accent, because he's from the South, but it does things to me that I've never felt before. It vibrates inside me, and when he says my name, it sounds so different. I used to loathe my name and had decided to change it as soon as possible. When I mentioned it, A said, 'Please don't,' with that tone in his voice that turns me into a complete mess. I suddenly love my name because it's beautiful to him.

If only he weren't married.

"It's him." Aeron whispered the two words she never thought she'd have a reason to say. "Sylvie?"

"I'm here." Sylvie's voice sounded thick.

"She's talking about 'A.' Aero. It's *him*. It has to be, doesn't it?" Aeron closed the diary. She couldn't bear to see any more of the neatly written pages right now. Her stomach had rolled up in a tight knot.

"It's a strong possibility. When is your birthday?"

"April twenty-fifth."

"They must have escalated their relationship in July, at the latest."

A spark of anger pierced Aeron. "She was seventeen and he was a grown man. I know. I'm grateful to be on this earth, but that doesn't make it right."

"She didn't tell him her age." Sylvie didn't sound shocked at the age difference or the fact that it was also a question of statutory rape. This thought hadn't struck Aeron before, and now she sat up straight and clutched the diary hard to her chest. "What if he's in prison?"

"What? Why would he be in prison?"

"If someone reported they were having sex and...she was under the age of consent."

"Oh, crap." Sylvie sighed.

Aeron had never heard Sylvie curse or use harsh language before. "My thoughts exactly."

"As you said, Maeve might have been deceiving him about her age, but he may also have disregarded it, and if that's the case, he's despicable."

That didn't sit right with Aeron. She wanted her father to be perfect. And here he was, starting to look way too flawed, too human.

Chapter Eleven

Sylvie gripped her cell phone tighter. Of course she'd had to be too blunt. Did she really have to remind herself why she had to keep the lines of communication open with Aeron? Yes, they had a contract, but it was still possible for their whole deal to go up in atoms.

"Aeron, listen. Your mother wasn't always the most truthful person. With me, yes, while we were alone. But with a handsome guy when she's just seventeen and used to the cliques and a tough climate at high school? I bet she told him she was over eighteen."

"Yeah?" Her voice raspy, Aeron sounded as if she might have been wiping tears only seconds ago.

"Yes."

"She wasn't very truthful with me either. This pink book may be the only way to find out the truth about her, what made her tick and who my father was."

"I'll help you any way I can." Sylvie meant it. Somehow, Aeron's pain tied in with her own, and she didn't want the next fifteen years of Aeron's life, and after that, to be anything like some of the stuff she'd gone through.

"You're far too kind to someone you never even heard about a few days ago." Aeron chuckled, but the sound wasn't entirely happy. "Then again, you have a vested interest in keeping me from going off the deep end, right?"

"There is that. I need you able to fly to Sweden, for one thing. My family alone can drive anyone crazy. Can't have you in some sort of pre-crazy state when we go there." Sylvie crossed her fingers that Aeron would get her warped sense of humor. Not all people did, and definitely not all Americans. To her relief Aeron gave a raucous laugh.

"Oh, God. I'd forgotten about that. Not completely, I mean, but right now. Go to Sweden. That sounds rather awesome. I've never been."

"It's great this time of year." Sylvie didn't intend to sound as if she were reading from a tourist pamphlet, but it felt good to move away from Aeron's heartache for a bit. "I'm expected to take part in my family's biggest holiday event, Midsummer Eve celebrations in the west-coast archipelago. It's in three weeks. The whole Thorn clan will be there with their respective entourages, and I usually suffer through it alone. This time you get to suffer right along with me."

What would her family make of Aeron's presence? Hopefully it would take some of the pressure off her. She planned to get the ball rolling when it came to resigning from Thorn Industries USA. If her parents weren't distracted enough, she wouldn't have any chance of slipping away to do this. Her father had a way of monopolizing her every waking moment when she was in Gothenburg. This time Aeron would have to work as her shield.

"You have to explain what the Midsummer celebrations entail so I don't make a complete fool of myself." Aeron actually sounded worried.

"Trust me. It's all about sweet pickled herring, schnapps, and mimicking frogs in a dance around the Maypole, which is an enormous phallic symbol, I might add."

"You're joking," Aeron said weakly.

"No. This is the truth. You'll also be able to stay up in daylight pretty much all night. The true midnight sun shines around the clock only up north, but even at our latitude, it's daylight for the most part around Midsummer." Like most Swedes, Sylvie grew nostalgic and proud of her native country when she talked about it to foreigners.

She found herself wishing Aeron would really see the magic in Midsummer Sweden.

"Actually, I'm starting to look forward to this. I might have to take work, as I have a deadline just about then for some edits."

"Your latest horror novel?"

"Yes. The first in a trilogy. My first trilogy. And my very first supernatural one." If this made Aeron nervous, Sylvie couldn't tell.

"I thought all horror stories were supernatural?" Sylvie tried to remember what little she knew about the genre. She actually loved genre fiction, though she had yet to read the type Aeron created. She had to admit she was curious.

"Not so. Horror can be very realistic. You know, being locked up in an asylum where a crazy staff is selling body parts—"

"Oh, goodness." Swallowing hard at the description, Sylvie knew she wouldn't want to read anything like that. "Please tell me you don't write the gory type?"

"I can safely say that the gore has never interested me. I like psychological horror stories, which can be even more frightening, but with minimum gore," Aeron said, sounding more enthusiastic now.

"Suspense I can deal with," Sylvie said and hoped she wasn't being overly confident. She was afraid of the dark, something she hadn't admitted to a living soul since she went off to university in her youth. Her illogical fear could hit when she was among people or alone.

"I can promise you'll be able to read my stories, unless you have a very strong imagination. I've heard from people who regretted starting to read after dark. So, on a sunny beach perhaps?"

Oh, God. Sylvie shook her head. "Sounds like a plan."

"All right then, I—oh damn! Look at the time. I didn't realize it was this late." Aeron cleared her throat. "Thanks for listening to my ranting...and to Maeve, I suppose."

"Hey, no problem," Sylvie said and meant it. "Contract or no contract, I'm interested in what happened to her." And to Aeron, she added to herself. She wanted to know what events in Aeron's life had molded a young woman who could be utterly fearless one moment and then so vulnerable and uncertain the next.

"That's…that's actually reassuring to know." Here was Aeron's unsure tone again, as if she couldn't fathom Sylvie could actually care on some level. Sylvie realized this had nothing, or very little, to do with her, but more to do with Aeron's experiences to date. Had she grown up thinking Maeve didn't care about her? So many variables were missing from this equation, and Sylvie ached to solve this puzzle.

Perhaps if she did, Aeron would find closure, which honestly was the most important aspect of their deal. Saving her own independence and finding her own type of closure from the father who towered over her, expecting her to fail and not wanting to miss a moment of finding he'd been right all along, was secondary.

"I'll see you in two days," Sylvie said, now eager to hang up as her emotions were about to get the better of her, something that rarely happened. That meant the floodgates might open, and nobody was allowed to witness that.

"Your spa on Madison and East 122nd, right?"

"Yes. It was the first one to open, and Maeve actually cut the ribbon for it."

Aeron remained quiet for a few moments, and Sylvie wondered if she was trying to compose herself. Then she heard the unmistakable sound of Aeron laughing. No. Giggling was a better word.

"She must've enjoyed that. That was so up her alley." Aeron snorted, a thoroughly charming sound coming from her.

"She did." Sylvie smiled as she recalled how Maeve had dressed as if it were a major Hollywood event and posed at any given opportunity. In retrospect, the way Maeve had kept referring to Classic Swedish Inc. as "our company," and rightly so, had been endearing. Had that perhaps been a pivotal moment for Maeve that had sparked her desire to spend her time doing other things than party her life away? It was anybody's guess, but Sylvie didn't think she was being conceited that the company she'd started had something to do with it.

"Good night, Sylvie." Aeron now sounded exhausted.

"Good night. Sleep well."

Sylvie thought she heard Aeron mutter something like "I wish" before they ended the call, but she couldn't swear to it. Carrying the now-empty brandy glass to the kitchen and placing it in the dishwasher, she remained motionless, hands shoved deep into the pockets of her loose lounge pants, her mind whirling. What was it about Aeron DeForest that kept her thoughts constantly returning to the few times they'd actually met?

Fourteen years her junior, Aeron was obviously of a different generation than Sylvie, who was only three years younger than Maeve. Still, she and Aeron had stumbled upon one thing after another where they connected in the most unlikely way, especially their respective issues with a parent. Dysfunctionality wasn't the ideal thing to have in common, but there it was. Also, the gossip magazines had a vested interest in them. Granted, Aeron had been kept away from the press both by sheer luck and her own wish for privacy, but sooner or later someone would leak the fact that Maeve DeForest, scandal princess and heiress to one of America's biggest fortunes, had a secret child.

Getting ready for bed, Sylvie pondered how many hands the DeForests, and later Maeve herself, had greased a palm to keep the press away from Aeron. The same went for hospital staff, school officials, and so on. Not that they couldn't afford it, but it must have sent a clear signal to Maeve, and later Aeron, just how shameful her mere existence was.

When Sylvie climbed into her queen-size bed, she only had to close her eyes to replay their phone conversation. What was it about Aeron's appearance that made Sylvie's stomach tighten and her heart race? Aeron was no classic beauty or stunning in that exotic way Noelle was.

Instead, she was pale, with tiny freckles and glasses. Her hair was amazing though. That particular dark-blond hue with golden highlights looked like the hair of a sorceress. Sylvie couldn't remember having reacted with such basic attraction to any woman before and certainly not to anyone that much younger. She hoped this infatuation that had taken hold of her would diminish with time.

No doubt Aeron's complete disinterest in her would do the trick. Sylvie wasn't one to pine for anyone who seemed indifferent. Life was too short.

Sleep had begun to claim her when a thought struck that made her instantly wide-awake. What if this wasn't just infatuation or simple attraction? What if the suddenness of it all meant it went deeper?

A cold sensation *flooded* her system, and she hugged one of her four pillows hard to her chest. No. That couldn't be it. She simply wouldn't *let* it be so. Sylvie could think of few faster routes to heartache than someone like her truly falling for a young woman like Aeron DeForest.

CHAPTER TWELVE

Aeron watched as the cab pulled up and Sylvie stepped out. Today she wore black ankle boots, charcoal slacks, and a black, waist-long leather jacket over a white cotton shirt. A sparkling hairclip held her side ponytail in place.

"Am I late?" Sylvie frowned and checked her watch that was the same as Aeron's.

"Not at all. I was early." Aeron didn't intend to mention she'd taken the subway. She wasn't a fool. For now she could move in complete anonymity, but once she was outed as Maeve's daughter, single and an heiress, life as she knew it would be over. The tabloid press would hunt her down. Perhaps that fact alone should encourage her to say good-bye to the DeForest empire?

Then she saw the cautious smile on Sylvie's perfectly shaped, wine-red lips. She wasn't sure what it was, but somehow the juxtaposition between the worldly, commanding CEO and this occasional shyness created a whirling sensation in her chest. Sylvie was stunning, obviously, but that wasn't what pulled Aeron in. It was Sylvie's contradictory nature, warm and cold, caring and distant, and yes, professional and uncertain.

"Let's go inside. I'll show you around and you can meet the staff." Sylvie motioned with her head to the understated entrance with a simple white sign, its black letters stating CLASSIC SWEDISH SPA—NYC.

"How will you introduce me?" They hadn't discussed this point.

"As Aeron, a friend of mine. Is that okay?" Sylvie pulled the door open and let Aeron pass her.

"It is." Aeron gazed around the first foyer that consisted of pine couches with white leather cushions and glass coffee tables. A marble floor helped sustain the luxurious feel. At the far end was yet another door, but this one was locked. "I did wonder how we could just walk right in." The glass wall toward the inner area of the spa was milky white and not see-through.

"We don't want our customers to stand outside in the rain and snow while we open the door for them. Also, when someone's picking up their friend or spouse after a treatment, they can choose to sit out here if they don't want to come inside for some reason."

"Good thinking."

Sylvie plucked a keycard from her purse and slid it through the code lock. The door not only unlocked but swung open automatically. In front of them stood a white and rose-gold counter. Two young women manned it, and when they saw their boss, they smiled widely.

"Sylvie! What a nice surprise. Welcome." The Asian-American of the two rounded the counter and extended her hand. "I haven't seen you in months."

"You do such a good job here, I'm obsolete," Sylvie said, then returned her attention to Aeron. "Michelle, this is my good friend Aeron. Aeron, this is Michelle, who manages the very first of the NYC spas. We have one on Canal Street as well, which is newer and larger, but as this is my first, it holds a special place in my heart."

Aeron shook hands with Michelle. "Good to meet you."

"I didn't have Thomas call ahead," Sylvie said, "because I wanted Aeron to see how professional and conscientious you all are whether you know I'm about to stop by or not."

"We strive for perfection. You know that, Sylvie." Michelle tucked her hand under Aeron's arm and began walking. "Why don't I show you the boring part first—the inner-office area?" She guided Aeron to a bright and airy room behind the counter. Aeron nodded politely toward the receptionist, who was busy assisting a customer. The office area was light gray and white, even the computer screens white, as were the desks and chairs. A standard gray rug kept the noise to a minimum as one man and one woman sat at opposite desks, answering the phones.

"We're as paperless as possible," Michelle said. "We scan all important documents and shred the originals when we've made certain we have at least five backup copies on different servers and in two clouds."

"How's that working?" Sylvie asked. "You were hesitant when I brought the idea up."

"I thought it would never work. As computer savvy as I am, I still thought it was an accident waiting to happen. I'm glad you proved me wrong. We save a lot of time not having to run to find a certain binder. The only pen on paper we utilize is the customer book at the front. When a client calls to make an appointment, we send the name, time, and date to our receptionist, and she enters it in the client book by hand. She has a code number for every returning customer and a temporary one for new customers and walk-ins."

"You get a lot of walk-ins?" Aeron's interest was stirred.

"We didn't use to, but after Sylvie was on the *Today* show, we get quite a few. We can't accommodate all of them, as we're usually booked solid, but we've begun offering minor services, like thirty-minute classic Swedish massage, pedicures, manicures, mini-facials, that can be done in a smaller room."

"Great idea." Sylvie pulled up her phone and tapped something onto the screen. "Have you communicated this innovation to Canal Street?"

"Not yet," Michelle said confidently. Her dark eyes sparkled. "We're evaluating a two-month trial right now and will bring it to you when we're done. No use for Canal Street to reinvent the wheel, as it were, when we're doing the test run for all of us."

"Excellent. I look forward to the report."

Michelle didn't exactly preen, she was far too poised for that, but her cheeks colored faintly as she smiled at Sylvie. Something in that smile hinted at adoration. Michelle looked like she was in her early thirties, and her body language as she guided them further suggested her interest in her boss wasn't merely professional.

"Want to try our facility, Aeron?" Sylvie suddenly asked. "I'm not sure if a single room's empty, but one of the couple's massage rooms might be."

"I'd love to, but I can't in good conscience monopolize a room that caters to two individuals." Aeron shook her head. "I might just make an appointment instead—"

"Why don't we share the room?" Sylvie asked.

Aeron gawked at Sylvie. Where had that come from? "What? No. I mean. Are you sure?"

"Of course. I have a hellish couple of days at the office to look forward to. I could use an hour massage." Sylvie raised her eyebrows in a clear challenge.

"But, I'm...Oh, all right. A classic Swedish massage sounds fantastic."

Michelle's glow had diminished somewhat, and she appeared indecisive for a moment before her professionalism kicked back in. "I'll arrange that. I believe the Norwegian twins, Mette and Marit, are working the couple's room today. If you have a seat, they'll come for you when the room's ready. It'll only take a few minutes."

Aeron sat down in a white leather armchair in the reception area. Sylvie remained standing as she listened to something on her phone. "Our flight tickets are taken care of. We fly on June 17. That will give us one day to kick the worst of the jet lag before the craziness begins on the 19th...What?"

"You haven't even checked with me." Folding her arms across her chest, Aeron focused her narrowing eyes on Sylvie. "I knew we had to leave around that time, but it'd still have been nice to check. Just because we have this contract doesn't mean you should assume you call all the shots." She could hear her own voice become icier by the second.

"That wasn't my intention. I don't feel I call any shots whatsoever. You're doing me a great favor by joining me on the trip to Sweden." Sylvie looked nonplussed.

"Yes, you do. You suggested this…this collaboration. You came up with the idea that I store all the documents in your condo. You set the schedule for all the business knowledge you're about to bestow on me. And I keep saying yes, like a fool, not putting my foot down even once."

Sylvie's blue eyes turned almost gray. "From where I'm standing, it sounds like you're angry at yourself rather than at me. I have nothing but the best intentions, and I wish you could see that."

"A lot of people have had my best interest at heart on many occasions. I've suffered through their efforts and tried to learn how to behave, how to please them so they don't abandon me like she did."

"She? Maeve?" Sylvie frowned and sat down next to Aeron. "I don't know the details of what happened to you once you decided to leave home."

"Decided. Hmm. Maeve sent me to boarding school when I was eight and allowed me back at the condo only for Thanksgiving, Christmas and New Year's, and Easter. I spent all the other holidays and weekends at the school. The people running the little kids' dorm were nice, but they weren't our parents. It was a small comfort that I wasn't alone. Several kids had parents who were ready to ditch them for an entire semester."

Aeron stopped talking, appalled at how the words had gushed out of her like a broken faucet. She hadn't meant to pour her past out on Sylvie, and certainly not in a public setting. Glancing around them, she found to her relief that they were alone. Even the woman behind the counter had left. Perhaps Sylvie had realized this wasn't for public consumption and motioned to the receptionist to make herself scarce. "Oh, God. I'm sorry." Feeling cold now, Aeron rubbed her palms against her thighs. "I'm not usually this…unhinged."

"You're in mourning. I think you're extremely composed." Sylvie's eyes had become a warm blue again. She took Aeron's right hand. "I must've hit a nerve when I kept steamrolling and just expected you to follow along. I apologize for being presumptuous."

This humble approach from the formidable-looking business-woman standing before her made Aeron's heart slow its hammering, and she could breathe normally again. "I suppose you're right. I've never felt this kind of turmoil before. Maeve wasn't a good mother. That's the God's honest truth. Still, I feel I missed out a lot and I have regrets."

"Also natural. Even people who've had amazing relationships feel they didn't do enough or say enough to their loved one."

"Love." For a long time, when Aeron was a young teenager, she'd been determined to hate her mother. In her mind it was better to be the one rejecting than being rejected. She opened her mouth to tell Sylvie this, but the receptionist came back and approached them. Her blinding smile was professional rather than warm. "This way, my ladies. Mette and Marit will be ready for you soon. I'll show you to the couple's room, where you can disrobe. Have you had massages before?" She motioned for Sylvie and Aeron to follow her.

"Of course," Sylvie said.

"Not really," Aeron added.

"No? Well, you need to take off as many items of clothing as you're comfortable with. Some leave their panties on, and others don't mind being naked under the towel."

Aeron didn't think she'd be comfortable with the latter. At least not during her first time.

"Then you climb onto the massage table and lie down on your back. Drape a bath towel over yourself so you don't get cold. The massage therapist will knock on the door to announce her presence, then ask you about your preferences before she starts. She'll use warm oil, and if you like, she has different aromas that she can add to the oil to either rejuvenate or soothe the senses."

"Okay." This sounded a bit complicated to Aeron, but as Sylvie was going to be there...now, wait a minute. Undress down to your panties and lie half naked on a massage table in the same room as Sylvie? Aeron's heart picked up speed again. The idea of catching glimpses of the slender figure stole her breath away.

"Here we are," the receptionist said and opened a door. "As you can tell, there are two dressing rooms. Then you can decide among yourselves which table you want." She nodded energetically and left.

"Goodness." Aeron scanned the large room. In the center stood two massage tables, looking very comfortable with thick mattresses, sheets, towels, and blankets. On an oak counter sat a plethora of bowls and bottles, which she guessed contained the aromatic oils and such. Inhaling through her nose, Aeron could detect a faint scent of pine, ocean, and sandalwood. Perhaps vanilla? It smelled divine.

"You like it?" Sylvie had removed her jacket and hung it to the right of the door. "We need to get undressed."

"Yes, I like it." Aeron hurried behind a drape in the far left corner, where she removed her clothes and wrapped a white terry-cloth towel around her. Padding out, she saw Sylvie enter, having attached her bath towel in a similar fashion.

"You look uneasy," Sylvie said. "Actually, you don't have anything to be concerned about. Mette and Marit are experts. I managed to persuade them to move to the US to work for me and haven't regretted it. On the contrary, I hear nothing but good from their customers. If you want them to go easier on you, or deeper, just say so."

"Okay." How could she explain to Sylvie that it had been ages since anyone had touched her, not counting a handshake or a quick hug from Annelie and Carolyn? She was by no means a virgin, but the last couple of years she'd kept to herself. Now a stranger would be touching her while she was in the same room as Sylvie, who'd penetrated more of her carefully constructed shields than anyone else.

Awkwardly, Aeron maneuvered up on the massage table. It was very comfortable, and she cautiously relaxed only to tense up when she heard a knock on the door.

"Yes, we're ready." Sylvie called from the other table.

The door opened, and two women in their mid-thirties stepped inside. It was obvious they were twins, but Aeron hadn't expected them to be of Asian descent since they were from Norway. Feeling a bit foolish for expecting blond women with blue eyes, as she hated stereotypical thinking with a passion, Aeron greeted them politely.

"I'm Mette and I'll be massaging you, Aeron." Mette warmed her hands. "Would you like scented oil or just plain?"

"Just plain, please." Aeron cleared her throat.

"Plain it is." As she arranged a bowl on the heater, Mette conversed with her in a low tone. "Have you had a massage before?"

"No. I'm sorry." Not sure why she apologized, Aeron squirmed. Perhaps this was a really bad idea after all.

"Then I'll start easy. If you want me to go deeper on any particular place on your body, just let me know. I'll start with your legs and arms. I'll move up to your upper chest, your neck and scalp, and then I'll tell you to turn over and do your back. You'll be all covered up the entire time except for the part I'm working on. If anything hurts or you don't want me to do that particular part of your body, just let me know. This is supposed to feel really good. No stress, no tension. Just relaxation."

"I understand. Thank you." Aeron began to relax marginally when Mette covered her with soft blankets, leaving only her right leg exposed.

A soft moan from her left made Aeron want to turn her head. Marit had begun working on Sylvie and was clearly doing a good job.

"I'm starting now," Mette said and began rubbing oil on Aeron's leg. She kneaded, pushed, and pulled on the muscles, and for Aeron this was close to a religious experience. Nobody had ever touched her like this—impersonal, but with strong, kind hands and great skill. Little by little, Aeron let go of her tenseness, knowing she was well taken care of. Before she knew it, a moan similar to Sylvie's escaped her lips. Aeron knew she blushed, but the muted light probably hid it. She didn't actually care. One limb after another received the same amazing treatment, and Aeron promised herself to keep getting massages, especially when she was this worked up about life.

"I'm going to hold onto the towel now so you can turn onto your stomach, Aeron," Mette said and held the towel like a tent above Aeron. Carefully she pivoted on the table, mindful to not fall over the edge, as she was a bit dizzy.

"You're shaking. Let me get your some sweet iced tea." Mette left for a moment and returned with a glass and a straw. "Here. Drink some. It's important you keep rehydrating throughout the day. This will help you rinse out the toxins we're freeing from the muscles."

"Are you all right, Aeron?" Sylvie asked in a low voice from her table. She'd also turned onto her stomach. "You're a little pale."

"I'm fine. Just not used to being massaged." Aeron drank gratefully from the straw. The delicious tea made from raspberries rejuvenated her almost instantly. "Much better. Thank you."

Mette put the glass away and folded the towel down dangerously low on the small of Aeron's back, who had her head turned to the side toward Sylvie's side of the room and saw Marit had done the same. Sylvie had the most beautiful pale skin. Her slender-looking frame gave the impression that she was delicate, but Aeron had learned better. This woman was strong. She met everything head-on. Aeron didn't know why Sylvie was so adamant about making it for herself with this spa chain, but she recognized her strength from how Sylvie approached their slightly odd business relationship. Like a low-key kind of warrior. Where did she find the tenacity?

Aeron raised her gaze to Sylvie's face and met her blue eyes. Sylvie was looking at her with a wholly unexpected intensity. She must have seen how Aeron studied her. Unable to tear her gaze from Sylvie's, she then noticed the other woman's gaze. Following the angle of Aeron's arms, and then down her side and back, Sylvie's eyes were like feathers against her skin. Small goose bumps rose as Sylvie scanned her.

❖

Sylvie couldn't take her eyes off Aeron. Her creamy skin, looking almost like mother-of-pearl in the dim light, the slight freckles over her shoulders, and the innocent expression in her eyes made Sylvie's stomach clench as Aeron kept staring at her.

Sylvie had already been on her stomach when Aeron turned around on her table. She'd fumbled a bit and the towel had slipped just a fraction of an inch, but enough to give a tantalizing view of a voluptuous outline of Aeron's breasts.

The flowing dresses or skirts that Aeron normally wore hid her figure to some degree. Now as she shifted beneath the towel, no, squirmed, she left very little to the imagination. Trying to get a grip on her sudden bout of hormones, Sylvie squeezed two fistfuls of bedsheet.

"Relax. You'll get all those knots in your neck right back if you keep doing that." Marit admonished her gently. "I bet you don't have time to stay here another hour for me to start all over again."

"You're right, as usual." Sighing, Sylvie closed her eyes, but that didn't work much better. Now she saw images of Aeron smiling reluctantly, glowering, and laughing. Her hair glimmered with the golden highlights among the dark-blond strands. The vision sent tremors through her body, made her grow rigid again. She pressed her legs together, and involuntarily her mind went forward into forbidden territory. New and decidedly more X-rated thoughts raced through her brain.

"Am I hurting you?" Marit was in the process of probing Sylvie's lower back but now stopped.

"No, no. Not at all. Please continue."

"Absolutely, but something is making you tense up like this. Try to cleanse your mind with each movement of my hands. Like a pattern, remember? Feel my hands repeat this pattern. Palm, roll, fingertips, pull. Palm, roll, fingertips, pull."

Sylvie latched onto Marit's monotone voice as the massage therapist worked the part of her back that always needed it the most.

Refusing to let her mind wander back to Aeron, Sylvie let Marit's words echo over and over. Palm, roll, fingertips, pull. Palm, roll, fingertips, pull. The distraction worked for a few minutes, but then her mind conjured up new images. Sylvie couldn't do anything about it. Every time she envisioned Marit's hands working, she automatically saw herself touching Aeron the same way.

Just then Aeron opened her eyes and gazed right into Sylvie's. She tried to harness her wayward thoughts, but how could that be possible when Aeron looked at her with such intensity?

As their eyes stayed locked for several moments, or it might as well have been hours, Sylvie knew she was in trouble. How would she be able to spend so much time with Aeron and keep a tight lid on her feelings? If she didn't, she'd jeopardize everything.

Chapter Thirteen

Aeron glanced at Sylvie, who looked uneasy where she sat in the passenger seat. "Are you feeling carsick?"

"What? No. Not at all. I'm just not used to riding in one of these."

She grinned. Aeron loved to drive and had been wonderfully surprised to find Maeve had kept her old pickup truck that she'd wanted for her eighteenth birthday. Not only had she kept it, but she'd given Paulina orders to keep it in good running order.

"You mean cars in general or pink pickup trucks in particular?" Aeron snorted now.

"Funny. Pickup trucks. I have a Porsche, but it's in storage back in Sweden."

"Ah. Totally different breed. And very close to the ground. So it's the altitude that gets you in this vehicle?" Aeron thought this silly joke would render her a lethal glance from Sylvie, but instead her passenger tossed her head back and laughed. The husky tone of Sylvie's mirth was new and very contagious. Aeron chuckled, which ignited more laughter in Sylvie.

"Thanks for coming with me. I mean, you must really have a lot of stuff to do other than accompanying me to the Adirondacks, no matter what we said earlier." Aeron shifted lanes and overtook a truck. "If I'm going to meet my deadline I need some of my hard-copy research material that I left behind, since I thought I'd be gone only a few days."

"I brought some work with me, mostly some video presentations created by our media department. I managed to cram in a few completely boring meetings earlier this week." Speaking casually, Sylvie still sounded cheerful.

"So that's why you weren't home the two times I came over to go through the boxes."

Sylvie frowned. "I'm sorry about that. Did you have any questions for me? You could've left voice mails if you did."

"No, no. I just found some dry legal documents having to do with my grandparents' will. I put them aside for later since I didn't understand all that legal mumbo jumbo. Perhaps you can have a look at them at some point?"

"Sure. Well, what I mean is, I'll have one of our lawyers have a look if you want. Remember, I'm a businesswoman so I know some about the law, but I rely heavily on our legal department."

Aeron nodded gratefully. "Thanks. That takes care of that."

"So, the Adirondacks. How did you end up there?"

"I went to summer camp there four summers in a row. When I found a cabin in roughly the same neighborhood, I just had to get it. It's right on the lake and far enough from the closest neighbor for me to not hear or see them, but we can still help each other in an emergency."

"You something of a hermit?

Chuckling, Aeron shook her head. "No. That would mean never seeing a living soul for years and years, right? I enjoy my own company, I need the peace and quiet for my writing, but I also like to socialize with friends, of course. I made friends with Carolyn, Annelie, and Annelie's little sister, Piper. They live about fifteen minutes by car from my cabin and are there almost all weekends, if Carolyn isn't filming. They really prioritize Piper. She's ten-and-a-half and quite precocious." Aeron heard her own longing. Had she ever felt as if Maeve prioritized her, sacrificed anything for her? Hardly.

"I've heard a lot of good things about them through Helena and Noelle."

"They're great. I hope you get to meet them during this trip. We did talk about having a barbecue soon."

Sylvie didn't answer at first, and Aeron took that as a sign that she wasn't interested in getting together.

"Why not?" Sylvie surprised her by saying after a while. "When in Rome and all that. I do enjoy barbecued vegetables. I can't remember when I barbecued last."

"Vegetables? You're a vegetarian?"

Sylvie nodded. "Yes."

"Good to know."

After a few moments of silence, Sylvie turned slightly in her seat toward Aeron. "About before. I can't remember laughing like that for a while. Hearing that must make me seem tremendously boring."

"A bit sad, perhaps, but who am I to judge why you haven't found anything as funny as you find me?" Aeron risked a glance at Sylvie, as they had just hit I-87 north and traffic wasn't too bad this early.

"Oh, I find you hilarious. A laugh a minute, as you say in America."

"Wow. You even have some of our idioms down pat." Aeron was actually impressed with how little accent Sylvie had. "When do Swedes begin learning English?"

"It can vary between schools, but third or fourth grade. It's one of the three subjects required for higher education, at a minimum. The others are math and Swedish."

"That's why most of you are so good at it." Aeron nodded. "When did you come to New York?"

"I was twenty-five. Fifteen years ago." Sylvie turned forward again.

"That's pretty young to take over as CEO."

"You're joking, right?" Sylvie gave a far less joyous laugh than she had before. In fact, it was acerbic.

"What do you mean?" Glancing at Sylvie, Aeron frowned. She hadn't been joking at all.

"My father considered me a failure and sent me here to learn the ropes because he actually realized I did even worse around him than in the presence of just about anyone else."

This insight was so unexpected, Aeron had to force herself to focus solely on traffic for a few moments. Anger radiated from Sylvie and filled the silence in the car. She didn't want to push for details, even if tons of questions crowded the tip of her tongue. What was Sylvie's father like if he could intimidate this woman like he did? Even if Sylvie had been only twenty-five, one year younger than Aeron was now, he'd still wielded some strange power over her. Then again, perhaps it wasn't that strange. Maeve reached for Aeron all the way from the grave.

"Daniel Thorn. You might as well know a few things about him," Sylvie said in a dark voice. "After all, you're going to come face-to-face with him soon enough, and he sniffs out fear or nervousness like a predator. Some would call him exactly that. His family has ruled the Swedish financial market for centuries. Banks, corporations, real estate, and lately, which he never mentions, refugees."

"What do you mean, refugees?" The latter astonished Aeron.

"There's a lot of money to be made providing housing to refugees seeking asylum in Sweden. I'm proud of my country for accepting so many people at our borders and showing them such support. My father sees the business opportunity and has bought real estate and also built some facilities that he rents to the state. It's good money. The state needs the housing, yet the fact that my father feels it's really beneath him makes my skin crawl."

"That's…unexpected."

"Which part?" Sylvie waved her hand dismissively. "Don't answer that."

"I can tell your dad seems like a hard-nosed businessman. But I don't get how you're such a success at Thorn Industries USA. You've even been on the cover of *Forbes* with Helena Forsythe and Eleanor Ashcroft." Aeron cheeks warmed. "I Googled you early on."

"You did, huh?" Oddly, Aeron's comment seemed to soften Sylvie's tone. "I Googled you and came up with pretty much nothing."

"That's reassuring. For now."

"I'll say." Sylvie went silent. "As it turned out, being away from my father and being allowed to blossom at my own pace was just the right way for me to learn. I employed my first assistant, Mark, using my own money, and his patience and loyalty made all the difference. Coming into this part of Thorn's with very little self-esteem also meant I wasn't a cocky, know-it-all boss's daughter, but someone willing to listen and learn."

"You came in with your cup empty."

"Excuse me?"

"Those who think they know everything and act obnoxiously cocky, their cups are already full. They don't have any room for new knowledge and never learn a thing unless they realize that fact." Aeron reached across the gearshift and was patting Sylvie's knee reassuringly before she realized her own intention.

"Thanks. That might have been why I got off to a good start." Sylvie's voice was strained, but she didn't say "hands off" or something similar, which was a relief. "Of course I ran into some people who thought I'd sailed in on a shrimp sandwich—what?"

"A what?" Laughing, Aeron covered her mouth. "A shrimp *sandwich?*"

"Ah. It doesn't translate well." Sylvie chuckled. "But you get the idea."

"I do."

"The one time I ran into serious trouble, it wasn't from anyone in power at the daughter company here." All joy seeped out of Sylvie's voice again. "It was from my father."

❖

Manhattan, 2006

"Have they lost their minds over there?" Daniel Thorn's voice boomed over the phone, making him sound as if he were in the next room rather than across the ocean. "How they can even contemplate making you CEO is beyond me. I won't allow it."

"I don't think it's up to you, Father." As a child Sylvie had called her father daddy, but that was a long time ago. Now, at age thirty-one, she stuck to the more formal way of addressing him. He probably didn't care one way or the other. *"The board of directors has voted."*

"That spineless Harry Stone. I'll fire him the first chance I get." Clearly seething now, Daniel growled. *"If I didn't know better, I'd think you'd slept with the lot of them."*

"Father!"

"Daniel!"

This was when Sylvie and her father realized Camilla was on another phone, listening in. Sylvie was grateful because, if anyone had any pull with Daniel, it was his wife. She'd grown increasingly less impressed with her husband's methods over the years.

"Camilla, I—"

"If I hear you talk to our daughter like that one more time, you won't know what hit you," Camilla said, her voice filled with icicles. *"What a foul thing to say to her, to anyone. You'll be lucky if she ever forgives you for that one."*

"But, Camilla, they've made her—"

"I heard. I heard everything." Camilla dismissed him with ease. *"Congratulations, darling. That's a tremendous achievement, and I think you're going to do the Thorn name proud. Perhaps even rectify some of the reputation your father has bestowed upon it by being less cordial."*

"Thanks, Mom." To hear this from her mother didn't erase the hurt her father caused, but it was still nice. *"Father, I'll talk to you as soon as I've reviewed all the reports my department managers are putting together."*

"And how's that going to happen? How will you possibly be able to?" Obviously, Daniel was trying to soften his tone, as his wife was still listening in.

"The same way I've made it work the last six years." She refused to share anything about Mark. He was leaving as her personal assistant, and she'd offered him a good position at the sales department, which he'd gladly accepted. Now she'd employ

two assistants, as one would be at her side, reviewing all documents with her, and the other running her office. Daniel didn't need to know any of this.

"Yes?"

"Yes."

"For heaven's sake, let her go, Daniel," Camilla said and sighed. "Sylvie, I'm coming over for my autumn shopping in a couple of weeks. We'll celebrate then."

"Uhm..."

"I thought it was a good opportunity, as your father's spending two weeks in China at the time."

Relieved, Sylvie began to smile. "Sounds good, Mom. See you then."

"I'll let you know in more detail."

"Good-bye, Father. I'm sorry this was such a disappointment for you." Sylvie had to say something.

"Hmm. Well. Perhaps if you're not a disaster, we can spin it to the press the right way."

Oh, God. Sylvie covered her eyes. "Bye." She hung up and placed the phone on the nightstand before she lost her temper completely and crushed it against the wall.

It was high time to put her plans into action. She couldn't put it off. She couldn't let her father make her a weird sort of "look what I managed to achieve in the face of adversity" poster child. He'd humiliated her once too often, and this last offensive remark was so hurtful and out of line, she needed an escape route.

Several old comments from Daniel echoed in her mind. "Why can't you just apply yourself?" "You'll be lucky to flip burgers at McDonald's." "I paid enough for tutors for you to feed a small country, and still you fail." "How you made it through the School of Business, Economics and Law, I'll never know. Must have been because they knew you were a Thorn."

Sylvie clenched her jaws and her fists so hard, it hurt. She'd been an average student at the university in Gothenburg, but she'd never cheated or been given any special treatment. To the contrary, she'd had to fight hard for every grade, and the only advantage she'd received was when she couldn't find the textbooks in audio format and someone was appointed to read to her. That and giving her exams orally could hardly be considered perks for being a Thorn.

Determined to be successful as CEO for Thorn's in the US while starting her own company based on her own painstakingly developed plans, Sylvie tried to disregard the hollow feeling in her stomach.

A very small part of her had hoped Daniel would finally recognize her ability and be proud of her. Clearly this would never happen.

CHAPTER FOURTEEN

Adirondacks—Present Day

"Finally!" Aeron's cheerful voice made Sylvie jerk and sit up straight. The rocking motion of the pickup truck as they drove along the winding roads in the Adirondacks had put her to sleep. Now she glanced around her and saw a vast lawn leading all the way down to a lake. To the left sat a log cabin, not unlike the one her parents had in the north of Sweden, but a lot smaller.

"God. That last part was murderous. When you have only another half hour to go, why does that half hour feel like half a day?" Aeron shook her head and stepped out of the car.

Sylvie did the same on her side of the vehicle, remembering at the last moment that she was climbing down from the door opening, rather than up like she did in regular cars. Her Porsche was so low, it actually hurt her back sometimes to get out with reasonable grace.

Outside, the narrow heels of her favorite ankle boots sank a few inches into the grass. Sylvie didn't care. She was busy taking in the beautiful scenery. The leaves on trees still had a light-green hue from spring, and the lawn virtually billowed down toward the lake. She thought she could spot a wooden dock at the edge of the lake and immediately thought of how long it had been since she swam in anything but a pool. As a child she'd always played in the lake not far from her parents' cabin. Nowadays, she did her laps in the pool at her gym located on the roof of her condominium building. Definitely not the same.

"Pity I didn't bring a swimsuit." Sylvie didn't realize she spoke out loud before Aeron answered.

"I have spare ones. You're taller than me, but I'm, uhm, curvier, so I think one of them might fit you."

The tone Aeron used when she spoke of her own curves made Sylvie swallow hard, and she had to fight off images of Aeron in a swimsuit. "Thanks," she murmured. "We'll see if we have time."

"The pace is slower here, so I bet we will. Let me show you the guest room. It's tiny, but it'll give you some privacy." She motioned toward the cabin and reached for what turned out to be a large, old-fashioned key, stuck to something underneath one of the windowsills. This truly was the countryside. Not even her parents were that casual about security. Their cabin had all the bells and whistles when it came to alarms.

As did Aeron, it turned out, when they stepped indoors. The key was only one way of opening the front door. Aeron tapped in a six-digit code on a touchscreen behind a weatherproof lid next to the door handle. The door clicked open and she held it for Sylvie to enter.

"Do I take my shoes off?" Sylvie asked, knowing that some Americans wanted you to do so, and others considered it downright weird.

"Either way's fine, but I suggest keeping them on if you didn't bring indoor shoes. I haven't gotten around to installing floor heating yet."

"I don't think they're dirty." Sylvie wiped her feet on the doormat one more time to be sure before she continued into an open-plan kitchen and living-room area, all very rustic with exposed pine logs and cabinets. Except for the stainless-steel appliances, the rest of the cabin boasted enormous log walls, but oddly enough it all went well together. The kitchen island with its dark-granite top looked well used and suggested Aeron enjoyed cooking and baking.

"To the left of the island." Aeron pointed toward a narrow opening that turned out to lead to an equally narrow staircase.

Upstairs, Aeron guided her to the guest room, which was indeed small but decorated in a way that fit the rusticity. A blue-

and-white quilted bedspread on top of the twin bed matched the white linen curtains with blue trim. The room contained only a small dresser and an exposed clothes rack in addition to the bed and nightstand.

"We'll have to share the large family-size bathroom up here, and there's a half bath downstairs at the foot of the stairs." Aeron shoved her hands into her pockets as if she was bracing herself against scorn or criticism from Sylvie. She obviously thought Sylvie was a hothouse flower, but she wasn't, and obviously, neither was Aeron.

"Thank you. I really like this room. Is yours across the hallway?"

Relaxing visibly, Aeron smiled again. "Yes. It's marginally bigger than this but at least can fit a queen-size bed. A girl's got to have her luxuries, you know."

"Damn straight," Sylvie said and returned the smile. It became increasingly easier to loosen up around this woman. Right now, Aeron stood leaning against the door frame, one leg bent in front of the other and looking a little tired after the five-hour drive with only a few pit stops, but still so attractive. "Why don't we go unpack the groceries we bought in that quaint little grocery store, and then maybe we can fire up your grill and make kabobs? I'll even cook since you did all the driving."

Aeron slumped sideways a little and her smile grew lopsided. "You're on. I'll go light the grill since I use the old-school type with real coals."

"Even better." Sylvie left her bags where they stood in the room and followed Aeron downstairs. As her hostess walked out on a deck via the back door, she made her way back to the car and unloaded the groceries. It took her two trips to carry everything back, and as she returned the second time, she met a frowning Aeron.

"You didn't have to haul all that. I would've helped."

"If you feel like helping even more, you can make us some iced tea or something. Nothing caffeinated or I'll be chatting your ear off all evening." Sylvie began filling the freezer with the new groceries.

"What? I find that hard to believe. You don't seem like the chatty type."

"Oh, you'd be surprised. Caffeine, or for that matter, wine or alcohol, can make me quite talkative." Sylvie peered at Aeron, who was busy running the faucet. "Someone told me once I have three stages. Chatty, nostalgic, and lights out."

Aeron guffawed. "Now there's some useful information. Nostalgic, huh?"

"Don't ask. I have no idea. Apparently I can become reminiscent with someone I've just met if I have a glass of wine too many."

"Wow." Aeron pulled something from the freezer and stirred it into the tall glasses of cold water. "Here you go. Some of Mrs. Gordimer's homemade lemonade. She freezes it so she doesn't have to add, and I quote, any funny stuff to make it last."

"Good thinking." Accepting one of the glasses, Sylvie tasted the pink beverage. It tasted sweet yet slightly acidic, all in all wonderful. Gulping half of it down, she sighed contentedly. "I have to send Mrs. Gordimer a thank-you note. That's amazing."

"She's a lovely lady of almost ninety. Her son owns the grocery store we shopped at. He's begged her to let him sell the lemonade in the store, but she claims that it's a gift among friends only."

"I like her even more." Browsing through some drawers, Sylvie found metal kabob sticks. After dicing mushrooms, peppers, onions, squash, and tomatoes, and slicing ears of corn, she pushed them quickly onto the sticks and put them on a tray. "If you want meat, you can add that to yours."

"No need. I'll slice some bread, and we can have that with butter on the grill and put some herbs on top. That should be filling enough."

They carried everything outside, where Aeron had set a picnic table with a white-and-red checkered tablecloth. "I know," she said and smoothed it down, "it's clichéd."

"It's clichéd for a reason. It's very pretty." Sylvie held her hand just above the glowing coals and judged they were hot enough. Placing the kabobs on the grill located at the far end of the table, she sat down next to Aeron, both of them with their backs against the table, and sipped her lemonade. "I wonder how I can befriend Mrs.

Gordimer enough for her to give me some lemonade." She was only half joking.

"No idea. I didn't think I'd done anything to deserve it, but two years ago, she gave me a jar. Last year I got two, and this summer, we'll see. If she gives me more than two, it might be enough that you're *my* friend. I can give you one."

Sylvie turned her head slowly toward Aeron, who looked entirely serious. "For real?" Had Aeron really meant it?

"For real." Her mouth stretching into a smile, Aeron's eyes were still guarded, as if she thought Sylvie might shoot this idea down. Or laugh. Or both.

"Then I hope I'll become a lemonade-worthy friend." She patted Aeron's arm, much like Aeron had done with her knee in the car.

They sat in the half-shade under the large maple trees, waiting for the kabobs to cook. The sun came and went behind small tufts of clouds, a soft breeze kept it from getting too hot next to the grill, and Sylvie couldn't remember feeling this peaceful in a long time. She adored the hustle and bustle of Manhattan and the world of business when it kept her on edge and ready to strike. Here she sat with a woman hardly anyone knew existed, or had forgotten about at least, and could actually breathe. Otherwise when life slowed down, old ghosts appeared and clung to her back, whispering of childhood pains and teenage traumas, which really should be over and done with by now, but weren't.

"I think they're done," Aeron said and rose. She poked a kabob with a fork. "Yes, they are." They got four sticks each and shared a sourdough baguette Aeron had grilled.

Sylvie ate with pleasure and could tell Aeron was as starved as she was. Aeron hurried into the kitchen at one point and returned with an entire pitcher of lemonade, which made Sylvie almost hug her. That was another strange reaction on her part. She wasn't the touchy-feely kind, but she kept finding excuses to pat Aeron, and this notion to actually hug her...she had to harness herself.

"Maeve never came here." Aeron spoke so quietly, Sylvie almost missed her words.

"No?"

"I know Paulina thinks I should've made more of an effort to invite her. You know? Be the bigger person or whatever. I've never told Paulina this, but I did invite her here, and she said she'd come. I worked like a madwoman, had everything all taken care of and was about to drive to Albany to be at the airport in time, when she called and said she couldn't make it."

"Why not?" Sylvie could easily hear the hurt still present in Aeron's voice.

"She was at a beach party in the Hamptons. As she put it, they'd just had margaritas on the beach when she remembered to call me. Ten minutes before I was to leave for the airport to pick her up! I just stared at my spotless cabin and my first book that I'd signed for her, as I wanted to surprise her. She had no idea I'd published a book. I'd made my bed with the type of bedding she loved, with a gazillion thread count and such, and planned on using the guest room, which wasn't as nice as it is now. I'd mowed the lawn, weeded around the house, and washed the outdoor furniture. I think I worked from morning till bedtime for four days. And she forgets she's supposed to come."

"She must've felt horrible." Sylvie hoped so.

"Not really. Not judging from how she was halfway talking to me and halfway giggling with some young guy, saying, 'Oh, Donnie, stop. There are people here, stop...'" Aeron gave a quiet sob. "I'm sorry. I'm being ridiculous for weeping over such old stuff now."

"No, don't say that. Go on. What did you tell her then?" Sylvie really wanted to know. This was her chance to see another side of Maeve.

"I told her she'd done this to me for the last time. I'd grown up with low self-esteem. This wasn't anything new. On rare occasions, Maeve would put her mom-hat on and we'd play house for a few hours at most, not very long but long enough for me, as a child, to get my hopes up. And this time, showing me where her priorities lay, she made it very clear—I wasn't the one she'd ever choose above everybody else. I was nothing."

"Oh, Aeron." Furious at the Maeve of several years ago, Sylvie rounded the table and sat down next to Aeron. Carefully she pulled her in for a hug. She wasn't surprised to find Aeron rigid and trembling. Such hurtful old memories tended to dwell in the muscle memory.

"So, I hung up and half-expected, or at least hoped, she'd try to call back, but she didn't. She was there in the Hamptons drugging, drinking, and screwing around with a young man named Donnie, and I was here. I remember burning the author copy I'd signed for her. I sat by the fireplace and watched the flames devour all the words I'd written, the story I'd created, and I promised myself that she'd never visit here. Ever. And that's how it turned out."

"I can only try to imagine how hurt you must've felt. I won't compare myself to you, since we all handle things differently, but I do know what it can be like to feel betrayed."

"Yes. I saw her a few times in New York after that, but during the last five years of her life, I talked to her only on the phone. Never in real life." Slumping sideways, Aeron hid her face against Sylvie's shoulder. "And now it's too fucking late anyway. She's gone. Not that she was mine before, but now she'll never be. She'll never learn about my modest success when it comes to my writing."

"I know it's hardly any consolation, but she was working toward all that. Her motives for trying to better herself aren't entirely clear, but I suspect it had a lot to do with you. She put together her will after she started paying attention to her family's business. Perhaps she feared you might be tempted to walk in her footsteps and wanted you to have options. Didn't she say something like that on the tape?"

"In other words, but yes. I suppose so." Aeron lifted her head. "I'm sorry for pouring all of this on you. You have your own wacky family member to deal with."

Sylvie had to chuckle at the idea of anyone calling Daniel Thorn wacky. "As I said, I want to hear about what happened to you. I really do want to help, contract or no contract." Sylvie was stunned at how true this was. No matter the deal they'd signed, she wanted to be of use to Aeron, so bruised by a thoughtless and selfish mother,

"Why don't we do the dishes and then have another look at the diary?" Sylvie suggested, wanting to redirect Aeron's thoughts.

"Yeah? You want to do that? You're not too tired?"

Sylvie snorted. "I may have fifteen years on you, but I'm made of quite sturdy stuff."

Aeron grinned. "I'll say. Sitting here with me drowning you in tears is no small feat."

"Don't mention it." Sylvie rose and began to gather the dirty plates and place them on a tray. "I'm famous for my unswayable courage."

Aeron got up to help, and together they carried everything back inside, after making sure the grill could be left unattended. Sylvie filled the dishwasher while Aeron placed condiments back into the refrigerator, and even if they didn't exchange many words, the ambiance in the cabin felt calm and the fresh air easy to breathe.

Chapter Fifteen

Adirondacks—Fall 2010

Curious where the path through the woods led to, Aeron strolled slowly while inhaling the crisp air. The sun seemed pale and distant, as it barely penetrated the clouds. She hadn't been farther than her garden, although that wasn't a good name for the overgrown lot where her cabin was built. She'd have to put in a lot of hours clearing the weeds and shrubbery.

Aeron walked for ten minutes before she saw another house through the pine trees. She didn't intend to start her life in the new neighborhood by trespassing, so she slowed down and tried to find some markings that indicated where these people's property started. Perhaps she was already trespassing?

"Hello there?" A husky voice startled Aeron, and she took a step back while trying to pinpoint where it came from.

"I'm sorry. I didn't mean to—"

"Hey, don't run away." A woman in her late forties, devastatingly beautiful, stepped out on the path about ten yards from her. "You're our new neighbor, aren't you?"

"Yes. I suppose so. I moved in a week ago. My name is Aeron. Aeron DeForest."

"Carolyn Black." The woman took off some work gloves and extended an elegant hand. "Nice to meet you, Aeron."

"Carolyn Black?" Aeron gawked at the woman before her. How could she have missed that? This was one of the most famous and popular actors in the US, perhaps even the world. Diana Maddox. Who hadn't read the books about the immensely popular lesbian criminal investigator? And here she was, in the flesh, in a manner of speaking. "Good to meet you too."

"Want to come over and say hello to Annelie? I believe she's making one of her famous apple-raspberry pies." Carolyn waved to Aeron to follow her. "You like pies?"

"I do." Annelie? That had to be the woman Carolyn Black had unexpectedly fallen in love with. It had been headline news a couple of years ago, and like most other people at her university, Aeron had devoured it. More and more lesbian celebrities had come out, and in Aeron's mind, they were all cool and brave for doing so. It had taken her quite a while to realize her own sexual orientation. Having people like Carolyn Black and Annelie Peterson as role models meant a lot.

She followed Carolyn quietly and saw the tall, blond woman before she spotted them.

"Look who I found skulking around." Carolyn walked up to her partner and kissed her lightly on the lips. "Our new neighbor, Aeron DeForest. This is Annelie, my fiancée."

Annelie tilted her head and looked thoughtfully at her. "DeForest," she said slowly. "Any relation to Maeve DeForest?"

"She's my mother. We don't see each other very often."

"I see. I've met your mother only twice, I believe, at some charity events in New York. Well, now that we've been introduced, I'm going to win you over by offering you a slice of my pie with homemade custard. You'll love it." Annelie smiled warmly and walked into the log cabin, three times the size of Aeron's. The interior was typical for this type of house, very rustic. Aeron longed to start renovating her cabin and decided to shamelessly steal ideas from this cozy home.

"Have a seat," Carolyn said and pointed toward a tall stool by the kitchen island. We usually have our meals here when we're not eating on the patio. A bit too nippy for that today."

"Thanks." Aeron sat and watched the interaction between the two women. Carolyn, poised and elegant, Annelie, at least ten years her junior, tall and lithe, and yet they were so clearly...one. Two individuals but joined in something that had to be love. Aeron had observed friends fall heads over heels, or so they claimed, and watched them crash and burn after weeks, months, or even years. To her it appeared that love was far too dangerous. She wasn't stupid. She was well aware of her well-founded trust issues.

"Coffee or tea?" Carolyn asked and moved to a futuristic-looking espresso machine. *"I can make anything you want with this baby."*

"Oh. Wow. Um. A latte, double shot of espresso?"

"A girl after my own heart," Carolyn said and looked triumphantly at Annelie, who snorted softly.

"I'm in favor of tea these days, but I'll have a half-espresso shot in my latte, Carolyn."

They sat down at the kitchen island, Aeron and Carolyn on one side and Annelie at an angle from them. When both her hostesses looked at her with such expectation, Aeron had to laugh.

"What are you thinking? Am I supposed to share my life history?" She grinned.

"It's a start. I want to know everything about you," Carolyn said. *"I'm not sure why, but as soon as I saw you among the trees, it was as if I knew you."*

The famous actor's frank words surprised her. She was pretty sure Carolyn didn't say something like this to just any stranger, in the woods or otherwise.

"I'm from New York. Manhattan. I'm a newly graduated English/history major and am writing my first novel."

The way Carolyn and Annelie leaned in when she talked opened the floodgates. Aeron told them about the main twists and turns of her childhood, and even if she didn't say how she felt about her decision to stay away from her mother, she got the impression they understood that too.

"Well, I for one think it was a blessing you bought the cabin next to ours. It's been under-utilized for the last ten years, or so we've heard."

"Twelve," Aeron said. "The garden, or what you might call the jungle, is proof of nature's ability to take over."

"Want some help?" Annelie asked.

Again she felt like she'd fallen down a rabbit's hole or two. "Sure, but you've seen it, right? It's pretty bad."

"I've seen it." Annelie nodded with an odd gleeful expression.

"You'd be doing her a favor. She bought a full set of different garden tools last spring and has whipped our garden into submission twice already." Carolyn ran the back of her hand along Annelie's jawline. "You're dying to use that brush cutter, aren't you?"

"Busted." Annelie took Carolyn's hand and kissed her palm.

Aeron blinked at the small tears rising in her eyes. This. This was what everyone who spoke of love wanted. This connection. She wanted it but was sure it wasn't for her. Aeron recognized that she was observing Carolyn and Annelie's interaction like she would a priceless painting at a museum. So beautiful and desirable...and out of reach. No money in the world could buy you this, and she was only too aware of that fact. Being friends with Carolyn and Annelie and basking in their interest would have to be enough.

❖

Adirondacks—Present Time

Voices boomed, echoed, and faded. Aeron tried to cover her ears, but her hands were stuck somehow, and she screamed for the people around her to let go. Instead, they held on harder, telling her to calm down, it would soon be over. Not sure how she knew they were lying, Aeron called out her mother's name.

"Aeron, please. Wake up." A gentle voice laced with concern filtered through the nightmare.

"Wh-what?" Aeron opened her eyes and saw the outline of a person sitting on the side of her bed. "No! You're dead! You died!"

"Aeron, it's Sylvie. I'm in your guest room, remember?" Sylvie's voice was even and reassuring, and the way her hands held on gently to Aeron's shoulders grounded her.

"Sylvie? Who...Oh. Of course." Groaning, Aeron rubbed a hand over her face. "For a moment..."

"You called out for Maeve. Did you think I was her?"

"Yes. Probably. Oh, God." Grimacing, Aeron shuddered and tried to clear the nightmare from her mind. She'd had it before, many times, but this time, waking up with a woman sitting on her bed, it had really rattled her. "I'm so thirsty."

"Wait. Let me help you." Sylvie reached over to the nightstand. "Watch your eyes. I'm turning on the light."

Closing her eyes briefly, Aeron opened them quickly again as the dream still seemed to hover at the edges of her field of vision, just waiting to reappear. She watched Sylvie pour some water from her pitcher and hand her the glass. "Here."

"Thanks." Drinking in slow, deep gulps, Aeron handed the glass back. "One more, please?"

"Sure." Sylvie repeated the process, and this time the water finally quenched Aeron's thirst.

"I'm okay," Aeron said, feeling awkward now when the light was on and embarrassment surged within her. What was Sylvie thinking? Was she sorry she'd come along to the Adirondacks? Did she think Aeron was too frail and weak to carry on with their agreement? Furious for second-guessing herself—and Sylvie— and creating new mind-ghosts when she had no reason for stupid speculations, she guardedly looked at Sylvie.

"I'm glad you feel better," Sylvie said and tugged at her dark-blue shorts as if this would make them cover more. She also wore a matching lace-trimmed tank top. "I was on my way back from the bathroom when I heard you."

"Yeah. Nightmares. Sort of a same old, same old." Aeron rubbed her eyes and squinted at the alarm clock. "Three thirty? Great. That's just a few hours of sleep. I'm going to look like a wreck tomorrow."

"What do you mean? Are you getting up?" Sylvie also looked at the clock. "Can't you go back to sleep?"

"No, not normally. What tends to happen is—" Feeling skinless, she stopped herself before she shared too much. "Just not a good idea."

Sylvie extended her hand and carefully took Aeron's chin between her thumb and index finger. With the lightest of pressure, she tipped Aeron's head back and met her gaze. Her scent bewitched Aeron's senses. "The nightmare keeps going, like in a loop?" she asked cautiously.

Aeron could hardly breathe but did her best to not let on how the gentle touch affected her. "Yes. Sometimes that happens. Often enough for me to not want to risk it."

"Because you're usually home alone?"

"Usually? Yes. Or always." Smiling wryly, Aeron pulled up her knees and hugged them to her chest under the covers. "It doesn't take a rocket scientist to figure out I'm a bit of a recluse."

"You and me both," Sylvie muttered and slowly withdrew her hand. "It's the strangest thing. Every time I think we're very different, you say or do something, or describe something that mirrors something from my own past or present. I won't tell you right now how all of this ties in to my own experience, since I'd rather you'd try going back to sleep."

"But—"

"I'm a light sleeper, and if you sound this distraught again, I'll hear you, and I'll come and wake you up. Perhaps not being here alone and having someone to talk to has caused you not to have to process whatever you're dreaming of right away?"

"Perhaps," Aeron said. "Okay, I'll try. If I have another one, I'll get up and be really quiet."

"Fair enough." Standing, Sylvie remained by the bed for a few moments while Aeron curled up on her right side.

"Thanks," Aeron said, yawning. "Will you be able to get back to sleep?"

"I think so." Sylvie didn't look entirely convinced. Did she also suffer from nightmares or perhaps insomnia?

"You know, I feel better knowing you're here." Aeron regretted her words at first, but when Sylvie gave her the softest of smiles, she was glad she'd spoken the truth. Something told her not a great many people ever saw Sylvie smile like that.

As Sylvie said good night and padded out of her room, Aeron was unwilling to turn off the light completely and instead put the dimmer on its lowest setting. Listening to the wind coming through the maples and sweeping along the windows, she hugged her pillow close, thinking of the reoccurring nightmare. Having gone through an invasive medical procedure at age nine, something she later learned Maeve pushed for and finally found a doctor to sign off on, she remembered crying for Maeve and Paulina. The staff did their best to console her, but she was in full panic mode, and the fear stayed with her for many nights over the years.

"And, you know what, Maeve?" Aeron whispered. "They never found anything wrong with me. All those tests, all that poking and prodding, and Dr. Burke was right the entire time."

Closing her eyes, Aeron let her mind leave the nightmare and the resentment that usually resulted from that particular nightmare session. Instead she thought of the amazing view she'd woken up to with Sylvie sitting on her bed looking at her with such concern. Her skin, so pale and flawless, made Aeron want to touch it to see if it was as silky as it appeared. Sylvie's long hair had flowed around her shoulders in an enticingly sexy bed-hair manner. This startling concept gave her pause. When had she begun to regard Sylvie as attractive? Probably the second time they met. But sexy? And not just a little bit, but more like gorgeously sexy.

Aeron had realized she was a lesbian about the same time she started her last year in college. Like a lot of other young women, she took advantage of her college experience to figure out if this was curiosity or the real deal. After going on a few dates with guys, she knew. Despite being great guys, they didn't catch her eye like the women did. She didn't fall in love with any of her female dates, but she did fall in lust a few times. However, she'd never responded to any of those girls like she reacted to Sylvie's presence. Yes, they'd been cute and pretty, some super-feminine and some decidedly on the butch side, as she wasn't sure if she was supposed to have a preference.

Now, with Sylvie sleeping—if she'd managed to go back to sleep yet—in the next room, Aeron had to clench her thighs and hold her breath to keep from gasping out loud. Her ever-agile imagination conjured up images of Sylvie offering to share Aeron's bed in case she had another nightmare. How would she have reacted if Sylvie had? Aeron wished she'd had the confidence to follow her desires but knew she didn't. As it were, that hadn't happened and never would. For now, Aeron would have to settle for enjoying Sylvie's company and perhaps a budding friendship.

❖

Gothenburg, Summer 1987

"Aren't you done yet?" Camilla strode into the library where Sylvie sat with her homework.

"I've finished the math stuff. That was easy." Sylvie hoped Camilla wouldn't ask too much about the essay she was supposed to write.

"And the essay?" Camilla walked over and glanced down at the desk. "But, Sylvie, you've written only a few sentences."

"I've got a good idea about what to write, but..." Tears formed and clung to her lashes, and she tried to force them not to fall. "I tried to write faster, but I have to find all the words in my textbook, and it takes so long."

"You're going to fail that assignment if you don't hand in an essay, honey." Camilla pulled up a chair and sat down next to her. "This is how we'll do it. You dictate to me, and then you copy what I wrote."

"Isn't that cheating?" Sylvie swallowed the last of the tears and looked questioningly at her mother.

"A little bit, but not where it counts. It's your essay, your words."

"But, Mom, they're going to know it isn't my writing. They're going to know someone helped me. That's even worse than failing the assignment." The idea of being found out before the entire class appalled her. They already had her pegged as stupid and slow, even if she was the best in her class when it came to math. "We can't do this, Mom."

"*Then it's about time I talk to your headmaster. You have the right to receive special classes and—*"

"*No! Oh, please, Mom. All the kids think I'm weird as it is. If you have them send me to the special class, I might as well forget about school. I won't go.*" *Her panic rose like bile in her throat.* "*I swear I won't.*"

"*What's this racket about?*" *Daniel stepped into the library.* "*Aren't you in bed yet?*"

"*Just finishing my homework, Father.*"

"*How can a sixth-grader have enough homework to keep her up past ten?*" *Daniel looked like he debated whether to go into one of his rants about the incompetent teachers in a failing school system. Thankfully he decided he needed a glass of scotch more and left the room after telling her to wrap it up and go to bed.*

"*See? I have to go to bed, Mom.*"

"*I know. But before you do, I have an idea. What if I speak to your teacher and explain how they can't demand you do the exact same assignments as the students who don't suffer from dyslexia. I want you to use this,*" *she reached into a drawer and pulled out one of her father's Dictaphones,* "*and record the essay in your room. If you get a sentence wrong, just press here and here and back up to where you want to start from.*" *She showed her the buttons on the machine. Then you take it with you tomorrow to school and show her. I know the school has alternative methods in place for students with your disability.*"

Disability? Really? Sylvie hadn't regarded the infuriating, hateful problem she had with reading and writing as a sort of disability. Now she grabbed the Dictaphone and hugged her mother.

"*Thanks, Mom. I'll try this. If she hates it, at least I tried to create more than a few sentences.*"

"*Exactly.*" *Smiling wistfully, Camilla cupped her chin.* "*No harm in trying.*"

Sylvie stacked her homework with the Dictaphone on top and was about to leave the library and return to her room when her father appeared, scotch in hand.

"About time. Good night—wait, what are you doing with one of my machines? Those aren't meant to be toys—"

"Daniel. I let her borrow it. It's for school." Camilla's voice was laced with iron, and even if Daniel normally ran everything, he pulled back the hand he'd just extended to take back his machine.

"School? A recording?" He looked suspiciously at them.

"Yes. You know her dyslexia is giving her more and more trouble. With this and some extra tapes, she can record her assignments and also record some classes where they're meant to take notes."

Daniel stood still in the center of the library, which Sylvie found rather fitting, as his empire, his entire world, always revolved around him. His word was law, and he never let anyone forget it. Camilla was one of the few who could oppose him.

"As long as the school agrees, I suppose the idea has merit." He nodded slowly and sipped his scotch. "That said," he added and pointed at Sylvie before she had the chance to mumble her intended 'Good night, Father' and slip out the door, "don't forget for a second that it's a form of cheating, and for a Thorn, that's not entirely acceptable. If it weren't for wanting to keep you from embarrassing us completely, I wouldn't allow it. I can tell you, my father and uncle would spin in their graves at the mere idea of a Thorn cutting corners like this—"

"Daniel!" Camilla growled from behind him, making him pivot. "You should know better than to have opinions when the topic is something you know nothing about. If you'd have taken the least bit of interest in the latest research regarding dyslexia, you'd know that the only way to judge the person in question fairly is to give them different tools to even the playing field. For heaven's sake, Daniel, even our King Carl Gustav has dyslexia, and you call him one of your dearest friends!"

His cheeks going a faint red, Daniel muttered something inaudible and emptied his glass. As he left the room, he didn't even look at Sylvie, which suited her fine.

"Is he mad at you now, Mom?" Sylvie whispered as they made their way up the stairs.

"Perhaps a little. It wasn't smart to argue in front of you, honey. Still, he's an intelligent man and now he knows he's wrong—or at least that I think he is. Your father is such a proud man, and not many people know him the way I do. In fact, after his uncle died, I'd say you and I are the only ones who see the true person."

This sounded horrible. If her father was his true self with her, then he must really think she wasn't much of a daughter. He criticized her a lot, and after observing other fathers she came across, she knew not all of them carried on the way Daniel did. Another thought struck her. If nobody but Camilla and Sylvie ever saw the true Daniel Thorn, he must be a very lonely person, having to pretend with everyone else. Sylvie knew quite a bit about loneliness. A twitch below her rib cage proved she could still feel sorry for Daniel, even if he intimidated her...frightened her, even.

Sylvie spent half the night dictating her essay, and when she finally crawled into bed, she was pleased with the result. She didn't like to hear her own voice—very few people did when they heard themselves on tape—but the story was good. She loved making up stories, but so far she hadn't been able to save any of them for someone else to read or hear. Now her teachers would know she could write, even if she could normally only crank out three or four sentences in an hour.

As sleep overtook her, she dreamed of how thrilled the teachers would be and how this would make Daniel finally see she wasn't stupid or lazy. She worked harder than most kids in her class, and if he were home more he'd know that. Perhaps if he realized she wasn't stupid, he'd ease up on the criticism and start seeing her the way other fathers saw their children. Then he'd be less lonely and so would she.

The teachers never did get to hear that particular story. Sylvie presented it proudly when it was time for Swedish class, but the teacher frowned and shook her head.

"I have to check with the headmaster, Sylvie. This isn't how you were supposed to return the assignment. Everyone else has had to think of spelling, penmanship, and so on. You can't expect us to give you special treatment just because you're Daniel Thorn's daughter."

Sylvie didn't protest. She tucked the Dictaphone into her bag and sat down at her desk. Fearing she might actually shed tears in class, she refused to blink. Her eyes burned from the dryness, and then she closed them hard.

"Hey, Sylvie?" Viktoria, the new girl, whispered to her while the teacher busied herself with some papers at the front of the class.

"Yes?" Sylvie whispered back.

"I want to hear that story. I bet it's good. You wouldn't dare bring a tape with you to school if it wasn't really, really good." She smiled in a guileless manner that surprised Sylvie. Viktoria had belonged to their class for only a couple of weeks, and Sylvie knew sooner or later the popular girls would suck her in. Right now, Viktoria's interest in her story was like balm on her frayed nerves.

"All right. Meet me at the girls' bathroom during our free period."

"Okay. Just the two of us?"

"If you tell anyone else, I won't share it." Sylvie was astonished at how stern she could sound.

"I won't tell a soul." Viktoria looked happy.

After listening to Sylvie's story, Viktoria was clearly impressed. "That's awesome. The teacher is stupid for not wanting to listen. I'd tell my parents if I were you."

"I'll tell my mom, anyway," Sylvie said. She had mixed feelings: devastated because of the teacher's reaction and thrilled that Viktoria liked it. Her father would hear of the teacher rejecting her way of delivering her essay. If he'd been like the other fathers she'd observed, he'd tell the teacher off and make sure the headmaster knew what was fair.

"Your mother's beautiful," Viktoria said wistfully. "My mom's nice and everything, but she's not anywhere near as pretty as yours."

Not quite sure how to deal with the change in topic, Sylvie thought fast. Her mother's face was often displayed on the cover of tabloid magazines. In some she was alone, and in others she was holding onto Daniel's arm. He in turn always looked handsome and distinguished. These pictures proved only one thing to Sylvie. Looks meant nothing. Her mother was beautiful on the outside and strong and kind on the inside. Daniel was handsome on the outside and impatient, arrogant, and ill-tempered on the inside.

"Want to come to my house tomorrow?" Viktoria asked. "My grandma's visiting from up North, and she's going to show me how to crochet."

Crochet? Sylvie had tried it a few times in needlework classes at school, but her lack of patience for such things made her ask the teacher if she could paint on fabrics instead. Still, it could be fun. She hadn't been invited anywhere for years.

"Sure. That sounds...interesting." She smiled cautiously at Viktoria, who merely looked thrilled at the idea.

On her way home from school, Sylvie dared hope that she might have a real friend who wasn't influenced by a parent who wanted to suck up to Daniel Thorn. If this turned out to be true, dictating that essay would be her best achievement yet.

Chapter Sixteen

Adirondacks—Present Time

"Please tell me you're a coffee person?" Carolyn asked. "Annelie has been staying away from this beverage of the gods lately." She stroked her auburn hair behind her ear and looked pleadingly at Sylvie.

Aeron had to hide a smile at how entranced Sylvie looked. No, dazed was a better word. It was one thing to know you were going to meet a world-famous actress and a whole different thing to actually do it. Yes, Helena and Noelle swore Carolyn was down-to-earth and very sweet in private, but all Sylvie could envision was how Carolyn portrayed Diana Maddox on the big screen—charismatic and commanding.

"I swear that wife of mine could persuade the most stubborn tea-drinker that they adored coffee instead." Annelie Peterson, publisher and film producer, shook her head with a loving expression in her eyes. "She seems nice."

"Good thing you married her then," Aeron deadpanned. She and Annelie sat at the other end of the screened porch, observing Carolyn and Sylvie.

"What? Oh, you're joking." Chuckling, Annelie pinched Aeron's side. "I meant your friend Sylvie, of course."

"Yes, of course." Smiling broadly, Aeron kept her eyes on the two over by the coffee station in their living room. "Sylvie's very nice actually. She hid just how nice she was from me at first, though."

"Smart move when you think about the cutthroat business she's in. She seems quite guarded even now. Maybe I need to rescue her if she really doesn't enjoy coffee?" Annelie asked.

"From what I've seen, she loves the stuff."

"Oh, thank God. But let's join them anyway. I want to know more about this woman." They strolled over to the other two and sat down in the two wicker loveseats, everyone with their chosen beverage.

"Annelie told me you're getting ready to film the next Maddox movie," Aeron said. "Last time I was over, you were still debating whether to do that or a one-woman play first." Aeron kicked off her shoes and pulled her legs up. Sylvie sat next to her, less relaxed but with a friendly expression. Her dark hair was arranged in a loose side-bun, and she wore jeans and a green golf shirt.

"I decided to do the movie first, since my producer gave me a chance to actually decide the time frame." Carolyn took Annelie's hand. "As we're on schedule for something else in our lives as well, it fit perfectly."

"What do you mean?" Aeron asked.

"We're going to be parents in five months." Annelie's eyes glittered.

"What? Oh, that's amazing!" Smiling brightly, Aeron pressed her hands against her cheeks. "That's the best news ever."

"Congratulations," Sylvie said. "I wish you the very best, both of you."

"I hope you make me an honorary aunt, and I have first dibs on babysitting." Aeron took Sylvie's hand and squeezed hard. She was so happy for the couple in front of them. They were such good friends and very loyal. They deserved all the happiness in the world. "What does Piper think? Where is she, by the way?"

"At the stables. She's completely hooked on horses of all kinds, but mainly the pony I told you about. Annelie bought it for her since the owner had to sell it, as they were moving." Carolyn turned to Sylvie. "We're Piper's guardians. She's Annelie's little sister, well, half-sister, and she's lived with us for two years now. Even if she's come a long way after losing her mother, she's still sensitive to loss. Going through something similar with her beloved pony might have become too much, or so we feared."

"I have a horse back in Sweden," Sylvie said, surprising Aeron. "I've thought of selling him, but one of my parents' gardeners has a daughter, Ingela, who rides him. And very successfully, I might add. She competes in dressage."

"I'm sure the kid riding your horse feels like she won the lottery. All the fun and none of the bills." Aeron realized she was still holding Sylvie's hand. She let go but patted it before she pulled hers back completely. "Don't sell him."

"I'll introduce him to you when we're there." Sylvie looked at Aeron with something entirely soft in her eyes. "I'm sure Ingela won't mind us riding him."

"Riding?" Aeron regretted taking a stand for the horse. She hadn't counted on having to ride.

"Oh, the look on your face..." Annelie laughed. "And you're going to Sweden, Aeron?"

"Yes. We plan to visit Sylvie's childhood home and her parents. Besides, you'd look just like me if you were going to climb some enormous animal for the first time." Aeron shuddered. "Can't it be enough if I give him a bunch of carrots?"

"Aw, come on," Sylvie said, clearly teasing her now. "You'll be fine. If you don't want to ride after meeting him, I won't nag you."

"Sure." Looking skeptically at Sylvie, she then returned her focus to Carolyn and Annelie. "Either way, I couldn't be happier for you regarding this baby. I can't wait to meet him or her."

"Same here." Annelie patted her stomach. "I'm not showing much, but yesterday I thought I felt the tiniest flutter. And don't tell me it's just gas." She glowered at Carolyn, who managed to laugh and look innocent at the same time.

"So, your agreement, which I understand you can't share a lot about, means you're joined at the hip?" Carolyn sipped her coffee and hummed with obvious pleasure as she studied Sylvie over the rim of the mug.

"When you put it that way..." Sylvie looked flustered. "I suppose it can seem like that. Maeve had some stipulations in her will, and we're trying to honor those. Actually, we're doing each other a few favors in the midst of everything. My parents are demanding, especially my father. Having Aeron with me as a distraction will help immensely."

"That sounds intriguing. Will you ever be able to share the details?" Annelie shifted and allowed Carolyn to stack a few pillows behind her. "Sciatic pain," she explained.

"I think once we've completed the conditions of the will and everything has gone the way Maeve stipulated, that shouldn't be a problem. If that's what Aeron wants." Sylvie glanced at Aeron. "The will mostly concerns you."

"Yes, of course. I didn't mean to pry," Annelie said quickly.

"Oh, God, I know that." Aeron spoke quickly. "You two are my best friends."

"I didn't mean to imply—" Sylvie looked mortified. "I'm sorry." She pulled away from Aeron and seemed to shrink into the corner of the couch.

"Hey, you're looking out for Aeron. That's a big plus in my book." Carolyn smiled gently. "Apart from a very small group of people, Aeron hasn't had too many people go the extra mile for her. When I ran into her in the woods between our properties, it was like a revelation. I had to bring up my siblings when I was very young, which I suppose gives me a protective streak. Aeron reminded me of my sister at that age—innocent and feeling rejected, albeit for very different reasons. Aeron let us in rather quickly, which was surprising, and after that she was simply family. A treasure. Annelie had met her mother, as they moved in some of the same circles at one point, in New York. This way we had some knowledge of Maeve DeForest before Aeron even told us. She did confide in us though, and I'm glad she did. She needed someone on her side. "

"Please. I'm sitting right here, and I'm not a frail little flower who can't make friends if I want to." Aeron pouted deliberately and found it rather fun that she managed to make them all look at her with the same startled expression. "After all, I'm the one here who thinks up all the scary stuff, right? That must mean I'm the toughest among us."

"Oh, you—" Annelie took one of the pillows and threw it at Aeron, who caught it and hugged it to her.

"But, all jokes aside," Aeron said, "you have a point. I don't let people in easily, and that has its reasons. It's nice to have friends that have your back. I hope you know I have yours as well."

"This is getting so emotional, I need more coffee." Carolyn rose and caressed the back of Aeron's head when she passed her. "We know, honey."

Looking furtively at Sylvie, Aeron was relieved to see she'd relaxed, at least marginally. What the hell had they said that made Sylvie react that way? Something had triggered her response, and Aeron was certain she'd never seen Sylvie look so forlorn.

"You okay?" Aeron mouthed as Annelie was busy retrieving the pillow from her and getting comfortable again.

Sylvie nodded briefly. "Yes, of course." The automatic reply didn't convince Aeron, but the fact that Sylvie slowly became less rigid did.

Carolyn took longer than they expected, but when she returned she had a young girl of about eleven or twelve years old with her. "Look who I found sneaking in through the back door."

"Sneaking in?" Piper snorted. "You're the one who says 'If I see any of those clothes you wear at the stables anywhere near the foyer...' and that's why I come in through the mudroom." She grinned at Carolyn. "And yes. I showered and placed the clothes in the washing machine. I didn't start it though. I can never remember how much detergent to put in. And remember when I forgot to—"

"Piper, we have friends visiting," Annelie said mildly. "This is Aeron's good friend Sylvie Thorn. She's from Sweden but lives in Manhattan. Sylvie, this is my little sister, Piper."

"Hello. I hear we share a love for horses." Sylvie extended her hand and Piper took it politely.

"You love horses too? That's brilliant! Do you have a horse in the US? Do you ride in Central Park? Can I—what?" Piper stopped talking as Carolyn placed a gentle hand on her shoulder.

"Why don't you save all those questions for dinner? Aeron and Sylvie are joining us, and you and Sylvie can discuss such things then. Right now, I need help setting the table."

"Sure thing. What are we having?" Piper waved at the other three as she followed Carolyn into the kitchen.

"Piper can eat anytime, not that you can see it. I think all her physical activities burn all the food." Annelie smiled, but with sadness in her eyes. "In the beginning I worried she might eat this much because she sometimes went hungry when her mother couldn't pay for groceries. She did her best, I know that, but..." She grimaced and shifted again.

"Her poor mother," Aeron said. "Such torment not to be able to put enough food on the table."

"Piper told us her mother would give her what food they had and go without, but sometimes that wasn't enough. It's unfortunately not that uncommon. Kids go hungry all over the country."

"Even in Sweden, though a lot less than here, I believe. I come from a very privileged background and can't fathom going without food." Sylvie spoke quietly. "I also have a loving mother, which no one should take for granted." She glanced at Aeron.

"My mother wasn't mature enough to have a child, but I'm still glad she had me, for obvious reasons. I never lacked for food." Only for attention, some sign that she mattered and that Maeve truly loved her.

"I grew up with a single mother." Annelie's smile was tender. "We weren't well off by any stretch of the imagination, but I was always well fed and clothed. She passed away when I was a teenager, and our neighbor took me in. My father wasn't in the picture. Later he was busy abandoning Piper like he abandoned me."

"That's hard on a kid." Aeron regarded Annelie with affection. "I wish I knew who my father was. Or is, as I assume he's still alive."

"Any news at all on that front?" Annelie asked.

"Not really. I'm debating whether to let a private investigator look for him, but I'm not sure yet. I mean, yes, I want to know, but not at any cost."

Sylvie tilted her head. "How do you mean?"

"He most likely has his life all sorted out. I have no idea on what terms he and Maeve parted. Perhaps she ended up hating him. Or he might have thought she was trying to trap him."

"Whoa. Those are quite some assumptions. He might not even know about you. What if he would love to get to know you? That's a possibility as well." Annelie sat up, made a face, and sank back against the cushions with a soft moan. "Damn this darn sciatic nerve, or whatever it is that hurts."

"You're pale," Aeron said, concerned now. "Do you need anything?"

"She needs to lie down." Carolyn stood in the doorway, her blue-gray eyes dark as she regarded her wife. "All those hours at the desk. Why can't you be normal and take your laptop to bed like everyone else?"

"Sorry. I will, I will." Annelie stood slowly. "I'm not even showing yet, and this darn back of mine is already giving me problems." She kissed the top of Carolyn's head. "Forgive me. I'm going to have to lie down now instead. I don't think my back can handle the dining-room chairs."

"Don't worry about it. I'll save you dinner and bring it to the bedroom. Piper and I'll entertain our guests."

"If you'd rather we leave…" Aeron said, but stopped talking when Carolyn looked mildly panicked.

"Oh, no, you don't. You're going to come to the dining room and have dinner with Piper and me. There'll be far too much food left otherwise."

"All right." Walking over to Annelie, Aeron kissed her cheek gently. "Go rest. We'll catch up more later. We're leaving for Manhattan tomorrow at noon, but I'll be back home here before you know it. You'll be tired of me."

"Never going to happen. We intend to stay here another month and then we'll go back to Manhattan while Carolyn's on location there. If all goes according to plan, it'll coincide with Piper's fall semester."

"Darling. Go—lie—down." Carolyn frowned slightly but mellowed when Annelie did as told.

As they went to have dinner, Aeron looked at the couple most of America adored. Carolyn had never been more popular in the entertainment business, and Annelie's companies grew exponentially every year. Piper was clearly thriving. A forbidden question—if she would ever meet the one who'd end up being to her what these two were to each other—poked through her defenses. She glanced in Sylvie's direction to see if she was taken with the obvious love and respect permeating the air in this house. She hadn't expected to see Sylvie standing by the window, her profile as if chiseled in granite. She was thinking of something somber, for sure. "Sylvie?" Sylvie didn't seem to have heard her. "Sylvie?"

"Yes?" Turning so quickly she startled Aeron, Sylvie pulled her arms down from where she'd crossed them over her chest.

"Dinner." Clearly, something had struck a chord with Sylvie, but if it was the child, the couple, the horse, or all the talk about parents, she had no way of knowing.

"Of course." Sylvie gave what Aeron now recognized as her professional smile—lots of teeth and a guarded expression in her eyes. "I'm starving."

CHAPTER SEVENTEEN

S ylvie couldn't sleep. Several of the topics from earlier in the day still haunted her, especially the talk about parents. Mothers who loved and sacrificed. Mothers who didn't. Fathers who were absent. Or in her case, a father who cast far too long a shadow on her life. Sylvie hadn't broached the topic of Daniel, as she couldn't bring herself to even mention him. When they had their dinner with Carolyn and Piper, they'd spoken about more pleasant things, such as horses, sports, and traveling. None of the other three had been to Sweden or any of the other Scandinavian countries, and Piper had a lot of questions. So many, in fact, that Carolyn had to intervene.

As Sylvie and Aeron walked home in the light of Aeron's large flashlight, they hardly spoke. The silence was quite comfortable, and Sylvie inhaled the sweet, fresh scent of the woods. Then, an echoing snap originating from the woods on Sylvie's side made her gasp and move closer to Aeron, grasping for her hand. "What was that?"

"Some animal stepping on a dry twig." Aeron sounded completely calm.

"Are you sure?" Feeling ridiculous for being such a city slicker, Sylvie still held Aeron's hand

"Pretty sure."

"I don't like 'pretty sure.' I like certainties." This was very true, and if Aeron used her keen mind, she'd figure this out.

"I'm fairly certain, though I don't mind you holding my hand. Trust me, I'd hold yours if we were passing some dark alleyway in New York." Aeron squeezed Sylvie's hand, but the laughter in her voice was obvious.

"You think I'm a silly coward," Sylvie muttered. "I can tell."

"I don't think any such thing. You're not a wilderness kind of person. You're bound to hear all kinds of sounds I don't pay attention to any longer. Like when an old houses develops its own sound pattern, and you get used to it and don't think it's haunted anymore."

"What do you mean? Your house? Did you used to think it was haunted?" Now this was beginning to really sound like…like too much.

"No, I mean in general. Didn't you listen to my house when you went to bed last night?" Aeron's hand left Sylvie's and began caressing up and down her lower arm.

"I fell asleep instantly, so, no." She chuckled. "And honestly, I don't believe in ghosts and I'm not afraid of them."

"Well, now, how could you be afraid of them if you don't believe in them?" Laughing, Aeron took hold of Sylvie's hand again. "Me, on the other hand, I'm on the fence about it. I think there's a lot we don't know and can't explain. You know, intuition, people who are sensitive to moods, unexplainable events."

"I agree this world we live in has many unexplainable things and events. I've even stumbled upon a few. As for intuition, I'm a firm believer in following your gut instinct when you've learned to listen to it at the right time. Usually doesn't fail me in business anyway."

"When does your intuition fail?"

"Can't you guess?"

Aeron was quiet for a moment. "Eh, at first I was going to say 'when you fall in love,' but that didn't feel right. So I listen to my intuition and it's not that hard. I think yours fails you whenever your father is in the picture."

"Correct. See? We're both right."

Stopping in the middle of the path, Aeron looked up at Sylvie, who could barely see the outline of Aeron's face in the faint light of the downturned flashlight. "I like being right." Aeron drew a deep breath. "What's more, I like being here with you."

"Likewise." Forcing herself to breathe evenly, Sylvie held on to Aeron's hand.

Aeron wrapped her free arm around Sylvie's neck. "May I kiss you?" she whispered, her lips a fraction of an inch from Sylvie's. "I've wanted to for days now. It's all I can think about right now." "Yes...Sure." Was she dreaming? Sylvie could hardly speak. The next moment, Aeron's lips pressed against hers. This was no dream. No dream had ever felt this real, this strong. Aeron's lips, full and firm, yet impossibly soft, claimed hers. Drowning instantly in wave after wave of arousal, Sylvie greedily drew in her breath through her nose. Parting her lips—she couldn't stop herself if she tried—she slid the tip of her tongue across Aeron's upper lip, tracing her Cupid's bow.

Aeron whimpered and sank into Sylvie. She parted her lips, reciprocating the kiss without hesitation. "Oh, my," she said, moaning. "I just had...to..." She kissed Sylvie again, who in turn pulled Aeron tight against her. Aeron smelled so good, and her fresh scent of wildflowers and something fruity blended with the crisp forest night. Sylvie pushed her hands under Aeron's light windbreaker. The T-shirt she wore underneath was yet another barrier, and though Sylvie ached to touch Aeron's naked skin, she harnessed any such premature notions. Instead, she escalated the kiss further, asking for entrance to Aeron's mouth.

"Mmm. Yes," Aeron whispered against Sylvie's lips before meeting her tongue with her own. Sylvie whimpered, a telling sign from her, normally the one always in control. She gently met Aeron's tongue, sliding it up and down, playing, dancing. She let go of Aeron's hand and slid her freed hand into her amazing hair. The silky feel of it made her moan into Aeron's mouth.

Aeron, trembling now, was clearly unable to restrain her hands as Sylvie did. She dropped the flashlight, leaving a pine tree well lit and themselves in darkness. Aeron slid her hands under Sylvie's linen jacket and then beneath the golf shirt. Hot against Sylvie's skin, they drew light circles, palms hot, fingertips cool.

Sylvie realized for the first time what the expression "drowned in her kiss" meant. Dizzy, out of breath, and unable to fight, she allowed the kiss to continue until her legs were about to give in. Pulling back, she inhaled deeply. She kept her arms around Aeron, not about to let go.

"I...I didn't count on that," Aeron said, her voice weak. "Damn."

Chuckling, Sylvie pressed her lips against Aeron's temple. "Me either."

"Should we perhaps walk the last little bit to the cabin? I mean, while I still have any strength in my legs?"

Sylvie nodded, even if she wanted to kiss Aeron again, right then and there. "Good idea."

After retrieving the flashlight, they walked the last stretch of the gravel road. Sylvie held her arm around Aeron's shoulders, and now her mind began to kick in—questioning, calculating, and reassessing. What had happened? How had they gone from tentative friends with a common goal to this...this explosion of a kiss?

When they reached the house, Sylvie let go of Aeron's shoulders. She waited in silence as Aeron unlocked the door and switched off the alarm. After resetting it, Aeron turned to Sylvie, and though it was impossible to judge her expression in the dimly lit room, Sylvie pulled back and pushed her hands into her jacket pockets.

"Sylvie?" Aeron took her gently by the elbows. "What's the matter?"

"Nothing at all. Just tired and ready for bed, really." A lousy cop-out if there ever was one. Especially when you considered how much she was ready to take Aeron to bed this instant. Hell, she'd have her right there on the floor where they stood if it wasn't so impossible. So much was against that, it was ridiculous. Maeve had entrusted her with Aeron in a sense. That was one thing. Sylvie had never felt so strongly about anyone before, and certainly not this fast. That was a warning sign of an imminently broken heart.

There were things about herself Sylvie wasn't ready to share. Intellectually she knew she had nothing to be ashamed of, but emotionally, the wounds had closed but never healed. Her father's contempt, to this day, pierced her soul, and it wouldn't take much poking or prodding for it to hemorrhage. If she let Aeron any closer, she'd find out that Sylvie was virtually illiterate. "I should get some rest. Long day tomorrow." Sylvie pulled back. She really wanted nothing more than Aeron's hands all over her body, but if she allowed that, she stood to lose so much. Business, heart, pride... sanity. She needed to return them to being tentative friends. How the hell would she be able to backtrack into that?

"It's only ten." Aeron's hands dropped from Sylvie's arms as if she'd burned herself. "Did I do something wrong?"

"Not at all. I'm just tired. Don't think I didn't enjoy our kisses. I did. You're a stunning young woman, but—"

"But now you're going to tell me how you really feel." Taking a step to the right, Aeron flipped a switch and the room was bathed in light from the ceiling lamp. "Go on." Crossing her arms over her chest, she was suddenly the defiant woman from her mother's funeral. Her green eyes sparkled, but not from joy or arousal.

"Aeron, please." Sylvie's stomach clenched into a tight knot. "You...I mean..." Hating how weak she sounded, Sylvie did what she always did when she felt cornered or lost. She turned into the ultimate business tycoon. "All right, if you insist. As lovely as kissing you was, we can't jeopardize our agreement. You want to find out more about Maeve and perhaps uncover clues about the identity of your father. I want to keep my business intact and avoid the risk of a hostile overtake in the future. If we allow personal... preferences to guide us in the middle of this, we risk losing sight of our objectives." She heard how callous and matter-of-fact she sounded, but it was all she knew how to do.

Aeron paled, only to blush a fierce crimson moments after. "You really can be an asshole when you feel like it, can't you? I kept telling Annelie and Carolyn how nice you are and how supportive you've been—and you have. I just didn't know you were such a Jekyll and Hyde. You really didn't need to lecture me. If you thought we were getting too intimate too fast, all you had to do was say so. Either you must consider me incredibly immature or fragile, or perhaps both, since you didn't think that was a possibility. How the hell can you first be the sensitive, if a bit aloof, woman I've known until now and then turn into...this? I don't get it."

Aeron gestured at Sylvie as if she faced something foul. "Don't worry. You're quite safe. I'm not going to accost you." Aeron stabbed the console with an angry index finger as she set the alarm code. "I'm going to bed. That should suit you since you're so tired. She strode up the narrow staircase, and then a door slammed shut upstairs. Sylvie heard the shower start.

Trembling now, Sylvie sank down on the third step of the narrow staircase. She'd blown it all: the joint business venture and the budding friendship, not to mention the memory of those hot kisses. She could still feel Aeron's hands against her. Whimpering, Sylvie slapped a hand over her mouth and pressed her forehead to her bent knees. "Why?" she whispered to herself. "Why couldn't I just level with her? What the hell's wrong with me? *What?*"

Chapter Eighteen

Aeron didn't like being back in Manhattan and having noises and smells forced upon her. Sylvie had been annoyingly correct ever since they had driven back from the Adirondacks and the whole mess that had ensued after the intimate moment in the woods. If it hadn't been for Aeron overhearing Sylvie's self-berating words on the stairs afterward, she'd have given up.

Sylvie had offered her to let her use one of her guest rooms, but the thought of spending days and nights with Sylvie was enough to make Aeron hyperventilate. Not that she wouldn't have loved to do that if the circumstances had been right, but not like this. Not with Sylvie walking around her like she was braced for impact.

She kept reading her mother's diary in between going with Sylvie to certain functions and meetings regarding Classic Swedish Inc. As it turned out, Aeron was such a fast typist, she replaced Thomas on a few occasions when he was taking care of his sister with Down syndrome. Slowly, as Aeron made herself useful and didn't mention their falling-out in the Adirondacks, Sylvie began to relax. She even smiled faintly a few times, which Aeron took as a good sign.

Their trip to Sweden came up faster than she realized as the weeks flew by. Aeron wanted to know what to take, and all she got out of Sylvie was "normal clothes, nothing fancy." She packed for several different occasions, as she knew Sylvie came from a rich, posh family, much like herself.

When they boarded the plane, Aeron realized they wouldn't be communicating on the flight as Sylvie donned her earbuds and began listening to the latest reports from Thomas and her next in command.

With a sigh, Aeron pulled out her mother's diary. Moving it back and forth between her hands as if it were hot to the touch, she debated whether to put it back in her bag or not. She had kept picking it up since she read from it last time, but something made her return it to her nightstand. Reading it while alone scared her. Perhaps it was because she could actually hear Maeve's voice with every word. Now when she was sitting next to Sylvie, even if they weren't on the best of terms, she might be able to keep reading.

The Hamptons—September 1988

I'm pregnant. I'm having Captain Aero's baby and am happier and more afraid than I've been in my entire life. I'm going to tell him tonight when we're at our favorite spot on the beach. I know he's married, but once he finds out he has a baby on the way with me, he'll choose me. I just know it.

I admit, I'm afraid he'll be angry. He's never shown any anger toward me before, but he might get the idea I've been out to trap him or something. I've had friends try this (of course they weren't really pregnant) to keep uninterested boyfriends, but that never works. Captain Aero must know by now how much I love him. I haven't actually said it, but I'm going to do that too, tonight.

The Hamptons—September 1988

I didn't tell him.
We never had a romantic date on the beach tonight. He started talking to me immediately in the car, telling me how bad he felt for leading me on, for not telling me the

whole truth. He's married, this I knew, but he never told me he has two little boys. That changes everything. I just clammed up and forced my tears to dry up and never fall. He asked me time and time again if I was all right. I told him I was fine. To make things worse, I laughed and called our times together a summer fling that didn't really mean anything. I think that hurt him, but I was in such agony myself I just couldn't bring myself to care right then. Now I regret saying that. Oh, my, do I regret it.

But I don't regret not telling him about the baby. I'm not going to have an abortion. I'm going to have this child, and it will be the only thing I have of him. That will have to do. Now I have to break the news to my parents before I start to show. I'm so nauseous that I've become quite skinny, so I may show earlier because of that. They're bound to blow all of their fuses and threaten to ground me for life. I won't change my mind about the baby no matter what.

Captain Aero is lost to me. I can't believe it. I don't want to believe it. I just want to rewind time to yesterday, when I didn't know about the pregnancy and was still happy and madly in love.

Now I'm crushed and still madly in love. How the hell will I survive this?

I'm sorry, little, tiny baby. I will have you, and I'll pour all my love for him on you, I promise. You'll be mine and I'll take care of both of us.

Aeron put the diary into her briefcase before she made her way to the plane's restroom. There she cried into a paper towel long enough that she was afraid she'd make herself sick. Maeve's pain was so real it pierced her heart. Her hopefulness for the future and her unrealistic thoughts of what it was to have a baby all helped to escalate Aeron's pain for her mother's sake. Poor little seventeen-year-old Maeve. What a child she'd been despite being so precocious.

Wiping her face with tissues, she hoped Sylvie wouldn't notice she'd been crying as she returned to her seat. She needn't have worried. Sylvie didn't even look up and just kept working. That suited Aeron fine. She pulled a blanket over herself and turned her back toward Sylvie, then promptly fell asleep.

❖

Gothenburg, which was actually called Göteborg in Swedish, judging from the road signs, turned out to be a lush city. As they passed through the city toward the area where Sylvie's family resided, Örgryte, Aeron saw parks and alleys everywhere. She remembered the article in the airplane magazine from Schiphol airport, Amsterdam, to Gothenburg saying it was Sweden's second largest city. Now when they sat in the backseat of one of Thorn Industries' company cars, she turned to Sylvie, trying to break the ice. "Why isn't your family based in Stockholm? Wouldn't the capital be the logical place for Sweden's first financial family to reside?"

"You can ask my father that later. He has a fascinating, ready-made speech on the subject that he loves to deliver." Sylvie didn't look at Aeron but instead raised a cell phone to her ear and carried on a conversation in Swedish. Aeron guessed Sylvie was talking with her mother. When she disconnected the call, Sylvie kept her gaze locked straight ahead.

"Everything all right on the home front?" Yet another question Sylvie might refuse to answer, which was ridiculous.

"Mom's fine. Father's at the office. He refuses to realize he's seventy-five and should be retired by now. He's lived most of his life in the fast lane and can't slow down."

"Can't say I blame him. Getting old doesn't sit well with most people. Someone told me once that we'll all get slower, drier, fatter, and colder with age. It's normal."

Snorting, Sylvie glanced at her. "Sounds lovely."

"Doesn't it?" Aeron smiled carefully. This was an almost-smile from Sylvie, which ought to mean progress, right? She'd been so cold and remote ever since the Adirondacks, even if she had dutifully listened to everything from Maeve's diary. The thought of the diary made Aeron hug her messenger bag harder.

The driver pulled onto an avenue with old trees. They drove for a couple of miles farther, and then the most beautiful old house appeared. It was more than a house; it was a mansion. Built from wood, it was painted a custard yellow with white trim around the windows and the corners and had a red-tile roof. A perfect lawn stretched for as long as Aeron could see around the building. Oak, birch, and copper beech trees grew about twenty yards apart throughout the park.

"It's stunning. How old is this?" Aeron gaped, but she didn't care. She'd never come across such a building in the US or in South America.

"It originates from the 1680s, but has been added to through the years. My parents put in the modern updates in the seventies. I think they added a pool ten years ago. It's in the back by the patio." Sylvie sounded like a tourist guide.

Aeron regarded the circular driveway where the driver now rounded the impressive flowerbed that encircled a marble statue of some Greek god or other.

"Who's the dude?" Aeron crinkled her nose. "He looks…well endowed."

Sylvie guffawed and gave her first real smile since the Adirondacks. "Oh, God, you have to promise to tell my father that. He'll be appalled, but it'll truly make my mother's day."

"If you insist." Aeron would do just about anything to have Sylvie warm up to her again.

"I do."

The car stopped, and a blond woman stepped out on the broad staircase. "Sylvie, honey. It's been too long. Far too long." She rushed down the steps and wrapped her arms around Sylvie. "I'm so glad you made it."

"You can thank Aeron. If she hadn't agreed to come and help ward off Father, I most likely wouldn't have." Sylvie spoke kindly, but with such a serious note in her voice, nobody could doubt she meant every word.

"Then I must take a look at this wonder woman." The blonde strode over to Aeron and extended a hand. "Welcome to Gothenburg. I'm Camilla Thorn, Sylvie's mother. I'm so glad to meet you. It's about time."

"As Sylvie said, I'm Aeron. Aeron DeForest." Aeron wondered about Camilla's last comment. What was about time? She didn't want to press on with questions right away, so she filed her inquiry for future reference.

"You look a bit young, but some mature faster than others, I gather." Camilla hooked her arms under Aeron's and Sylvie's, pulling them with her up the stairs.

"My bags…" Aeron tried to free herself, but Camilla would have none of that.

"Never mind the bags. Lars will take care of them and put them in your room. Now, I want you to meet everyone. Come on."

"Everyone?" Sylvie sounded suspicious.

"A little luncheon. A small gathering of your friends and some relatives. This is what you get for not being home often enough. It sort of becomes an event."

"Mom, what did you do?" Sylvie's eyes darkened. "Aeron and I are tired from the flight and want to have a shower and rest—"

"Nonsense. You're young, Aeron obviously even younger. What's a little flight across the pond for the two of you? Besides, you look wonderfully well dressed, both of you. No excuses. Everyone's on the patio since we're having a virtual heat wave."

Aeron stumbled at Camilla's side and felt anything but well dressed and rested. She was wearing her Tommy Hilfiger leisure suit, which was stylish enough to walk around the Hamptons in, but she hadn't even had time to brush her hair. Thank God she'd brushed her teeth on the airplane before they landed.

"Mom, we're going to discuss this later." Sylvie growled and then sent an apologetic glance toward Aeron, who merely shrugged.

As they passed through the house, Aeron was so nervous about the waiting crowd, she barely registered antique furniture with curvy legs, golden dressers, and tall clocks as Camilla guided them. When they walked through the tall double doors to the patio, she noticed that she and Camilla had completely different criteria for a "small gathering." At least fifty people sat and stood with a drink in their hands, and they were all turned toward the newcomers.

"Look, everyone," Camilla called out in English. "Sylvie's finally here with her girlfriend! Her name is Aeron DeForest, and now we must all make her feel very welcome so she can persuade our wayward daughter to visit more often."

Sylvie flinched visibly, and Aeron stood as if lightning had just gone through her entire system. Did Camilla mean girlfriend in a romantic context or girl*friend* as in a buddy? How the hell could she be meant to decipher the Swedish subtext?

"When's the wedding, Sylvie?" a young man shouted from the far end of the patio.

"Oh, my God." Sylvie gasped and freed herself from her mother. "Mom, tell me you didn't just out me *and* our guest?"

"I did nothing of the sort. Everyone already knows you're gay, honey. That means I didn't out anyone. Come on. Have a mimosa and relax."

"Oh, my goodness," Aeron muttered to Sylvie. Jet-lagged, starving, and then alcohol.

"Don't worry. I'll help you pour most of it in the flowerbeds."

It was Aeron's turn to snort at the outrageous suggestion. It didn't matter to her if anyone here thought Sylvie and she were an item. She didn't budge from Sylvie's side during the long, agonizing meet-and-greet. Only once did she see true happiness in Sylvie's eyes.

"Still running the gauntlet for dear mommy," a low, teasing female voice said.

"Viktoria! What a surprise." Sylvie flung her arms around the petite woman in front of them. "I can't tell you what a relief it is to see an actual friend here."

"As it happened, I was in town and heard you were doing one of your rare bow-in, stay-three-days, bow-out things." Viktoria grinned and looked up at Sylvie's eyes. "I can see your mother isn't exaggerating this time. She's almost given up hope of you ever falling for someone for real. Thank God it happened, finally."

Sylvie grew rigid and took a step back. She looked so trapped, Aeron had to act.

"Hi, I'm Aeron." She extended her hand, but before she knew what Viktoria meant to do, she found herself wrapped up in a firm hug.

"You're gorgeous. And you look like the perfect woman for Sylvie. She's not easily charmed, our girl, but I can tell you're like made for each other."

"Thank you. We haven't known each other for very long, but Sylvie is a wonderful person, and I count myself lucky to be her girlfriend."

"She's just as lucky." Viktoria wrapped her arms around their waists and held on.

Just as they started walking, another voice virtually erupted behind them. "And here she is, my long-lost daughter. Sylvie, don't I get a hug as well?"

Sylvie's muted gasp didn't escape Aeron. Daniel Thorn had arrived.

❖

He stood there in his usual arrogant lord-of-the-manner style, the usual smirk in place.

"Father," Sylvie said and met his eyes without flinching anymore. "You look well."

"Why, thank you, Sylvie. As do you, despite jet lag and, what was it, starvation?"

Had he been spying on them as they arrived and walked through the house?

"Yes," Daniel said as if he read her mind. "I was on my cell by the fireplace when Camilla hauled you and Erin, was it, through the living room."

"Aeron DeForest." Aeron couldn't make herself force warmth like she had with Viktoria and Camille. Now the man that had hurt Sylvie so badly over the years stood there with smug look, as if he knew something they didn't and was about to drop a bomb on them. Gleeful. That was a good word to describe his expression. "I've heard a lot about you."

"I bet you have, but I promise I don't bite—much." Daniel Thorn chuckled.

God damn it. Did he have the audacity to flirt with her? Didn't he think she was his daughter's girlfriend too? Then it hit her. He was goading her. It was the classic "I know that he knows that I know" situation. Daniel Thorn wanted her to come at him in front of the family's friends and in his own house. He planned to make her act out, say something that would embarrass her, and him, thus weakening her in the eyes of the spectators. What a conniving, shrewd thing to do.

Thinking fast, Aeron put on her best innocent expression. "You may not bite, sir, but I do. You're lucky I have standards and don't chew on senior citizens."

It was quite interesting to watch Daniel Thorn become flustered. His eyes would have incinerated her if he'd been able to unleash the fire she saw there. Instead, he decided to laugh her comment off, only he took a little too long and that made all the difference. Aeron didn't think anyone among the guests bought his sudden joviality, even if he could probably intimidate them if need be. Daniel took his wife's arm and headed toward the bar over by the pool, where he poured himself a drink, and Aeron could see him speaking fast and pointedly, even if she couldn't hear his ranting from where she stood. Camilla looked increasingly annoyed, and eventually she snatched a glass from the counter and left him standing there.

"That was quite something," Viktoria said, her eyes still wide at the exchange. She pulled Aeron and Sylvie with her to a remote corner of the patio where they wouldn't be overheard. A planter with tall lilies and artfully added grass kept them partially obscured as well. "You rock, girl, taking on that old bull! Wow."

"He tried to belittle me. It's not the first time that's ever happened, but I sort of had to take him on because of what Sylvie has told me of her childhood."

"Well, since the two of you are the new it-couple from now on, it's important to stand your ground," Viktoria said, looking thoughtful. "The tabloids scrutinize this family every week like they're fucking royalty, so they'll make you the poster children for gay women. We have quite a few these days, but at this level, it's almost as if one from the royal family came out."

Aeron began to realize she might have stepped into something she had absolutely no clue about. "Really?" she said, her voice little more than a squeak. "I mean, why would they care about me if it's Sylvie—"

"Because Sylvie is Daniel's daughter and heir. Heiresses to that type of fortune don't grow on trees. I know you've never hidden your sexual orientation, sweetie." Viktoria patted Sylvie's back. "But since you've kept your relationships secret even from me, the press is going to find this yummy. Even the evening papers will want their part of the cake."

"Fuck," Aeron whispered.

Sylvie had been pale and quiet during the small drama, but now she put her glass down on the stone banister hard enough to snap off the foot. "He's gone too far. We're not staying here, Aeron. Screw the stockholders and Midsummer. I—"

"Sylvie. Calm down. Honestly, I'm okay." Aeron risked being pushed back and edged closer to Sylvie. "He's exactly as you described him. Surely you can't be surprised? He's a business tycoon with a God complex. You knew that."

Slowly, Sylvie relaxed. "Yes. Yes, I did. He can get under my skin and he knows it. I used to fear it, and the last few years, it's more of a constant annoyance."

"Has it really escaped his attention that you're your own grown-up person at the ripe age of forty?" Viktoria snorted. "He's such an old fool. And you're stuck in the trap of seeking his validation, or his recognition."

"I know. It's sick."

Aeron still stood close to Sylvie, who didn't seem to mind. After their falling-out in the Adirondacks, she was afraid of doing something wrong to push Sylvie completely away. Almost walking on broken glass around the woman she'd come to adore made for an unequal relationship, but if that was what it took…

"What do you think, Aeron?" Viktoria said, nudging her.

"Excuse me. I got sidetracked."

"I could tell. I was just asking if you guys need a place to crash. I'm returning to Stockholm later today, and my overnight condo will be empty. It's not very big, but it's right next to Slottsskogen."

"What's that?" Aeron asked.

"A big park where they also keep indigenous animals in a small zoo."

"Thanks, my friend," Sylvie said, looking determined. "I won't need it as long as it doesn't get worse around here. We're only in Sweden for four days, and unless things become unbearable, we should be all right. But if the situation with Father deteriorates, we might take you up on the offer. Thanks."

"No problem. Same goes for you as well, Aeron. The Thorns are mostly good people, unless the biggest drama queen of them all creates more drama." She laughed and squeezed both their hands. "Now, please excuse me, but I need to go mingle. I saw potential clients at the other end of the patio. Can't let such a good opportunity pass."

"What does she do?" Aeron looked after the diminutive woman who walked with confident steps toward two men and a woman.

"She's a corporate lawyer. Don't let that girly attitude fool you. She's a shark." Sylvie shook her head and smiled faintly. "She was my best friend from middle school onward. We lost touch for a bit after we went on to university. She studied at her parents' alma mater in Uppsala, and I went on to the one in Gothenburg. Once I moved to the US, oddly enough, we started emailing and rekindled the friendship. She's engaged to one of Stockholm's most renowned bankers."

"And you? Why's everyone on your case about finding the right person and so on? That ought to be your business and not anybody else's."

"You'd think so, yes. And on that note, I need to mingle some too, no matter how I detest it." Sylvie hesitated and fiddled with her bracelet. "Will you join me? I don't have the right to ask—"

"Sylvie." Aeron put a hand on Sylvie's arm. "Of course I'll mingle with you. I'll draw some of the attention away from you, I'm sure." She wanted to show Sylvie she could be there for her. Even if Sylvie wouldn't dare—or want—to explore the attraction and feelings so clearly there between them, Aeron wanted her to know she had her back.

"Thank you." Sylvie began walking toward the guests, her professional smile in place. Aeron chanced taking her hand and winked at Sylvie when she flinched.

"We're the next big thing when it comes to lesbian love, remember?"

Sylvie snorted, but it turned into a cough as they neared an elderly couple. "Uncle Fredrik, Aunt Carola, so nice to see you again. It's been far too long."

As Sylvie asked about cousins and their offspring, Aeron stood smiling, holding her hand and telling herself not to wish for the moon. Such wishes, in her experience, only led to a broken heart.

Chapter Nineteen

Gothenburg—1998

"Congratulations, honey!" Camilla rushed toward Sylvie as she told some of her friends good-bye outside the main auditorium.

"Hi, Mom! I'm so glad you could make it." Genuinely happy, Sylvie hugged her mother. "I didn't think this day would ever come. Imagine that, huh? I've completed a university program, and at the same time as the other students." Her cheeks hurt from smiling so much. Tears waited in the wings, but she didn't want them to show.

"I know. You should be very proud of yourself, Sylvie." Camilla obviously had no need to hide any tears as they flowed freely down her perfectly made-up face. "You showed all those pessimists and prophets of doom that you could do it."

That had been half of Sylvie's motivation in the beginning. The other half was to rub her father's face in it when she completed her education, but as it turned out, he wasn't present for any nose-rubbing. After the first year, which had been a long period of acclimatizing, Sylvie had come back after working as an intern at one of the Thorn banks, realizing she enjoyed her studies. Instead of imagining her father's reaction when she succeeded, she threw herself into university life and finally was able to embrace the fact that she loved women. Now she looked at her mother, the one person who did her best to communicate Sylvie's rights to have the technology available for people with dyslexia.

Sylvie felt someone tap her shoulder and turned around. Professor Marika Hjälm stood there, looking almost as moved as Camilla. Considering how feared the woman was on campus, this was something of a shock.

"Sylvie. Mrs. Thorn." She shook hands with both of them. "I wanted to congratulate Sylvie on her accomplishment. Your four years here has showed us how a true fighter takes on what looks like an overwhelming obstacle and turns it into a success."

"Thank you, Marika." Sylvie did an out-of-character inward twirl, mainly because she was so relieved to have passed all her courses despite her dyslexia. For the first time, nobody had debated the fact that she needed some texts recorded by an assistant to be able to study at the required pace.

"I know you've had many offers, Sylvie. Have you decided which ones you're mostly interested in?" Marika Hjälm asked.

"Actually, my father has asked me to join him at the headquarters in Gothenburg. Work myself up and earn my promotions like everyone else." Sylvie's stomach constricted at the mere thought, but she knew this was her path. It had been instilled in her as a child, even if her father had constantly expressed his doubts. Perhaps this had been the force behind her relentless drive to make it through school and university.

"I see. For a while I thought you might go for the Bank of England, where you did your internship?" Marika Hjälm frowned as if she tried to remember. "You got excellent references as I recall."

Sylvie had loved living in London for four months. She'd discovered she could read marginally better in English, which was mystifying. Her assistant thought it might be because it was a learned language and perhaps processed elsewhere in the brain than her mother tongue was. Sylvie found that explanation as good as any and enjoyed being able to make it through shorter documents all on her own. When it came to math, she excelled and impressed her instructors.

"I did, and I hope that might take me abroad for Thorn Industries at one point."

"Camilla! Sylvie!" Daniel's voice, springing from the conversation as if he'd magically appeared if you spoke his name, boomed across the yard. "Damn it, I missed the ceremony." He actually looked disappointed as he strode toward them. Dressed in a slate-gray three-piece suit, despite the warm early summer day, he was still a very handsome, charismatic man.

"Darling, this is one of Sylvie's professors, Marika Hjälm. Professor Hjälm, this is my husband and Sylvie's father, Daniel."

"Of course I recognize Mr. Thorn." Marika offered her hand briefly. So briefly, in fact, Sylvie barely saw her father touch it. "We've met before."

"We have?" Daniel said, and Sylvie wondered how such a smart man could sometimes be so socially clumsy. "Pardon me, Professor, but I don't remember. I meet very many people." His self-satisfied smile clearly didn't affect Marika at all. She merely smiled wryly.

"I'm sure this is true." Pausing as if debating whether to explain how she'd met him, Marika hoisted her heavy tote bag higher up on her shoulder. "You're forgiven, as it was many years ago. I'd just started teaching here, and I believe you attended a distant relative's graduation. 1974, I believe."

Camilla grew rigid next to Sylvie and cast a glance at her father. He looked like something was slowly dawning on him. "Hmm. Yes. Now that you mention it. That might be it. As you say, long time ago."

Now Sylvie knew something was wrong. Her mother's lips were compressed into fine lines, and Daniel's smile was far too broad to be natural.

"Congratulations again, Sylvie. I wish you the very best, no matter whom you choose to work for. Who knows. You might just start your own company at one point. I can actually picture you doing that quite vividly." Marika Hjälm surprised Sylvie by kissing her cheek. "Stay strong," she murmured in Sylvie's ear before she nodded and told them all good-bye.

The ride home in the car was torturous. Daniel tried to keep a conversation going, but Camilla sat half-turned away from him, impossible to reach. Sylvie wished she were anywhere but in the car with her parents. Eventually Camilla rounded on Daniel so fast, Sylvie jumped where she sat in the backseat.

"It was her," she said, her voice a mere hiss.

"Camilla!" Daniel growled. "Not now."

"Of course not now. Not ever, if you get to decide, but this time you're going to tell me everything when we get home. If you don't level with me—" Camilla glanced at Sylvie. "When we get home."

"Fine." Daniel gripped the steering wheel hard.

"Daniel..."

"I said fine."

Sylvie wondered what her graduation would have been like if they hadn't run into Professor Hjälm. Perhaps at this point, they would have actually been talking about her, her future and her options. Instead, they spoke in code, hissed at each other, and left her in the dark. Sylvie sighed. It was no use to wish it would be different. This was what passed for normal in her family.

❖

Gothenburg—Present Time

Sylvie had had enough of her parents' bickering at the dinner table. Daniel had tried to stealthily insult Aeron twice, and Camilla had worked the wineglass a bit too much, which had to be a new habit. Was life with Daniel Thorn so bad now she had to numb herself? Sylvie hoped not.

"I don't know about you, but I'm exhausted," Sylvie said. "Jet lag going from the US to Europe is always worse for me."

"I'm pretty tired too." Aeron looked gratefully at Sylvie. "Isn't it tomorrow we're supposed to pick flowers or something?"

"Yes. For the maypole. We need to catch up on our sleep before that. If I know Mom right, we'll have to be up early to help with that and the tables in the park."

"Exactly." Camilla chimed in and wiggled her half-empty glass of white wine at them. "I have a checklist in my office."

"We'll be up early to help." Sylvie rose. "Which room is Aeron's, Mom?"

"What do you mean? Oh, you don't have to worry about us. We know you sch-sleep together." Camilla smiled endearingly. "Young love. So precious. Doesn't matter that it's two pretty girls together. So precious."

"Dear God, you've had enough of that stuff." Daniel took the glass away from Camilla, who looked only mildly affronted. "I can't say I find it natural, but these days only a fool runs his mouth against gays if he wants to keep his business. I appreciate that you're not too demonstrative."

Sylvie refused to dignify that remark with a reply. Her father was no homophobe per se, but he did have some problems with her sexual orientation being bad for business. Hopefully he wouldn't have to worry much longer. As soon as she could prove how successful Classic Swedish Inc. was, she'd be as demonstrative as she damn well pleased.

"You have a queen-size bed in your old room. You girls just snuggle up there and sleep tight." Camilla waved them off with a flick of her wrist. "Night, night."

"Good night, Mom."

"Good night, Camilla." Aeron stood and, in Sylvie's eyes, quite deliberately took her hand and raised it to her lips. "Lead the way, gorgeous."

Sylvie was about to attempt to object one last time, but Aeron's words burrowed under her skin, and she guided Aeron from the dining room and into the vast hallway. Her old room was on the second floor at the far end of the left corridor. For some reason Aeron held Sylvie's hand all the way as they walked toward it.

"I'm sorry for my father's crude words." Sylvie's lips tightened. "He can be a total jerk."

"He does seem to have some unusual qualities." Aeron spoke with a slightly high-pitched voice. "So we're sharing a room, huh?"

"Looks like it." Sylvie stopped just outside the door, looking down at their joined hands. "If you'd rather not, I'll find Jeanette, our housekeeper, and ask her to make up one of the guest rooms."

"Is that what you'd rather do?" Aeron looked down at the floor but then raised her gaze, her green eyes darker than usual.

Sylvie's heart thundered. What was it about this woman that made her melt at a mere glance? She'd known her only a few weeks, and she'd taken over Sylvie's thoughts and entered her dreams. "No. That's not what I'd rather do. I just want you to know my parents don't dictate who's in my bed. I do."

"Good to know. It could be awkward if they sent more people in there." Aeron grinned. "I'm not *that* adventurous."

Chuckling, Sylvie relaxed marginally. "Me either." She opened the door and motioned for Aeron to step inside.

"Oh, look. My bags are already here. Seems this was meant to be." She let go of Sylvie's hand and walked over to her suitcase that sat on a rack over by the far wall. Opening the lid, she pulled out her toiletry bag and a shirt. "I'm dying to take a shower. May I go first?"

"Absolutely." She pointed at the door to the left of Aeron. "En suite's there."

"Thanks." Aeron disappeared into the bathroom, and soon Sylvie heard water running in the shower.

Gazing around her, she realized she hadn't taken the time to really see her old room during her few short visits with her parents. Her mother had had the wallpaper changed into an intricate pattern of white, yellow, and gold. The hardwood oak floor was well kept, the bed was only a few years old, but the desk and bookshelves were the same. She walked along the bookshelves, most of the contents audiobooks, and ran her fingers along their spines. Children's books, books for teens, young-adult novels.

The desk was clear of clutter, of course, but for her inner eye she could envision it covered in one draft or another when she'd tried to get her assignment done right. So many times she'd felt such shame. And when she'd succeeded with a particular homework that involved reading and writing, a few times she was accused of cheating. At one point, a clueless teacher had lectured Daniel about how detrimental it was for Sylvie if her parents did her homework for her. That teacher had switched schools shortly after, and Sylvie was still certain her father had something to do with that.

Daniel was a brilliant man in many aspects, and one of them was being well connected in all socio-economic groups. He wasn't snobbish in the sense some people at his level on the social ladder were. He could easily meet anyone and make them eat out of his hand, if that served his purpose. His connections reached all social strata, and if he'd told the principal to get rid of that particular teacher, that teacher would find himself transferred so fast, his world would tilt for weeks.

"Your turn." Aeron's voice from behind startled Sylvie so much she gasped out loud. "Whoa. Sorry. Lost in thought?"

"Pretty much." Turning, Sylvie inhaled sharply a second time at the sight of Aeron in a thigh-long brown T-shirt. An almost washed-out print on the front said, I RIVER RAFTED IN 2013.

"Sylvie?" Waving her hand in front of Sylvie's eyes, Aeron laughed, which also made Sylvia jerk slightly. "You're jumpy tonight."

"When you look like that, what do you expect?" Sylvie tried to chalk her honest words up to jet lag, but Aeron's presence, looking so sexy and cute in that shirt, was the real reason.

"You like?" Pinching the hem on either side of her legs like she was holding on to a skirt, Aeron twirled. "It's a very important T-shirt. First and only time I ever river-rafted. Horrible experience, but I'm proud now. At least I did it, even if it scared me shitless."

"You're brave. I'm not a water creature if it isn't about doing laps in a pool. I hope that doesn't make me too boring. It does sound dreary, though, when I mention it."

"Nah. I'm the same way. I have branched out into swimming in the lake back home. It's really clean and nice, better than any pool."

"Perhaps if I don't make an idiot of myself, I may get invited back?" Her own audacity stunned Sylvie.

"I'd love for you to come back to the Adirondacks. We don't get many do-overs in life, and I'd like for you to share my room there. Tit for tat, as they say."

"They do? Does anyone really say tit for tat? To a Swede that sounds really...naughty, in a funny and quirky kind of way." Sylvie stepped closer. "I should hit the bathroom before I fall asleep standing up."

"Please come back before I'm out cold, okay?" Aeron pulled the covers back and was about to climb into the bed when she stopped herself. "Which side do you sleep on?"

"Any. Usually in the middle."

"Wow. Okay. I'll just pick my favorite side, on the left, and wait for you."

"All right." Sylvie walked into the bathroom and also didn't recognize her reflection in the mirror. Instead of the weary, annoyed, and reluctant woman she usually saw, she gazed at someone with startling blue eyes, glowing complexion, and a tremulous smile. Part of her couldn't wait to get back to Aeron, and the other part feared the strong emotions rampaging inside her.

Sylvie showered and brushed her teeth. Then she realized she'd forgotten to bring any sleepwear in with her. Muttering, she wrapped a bath towel around her and padded out into the room.

CHAPTER TWENTY

A eron had never seen anything as enticing as the sight of Sylvie Thorn entering the room wearing only a towel. Little drops of water still clung to her shoulders, and her toweled hair lay in messy ringlets down her back. She muttered something barely audible.

"Is that Swedish you're speaking?" Aeron laughed and looked up from her cell phone. Her breath caught, and the hand holding her phone fell down on the bed. "I—I'm just asking because I can't understand a word."

"Probably. It's a saying. What's not in your head, you have to have in your feet. Approximately."

"And it means?" Now Aeron devoured her with her eyes, and the green fire in them made Sylvie's thighs tense.

"That I forgot my nightgown." Sylvie shook her head at herself and picked out one in indigo satin, then returned to the bathroom. She came back only moments later. Aeron's mouth dried until it was impossible to swallow because of how stunning and, yes, hot Sylvie looked in the nightgown that was about the same length as her own river-rafting T-shirt.

Sylvie rounded the bed and took a moment to plug in her phone to the charger. "I have another cord here. Does your phone need charging?"

"Yes, thank you." Handing over her cell phone, Aeron realized how little it took from Sylvie for her to ignite, as the mere touch of fingertips against her hand gave her goose bumps. Sylvie looked completely unaffected, but then again, she was the one who'd kept gasping at the sight of Aeron before, so perhaps she'd just reeled herself in while showering.

Sylvie crawled into bed, pushing and moving pillows this way and that. Was she nervous? Or was she a fussy sleeper? Aeron didn't mind. Scooting down, she reveled in the soft pillows and smooth bedsheets. "I like your bed."

"I'll tell Mom you said so." Yes, definitely a blend of humor and nerves in Sylvie's voice.

"What a crazy day, huh?" Aeron wanted to slide closer, to regain the connection, but was afraid that Sylvie would throw herself out of bed on the other side and break her neck or something.

"That's the Thorns for you."

"I really only care about one Thorn." There. It was out. The words passed her lips without effort, and now Aeron did her best not to hold her breath.

"Really?" Sylvie rose onto her elbow and leaned toward Aeron. "I'm not an easy person to care about sometimes, as you've noticed. I have enough insecurities and hang-ups to share with the neighbors. You can't say such things flippantly. You realize that, don't you?" Her blue eyes were almost violet in the dusk.

"Sylvie. Calm down. It's me, Maeve's screwed-up daughter, you're talking to. Neither of us had a perfect childhood—or even close to it. But I had Paulina and you had your mom. We survived. We made a life. We can carry on turning our lives into what we want. You're almost there with Classic Swedish Inc., and I'm making a decent living from my book sales. That's my fuck-off money. I don't need a life of luxury with everything the DeForest fortune entails. Honestly, I don't want it. I only agreed to our deal because Maeve was honoring a promise to you—and even if part of me is jealous that she didn't do the same with anything she promised me, I still want you to reach your dream. Also, I'm dying to get to know

Maeve, and having read half her diary with her thoughts, I'm getting there. But please, don't think you're any worse off than I am. We're both pretty damaged in some ways."

"That just goes to show it doesn't matter that I'm forty and you're twenty-six. You're still smarter and more mature than I am." Sylvie pushed a persistent strand of hair behind her ear. "Want the naked truth?"

"Is that a trick question?" To lighten the mood, Aeron wiggled her eyebrows.

"I've wanted you from that first day at the lawyer's office."

Aeron closed her mouth, opened it to speak, and closed it again. "You…what? Even in the Adirondacks?"

"Especially then."

"I'm stunned. I mean, I knew you found me attractive, judging from the kisses and the looks you gave me, but even before then? Wow." Aeron shook her head, trying to clear her mind. "Just wow."

"Wow? Such eloquence from a writer." Clearly Sylvie's mood was going in the right direction. She scooted closer. "Did I hurt you beyond repair?"

"No. I have something to confess."

Sylvie had raised her hand as if to caress Aeron's hair, or forehead, but now she let it hover for a moment and then put it down again. "What?"

"I overheard you berate yourself on the staircase, and that made me realize I was taking something personally that had more to do with you and your experiences than with me. I was pretty arrogant to put me and my insecurities first, as I did feel rejected—which is the theme song to my life story so far, as you can imagine."

"You're too hard on yourself. I guessed that was part of how I'd hurt you, yet I kept pulling back more and more."

"Hence us being damaged goods. That said, I still care about this particular Thorn. I can't help it." Aeron's voice sank to a whisper. "And I've dreamed of kissing you again, Sylvie. That and more."

Sylvie gasped, and then her mouth pressed against Aeron's and sucked her lower lip in between hers.

Groaning, Aeron wrapped her arms around Sylvie's neck and her damp hair tickled Aeron's arms, sending shivers up to her scalp and down her spine. "Oh, damn," she moaned against Sylvie's lips. "This…you feel amazing…so hot…"

"And you're gorgeous. And sexy. Ah yes, and hot too. Scorching." Sylvie raised her head and smiled down at Aeron. "And I can't believe you're here."

"In Sweden?"

"In Sweden. In my bed. And in my arms." Sliding one hand up under Aeron's T-shirt, she cupped her right breast tenderly. After massaging it gently, Sylvie plucked at the hardening nipple with her fingertips, all the time looking into Aeron's eyes as if searching for something. "I want to see you."

"Then push my shirt up." Aeron let go of Sylvie's neck and reached back for the headboard with both hands. This movement arched her back and pressed her farther into Sylvie, who was now busy shoving the shirt up above her breasts.

"You're stunning." Sylvie lowered her head and drew circles around Aeron's breasts with her tongue. "And you taste exquisite."

"I want to taste you as well." Aeron rubbed her thighs together and wondered if Sylvie had noticed how drenched she was between her legs. Her lace boy briefs were already soaked.

"You will, but right now, you're mine." Looking up with a devilish gleam in her eyes, Sylvie was gorgeous. Her long hair lay around her shoulders like a damp, wavy mantle. The way her eyes had darkened made her complexion look even paler, except for the redness of her cheeks. Her lips, half-open and swollen, looked so tempting, Aeron had to force herself not to reach around Sylvie and kiss her again. Aeron wanted Sylvie to do anything she wanted right now, to take charge. She yearned to know what Sylvie wanted to do to her and what making love with Sylvie Thorn would be like.

Sylvie moved up and latched on to Aeron's neck. She licked a blazing trail from Aeron's clavicle to her ear. As if she knew Aeron's preferences already, she refrained from sucking on her earlobe or sticking her tongue in her ear, but instead she very lightly outlined the sensitive shell.

Shivering, Aeron slid her legs up around Sylvie. Now she knew Sylvie could feel the dampness between her legs, but she didn't care. She just wanted to have this wondrously amazing woman as close as possible. Aeron closed her eyes. It was as if their skin fused and the blood in the veins sang the same song. Sylvie's scent of soap, lotion, and sex was enough to drive Aeron crazy. She abandoned the headboard and pushed her fingers into Sylvie's hair.

"You feel so good. So damn good." Aeron groaned and undulated against Sylvie's stomach. "I want you so much. I have since…even before the Adirondacks."

"Me too. I wanted you even before you started looking at me that certain way you do."

"I do?"

Sylvie raised her head. "Yes. You do."

"Come to think of it, Sylvie, so do you. You've looked at me like you wanted to devour me sometimes."

"Astute observation." Sitting up, Sylvie tugged her nightgown off and then Aeron's T-shirt. Their panties went the same way, and now it was Aeron's turn to discover just how wet Sylvie was. Groaning, she flipped them over, unable to resist the urge to do some devouring of her own.

❖

Sylvie melted into the soft bed as Aeron's tongue explored her mouth in one long kiss after another. As Aeron rested on one elbow, her free hand found Sylvie's right breast, cupped it gently at first, but soon rolled the nipple between her fingers.

"Oh, God, don't stop," Sylvie said against Aeron's lips. "No matter what, don't stop."

"Trust me. I have no intention of stopping." Aeron spoke calmly, but her voice trembled.

"Thank God." Sylvie took a deep breath. "Please. Use your mouth."

And Aeron did. As if Sylvie's wish was all she needed to hear, Aeron explored every inch of her body with her tongue. Parting Sylvie's legs, Aeron slid down, nipping at her inner thighs with her lips. "May I?"

"Anything," Sylvie whispered. "I want you so much."

"Oh, sweetie." Aeron blew gently at the damp curls between Sylvie's legs. "I *crave* you."

Sylvie couldn't breathe. Aeron's words, together with her tongue parting Sylvie's slick folds, were enough to send convulsions throughout her. The fire, because there was no other word for it, erupted, spread, and when Aeron pushed her tongue flat against her clitoris, she cried out, belatedly muffling herself with a hand over her mouth.

"Yes," Aeron said against Sylvie's pulsating folds, "you must be quiet. So very quiet."

Whimpering behind her hand, Sylvie wondered if that was at all possible. The orgasm was already building with startling momentum. It traveled through her system, and when Aeron sucked the small ridge of nerves into her mouth and let her tongue flick rapidly against it, she whimpered Aeron's name over and over. She came so hard, the release bordered on painful. Curling up around Aeron, she forgot to be quiet as the convulsions rolled over her, one after another. She sobbed, feverishly stroking Aeron's hair, and another orgasm erupted, though not as strong but longer, sweeter. Sylvie eventually relaxed and went limp.

Aeron kissed her way up Sylvie's body until they lay face-to-face on the pillows. Pushing Sylvie's hair out of her face, Aeron smiled gently. "Are you all right?"

"Mmm-hmm." She felt afloat. Sylvie couldn't remember ever feeling like this after having sex. This was more than a physical release. She wasn't sure what made it so different...oh, God, who was she trying to fool? Of course she did. The difference began and ended with the woman next to her. Still feeling rather weak, she raised a hand and cupped Aeron's right breast. "Now where was I?"

"When I so rudely interrupted you, you mean?" Aeron snorted.

"I think you were paying attention to my—oh, my..."

Sylvie bent forward and took the pebbled nipple in her mouth. Sucking and gently chewing, she made it grow diamond hard. Not until Aeron whimpered a "no more, please" did she let go, and then only to roll Aeron onto her back so she could reach the left one.

As it turned out, Aeron's smooth skin was delicious. Sylvie sampled one area after another, licking, nipping, and when she reached Aeron's hips, she carefully nudged the slender thighs apart. "You're beautiful," Sylvie said with a catch in her voice. "You're irresistible."

Aeron was squirming beneath her. "Please..." She trembled as she pulled her knees up, looking at Sylvie with such trust, she could barely breathe.

"You don't have to beg. Ever." Sylvie cupped the swollen folds, ran her fingers deeper and deeper in between them, and found Aeron's clitoris to be as big and hard as her nipples. Running her fingers on either side of it, she used her other hand to explore the opening just below. "Inside?" she asked quietly.

"Yes. Yes!" It was Aeron's turn to cover her mouth to stay quiet. Muted whimpers escalated when Sylvie entered Aeron with two fingers.

"Like this?" Sylvie bent over Aeron, greedily absorbing the expression on her face. The light in Aeron's eyes burned so brightly there was no reason to doubt how this was affecting her. Sylvie began a deep thrust with her fingers and buried them to the hilt every time she reentered Aeron. The silky feel of Aeron made her own arousal return to life. "Raise your right leg," Sylvie said, so out of breath at the sexy, beautiful sight before her, she gasped between each word.

Aeron pulled her leg up as Sylvie moved, making it possible for Sylvie to slide her wet sex along Aeron's smooth thigh. "Fuck, Sylvie...you're, you're driving me insane. I can't wait...I just can't..."

"Don't be silly. Just come. Come with me, darling." Sylvie pressed herself harder against Aeron's thigh and increased the speed of her fingers pumping between her legs.

"Yes!" Arching off the bed, Aeron now had both her hands over her mouth. "Oh, fuck, yes, yes, yes..." She ended her words with a long, soft wail, shaking before she collapsed beneath Sylvie, who reached yet another smaller orgasm that kept going until she grew so weak again, she had to push herself to the side not to crush Aeron.

"Shit..." Aeron clawed for Sylvie and pulled her closer.

"Not a very romantic word, but it does aptly describe how I feel as well. Shit indeed." Sylvie pressed her lips against Aeron's.

They both smelled of luxurious soap and sex, which Sylvie greedily inhaled. Never in a million years had she thought she'd give in to another woman as she'd just done to Aeron, nor feel so free the very first time making love.

"It was the first one that came to mind without having to go through every superlative I know...but then again, you deserve all of them."

"Next time we can bring a thesaurus." Sylvie kept giving Aeron little kisses and caressed her in slow, small circles with her hands.

Aeron rested her head against Sylvie's shoulder, with one hand against her breastbone.

"Good idea." Aeron tipped her head back and kissed her neck, just below her earlobe. "I can feel your heart starting to slow down."

"Hmm. That can easily change."

Chuckling, Aeron took one of Sylvie's hands and pressed two fingertips to her neck. "You're not the only one climbing down from that mountaintop we ended up on."

"We sure did fly, didn't we?" Sylvie could feel the slowly diminishing flutter under her fingertips.

"Yeah, we did."

Sylvie wanted to talk more, really make sure Aeron saw how important this was and not just an enjoyable one-night stand, but her eyelids refused to stay open. As she sank farther into the bed and sleep began to overtake her, she heard Aeron murmur something.

"What?" Sylvie struggled to remain awake.

"Never been like this. Ever."

Sylvie drew a deep, trembling breath but was still too exhausted to open her eyes. "I know," she murmured and hoped Aeron heard her. "Same here. You. Special."

And then she slept.

CHAPTER TWENTY-ONE

The fifteen-meter-tall maypole, clad in birch twigs and branches, stood against an indigo sky. Earlier that morning, men and women had pulled at ropes, shouting in Swedish to each other as they secured it in place. Around them, other adults had kept children out of the way and called out what had sounded like not-so-helpful advice, judging from how it was received.

What amazed Aeron the most was watching Daniel Thorn in the thick of it, pulling at one of the ropes with all his might. His face was red from the exertion, but he smiled broadly and cheered everyone else along. Even now as he joined in the dance around the maypole, he seemed tireless. He had one child on each side of him, and they were doing some odd movements to what sounded like some folklore song. The lawn was filled with hundreds of people of all ages—dancing, sitting at picnic tables, or lounging on blankets like Sylvie and she did.

"He loves this. It amazes me. Not that he's all that high and mighty about many things, but he's not terribly fond of kids—except at Midsummer and Christmas." Sylvie handed her a plate covered with strawberry cake. "Here. I bet you'll enjoy this more than you did the sweet pickled herring." She bent closer to Aeron's ear and kissed her earlobe. "I swear, the look on your face..."

Aeron tipped her head back and laughed. "I know. I wasn't sure what I expected the Swedes to eat at their most beloved holiday after Christmas, but surely not almost-raw fish and sour cream. I did like the chives and new potatoes though."

"That's always something. You'll love this cake. Our cook makes it from scratch." Sylvie took a bit of her own. "Mmm, smooth. Love it. Just like I loved something else last night. It was even smoother."

Aeron merely nodded regally, refusing to blush, but then she began to laugh. Waking up in Sylvie's arms had been the single most fulfilling experience in her life. Aeron grinned and tasted the cake. It was wonderful, definitely a keeper. She resolved to hunt said cook and ask for the recipe. As they sat on their blanket on the lawn of the park, she felt bone tired after their long night of making love instead of getting much-needed sleep.

Earlier in the morning, they'd picked flowers and cut birch tree branches, and Aeron had thoroughly enjoyed it even if her body had screamed for a soft bed. Another highlight had been watching Sylvie mutter over the sap from the trees and the small bugs crawling among some of the flowers. They'd dressed the maypole, which was formed like a cross with two large flower wreaths dangling from it on the other side.

"I see what you mean," Aeron said now. "Phallic symbol."

"Yup. But truthfully, people only started to make that comparison during the 1800s. I read somewhere it was due to some Freudian influence. I believe they used to save the wreaths to put into their Christmas bath."

"Whatever for?" Aeron eyed the wreaths. Surely the old wreaths had to have been smaller? With these you'd need a swimming pool.

"Good health during the winter."

"Considering people died like flies from the flu and pneumonia back then, who can blame them from jumping into a bath with one of them?" Aeron wrapped her arm around Sylvie's waist. "Although I prefer to think of jumping into a bath later with someone rather than something."

"Is that so?" Sylvie's voice held a low timbre that made Aeron's knees wobble.

"It sure is. Can I interest you in something that frivolous?"

"I'll do your back if you'll do me…mine." Sylvie chuckled as she leaned over and whispered into Aeron's ear.

"A Freudian slip?" Aeron giggled.

"Nobody's slipping anywhere. In fact I—Oh, no." Sylvie cast a glance over Aeron's shoulder.

Aeron turned to see what had caught Sylvie's attention. "What?" She saw Camilla wave at them to join her.

"It's time for the darn frogs." Sylvie stood. "Most of the time I refuse to join in the dance, but Mom said it would be a crime if you didn't get to dance around the maypole at least once. Sorry. I was weak. I promised."

"I'm perfectly able to run around in a circle with kids. "

Sylvie chuckled. "Oh, my dear, you have no idea."

As Aeron watched people line up in several big circles, hands on their hips, she wondered what could be so bad about dancing in a circle.

"Get behind me and do as I do. If you tell anyone back in the US about this, I'll have to shoot you." Sylvie gave her a stern glance.

"All right." Aeron snorted.

The music began, a march-like tune, and the people began to sing and jump forward. Then they stuck their thumbs in their ears, waving their hands, only to move their hands to just above their bottoms and wiggle them there. And then the song lyric turned to something like "coo-ack-ack-ack," and Aeron was now laughing so hard, she could barely move. She saw the posh Camilla and her intimidating husband do the same dance with children around them. When the song finally ended, Aeron was breathless with laughter and clung to Sylvie for support.

"I knew this would be a mistake. I take it I don't have to worry about Facebook pictures of my derriere and flopping hands?" Sylvie laughed as well.

"I wish I'd thought of that—"

Loud voices echoed across the field behind the Thorn mansion. Camilla's shrill voice rose above the rest.

"Daniel? Oh, God, Daniel! Please, help him!"

❖

"Mom?" Sylvie began to run, and Aeron was close behind her. Pushing her way through the crowd, Sylvie growled at them to move. Her heart pounded painfully and it was hard to breathe. Her mother's voice had been so filled with dread. "Mom?"

They reached Camilla, who was on her knees in the grass, holding Daniel close to her. Sylvie threw herself to the ground, bruising her knees but couldn't care less. "Mom, what happened?"

"He staggered to the side and fell." A voice from behind them spoke, out of breath. "We kidded with him that he shouldn't have started on the schnapps so early when we realized…something was wrong."

"Call 112." Sylvie ordered, slipping into her CEO persona seamlessly. She regarded Daniel, noting the slackness of the right corner of his mouth, his listless right arm and confused expression. "Tell them it might be a stroke."

"What?" Camilla's eyes snapped up to meet Sylvie's. "Why do you…?" She looked down at her husband of forty-two years. "Oh. Oh, of course. Darling, can you speak. Say something, Daniel?"

"Krr…ng…ng…" Daniel tried to communicate, but only gurgling sounds came out. His hair lay ruffled and he had grass stains everywhere. Sylvie could hardly believe that she'd seen him direct the erecting of the maypole just moments ago. Now it stood there, firmly attached to the special foundation made for it and the tree at Christmas. It towered over the fallen lord of the manor like some dramatic scene in a film.

"Here. Some blankets. I asked one of the staff." Aeron joined Sylvie, who hadn't even noticed Aeron's absence.

"Oh, thank you, dear." Camilla took one of the blankets and wrapped it around the now-shivering Daniel. Aeron tucked another one around his legs.

"Yes, thank you." Sylvie squeezed Aeron's hand quickly. "You think fast."

"How is he?" Aeron rubbed Sylvie's back. "The EMTs on their way?"

"Yes. We're not far from the major fire station in Gårda. Ten minutes, if they step on it and traffic isn't screwing around."

"Schy-vi…" Daniel waved his unaffected arm. "Schy—"

"He means you," Aeron whispered in Sylvie's ear.

Her mouth dry, Sylvie took Daniel's flailing hand. "Father? Just relax. The ambulance is on its way. You'll be at Sahlgrenska before you know it."

"N-no…Sch…g-guss…" Sweat dripped from every pore on Daniel's face from the effort of making himself understood. When Sylvie still didn't understand, he closed his left eye hard. The right eye only closed partially, which gave him a drugged appearance.

Sylvie looked up and found the chief caretaker of the mansion. "Olle? Make sure the guests don't get in the way when the ambulance arrives. Keep the press by the fence. I saw quite a few of them hovering over there earlier." She pointed at one of the side gates.

"No problem. I'll take care of it."

"What's going on? Can I help?" Aeron asked, and Sylvie translated, explaining quickly, and Aeron nodded before standing up "These people need to give Daniel room to breathe as well." She raised her voice, assuming most of the guests understood English. "Listen up. Everyone needs to take ten steps back. Yes, that's right. Ten steps!" She shooed them backward, not giving anyone a chance to object. "Let's keep an eye out for the ambulance and make sure it reaches Mr. Thorn quickly. Thank you, everybody." She made sure everyone did as told before she sat down again.

Camilla looked at her with tear-filled eyes. "Thank you."

"Anytime, Camilla." Aeron tried for a comforting smile, but fear for the outcome of Daniel's potential stroke made her lips tremble.

Time slowed, it seemed, but after a few minutes more, a yellow ambulance rolled across the lawn. The guests pointed in Daniel's direction. As the ambulance stopped a few yards from him, Sylvie and Aeron stepped aside to let the nurse and paramedic do their job.

It all went very fast from then on. Camilla rode in the ambulance with Daniel. Sylvie enlisted a few cousins to take over the responsibility of the festivities and hurried to change clothes. "You don't have to come. You'll miss all of Midsummer." She glanced at Aeron as she pulled at her jeans. "Honestly."

"I want to be there. Daniel needs you and Camilla now, and I'm conceited enough to think you need me." Aeron stepped closer and hugged Sylvie. "Please?"

"You...are you sure?" This wasn't what Aeron had signed up for when accompanying Sylvie to Sweden. She really couldn't ask this of her.

"I am. And I'm not about to crowd you. I can be useful. Fetch coffee, check the parking meters, what have you." Aeron kissed Sylvie quickly. "I'm going to hop into some clean clothes too. You have your car here?"

"Yes. It's in the garage." Sylvie buttoned her shirt and pulled on some linen trousers. "You ready?"

Aeron nodded, and they grabbed their purses and hurried out the door. Several people tried to stop Sylvie to ask questions as they exited the front door, but she didn't even break stride as she headed for the garage that hosted the multitude of cars her father collected as well as her Porsche. She debated letting Aeron drive since she was feeling so agitated, but Aeron wouldn't know her way around so it would take them longer to reach the hospital.

They entered the garage from a side door, and Sylvie was relieved to see her car sitting right inside. She opened the driver's door and slid inside, the new-leather look maintained by the garage foreman so familiar. Aeron slid into the passenger seat. As soon as they were buckled up, Sylvie pressed the button on the dashboard and the garage door rose. She slid into first gear, and soon they roared down the road leading to the center of Gothenburg toward the Sahlgrenska University Hospital.

❖

Aeron could tell from Sylvie's expression that it was going to be bad news. Camilla was still in the room where they'd taken Daniel at the stroke unit. Now Sylvie approached her slowly, walking as if she'd injured something vital. Getting up, Aeron hurried toward her. Just as she reached her, Sylvie sagged against the wall, her tears quivering where they clung to her lashes for a moment and then fell.

"Oh, Sylvie. Come and sit down." Aeron guided her to the area where she'd been sitting. They almost fell down on a couch, Aeron still with her arms around the trembling Sylvie. "Can you tell me?"

"He's had a stroke, like I thought." Sylvie sounded hollow but composed. "It affects the left part of his brain, including the speech area. They're giving him medication. Thrombolytic therapy."

"I'm so sorry." Aeron kissed Sylvie's cheek and pressed her forehead gently against her temple. "How's Camilla?"

"In shock. In denial." She shook her head. "Much like I'm feeling, actually."

"I can imagine that's normal when someone close to you becomes ill out of nowhere." Aeron wanted to erase the tension around Sylvie's eyes. "What can I do to help?"

"I don't think there's anything anyone can do, other than the stroke team. Mom is going to stay here at the hospital—she insists. She's already called the housekeeper to bring her an overnight bag and arrange for meals to be delivered to her. In shock or not, my mother's efficient."

"I'll say." Aeron laced their fingers together. "So, practicalities are dealt with, I get that. I still think you need someone in your corner for when you feel you need it."

Sylvie rested her head against Aeron's. "Thank you. I do need to feel you near me. When I sat with Mom next to Father's bed, I felt ashamed at how much I wished you were there to hold my hand. I was supposed to support Mom, and I damn near crumbled."

"Hey. Don't berate yourself. He's your dad."

"That's just it. He's my father, not so much my dad. I stopped saying Dad about the time I started school as a child. In my mind he's Father or Daniel. As I see it, Dad is a word that signifies closeness. We're not close."

Aeron didn't state the obvious. She'd give her right arm to have a father in her life. Or at least know who he was. Captain Aero was a mystery, and now, watching Sylvie's agony, she wondered if she might be setting herself up for major disappointment if she went ahead with hiring an investigator. "That doesn't mean you can't help him and, most of all, your mother. As beautiful as she is, Camilla's no kid anymore. She's bound to get tired."

"I know. She's awfully tired and pale already. I hope they keep an eye on her here so she doesn't get ill as well." Sylvie shuddered. "I have to go in to headquarters. The next-in-command and I need to address the major shareholders. We also need to issue a press release. Mom reminded me I should call the prime minister as soon as possible." Flinging her arms around Aeron's neck, she hugged her close. "Will you come with me? I know you'll be bored out of your mind, as all of this will take place in Swedish, but…"

"You don't even need to ask." Aeron hugged Sylvie and ran her hands up and down her back. "You'll do fine. I saw you slam on your command persona when you issued orders on the lawn. Do that when necessary, and then you can return to me and be yourself."

"It sounds so tempting." Sylvie let go of Aeron with a wistful sigh. "I guess I better go back to the house and change clothes—again. You're fine the way you are, but I need to look the part."

"Ah. You mean power suit and the whole shebang?"

"Exactly." Wiping at her damp lashes, Sylvie stood.

Aeron rose as well and took Sylvie's hand. "Just think of me as your very, very personal assistant," she said softly. "I'll help you through this."

"Thank you, darling. I'm actually quite certain you know how much that means for me to hear."

"I do, if it's anywhere near how it feels for me when you listen to me read a passage from Maeve's diary."

"I would imagine so, yes." Sylvie glanced at the door leading in to her father's room. "I should let Mom know I'm leaving. Want to join me?"

Aeron wondered for a moment if this was yet another attempt to keep up appearances, but she scolded herself for having such insecurities and suspicions. "Sure. Might do Camilla good to know you have someone looking out for you."

The room was full of machines monitoring Daniel's condition. Bags containing enigmatic content hung around him in a semicircle. The formidable man looked suddenly his age and then some, where he lay propped up against the pillows, his mouth lopsided, his arm tucked neatly against him.

Camilla sat holding his other hand, her eyes closed and her head slightly tipped back.

"Mom?" Sylvie murmured. "How's he doing?"

Camilla slowly raised her head and opened her eyes, answering in Swedish. When she spotted Aeron, she automatically switched to English. "He's asleep, I think. Or at least I hope sleep is all it is." She drew a deep breath. "Aeron, dear. What a disastrous Midsummer Eve celebration for you."

"For *me?* Nothing else matters as long as Daniel recovers." Aeron let go of Sylvie and rounded the bed. She bent and kissed Camilla's cheek. "And from what I know about Swedish health care, he's in the best place right now, given the circumstances."

"I'm so glad Sylvie's found someone like you," Camilla said huskily. "She's been alone far too long."

"Mom." Sylvie shook her head. "Anyway, I'm going to take care of HQ, the prime minister, and the press release."

"Thank you. I could've done it, I suppose, but I don't want to leave him." Stroking back her husband's mussed hair, Camilla's hand trembled.

"Don't worry about Thorn Industries, Mom. Just take care of Father, and I'll be back to let you know how it all went later. Aeron's coming with me as my moral support."

Camilla smiled faintly toward Aeron. "I knew you'd be a blessing."

As they walked toward where they parked, Sylvie let go of Aeron's hand and began tapping away at her phone. Only when they reached the Porsche did she tuck it away. They drove toward the Thorn mansion amid silence, and Aeron knew Sylvie had already slipped back into her professional role.

It was as it had to be. If this was what Sylvie needed to stay strong at the headquarters later, so be it. When they were either back at the hospital or at the mansion afterward, the Sylvie Aeron knew would reappear. At least that's what Aeron had to believe.

Chapter Twenty-two

Sylvie stood in her father's office at the Thorn mansion. How many times had he called her in here, having her stand almost at attention at the other side of the desk while informing himself of her test results and grades? While Camilla was always thrilled for Sylvie to pass the subjects that required reading, Daniel wasn't as understanding. He considered dyslexia little more than a character flaw for a Thorn.

Now Sylvie unlocked the drawers with the key her mother had given her.

"You're the Thorn in command right now," Camilla had said before Sylvie left the hospital for the second time that day. She'd returned to report to her parents about the measures she'd taken and what protocols she'd put in place to help the staff handle the crisis. As it turned out, her father was still asleep and Camilla looked completely drained. She told her mother the most important details, received the keys, kissed Camilla's cheek, and then returned to Aeron.

Aeron had been like her quiet, supportive shadow all day, whether at the Thorn Industries' headquarters or when Sylvie was on the phone with Prime Minister Löfvén and the Minister of Finance, Andersson. Her presence had helped ground Sylvie and made it possible for her to take the helm.

The envelope her mother had talked about lay right in front of her in the shallow middle drawer. *For Sylvie and Camilla when required.* Inside, Sylvie found a key chain with at least ten different keys to deposit boxes. There was also a thick folder of documents she required to run the company in her father's absence. The weight of responsibility crashed down on her shoulders, and she resorted to her childhood rigidity, something she'd need to pull this off. She pressed the heel of her hands against her eyes. Sylvie knew she had to stay in Sweden. For how long, she had no idea. Thorn Industries USA would have to make do with her second-in-command until she had the chance to fill that position.

Sylvie swallowed hard when she thought of Classic Swedish Inc. This wasn't going to happen the way she'd planned for so many years. Michelle would run the company with a sure hand; Sylvie knew this. As much as Michelle would report everything worth Sylvie's attention, it wouldn't be the same. For the business to work and thrive, she'd have to let go of the control she had now. She'd no longer be able to set aside the hour, or even half an hour, every day, like she'd done while working in the US, to devote to Classic Swedish Inc. Michelle would become CEO, and as wonderful as she was, they were completely different people. This was bound to have a direct impact on how the company was run. However, Sylvie wouldn't dream of putting anyone else but Michelle in charge in her absence.

"Sylvie? You okay?" Aeron asked softly from the doorway.

"Come in." Steeling herself, Sylvie knew this would be hard. So hard she wondered if she could pull it off. This was Aeron, after all. The woman who'd reached her in a way nobody else ever had.

Aeron scanned the room. "Wow. Impressive."

It was a magnificent study, with cherrywood, built-in book-shelves from floor to ceiling. "I suppose they reflect my father."

Shoving her hands into the back pockets of her jeans and swaying back and forth on her heels, Aeron looked over at Sylvie through her eyelashes. "I'm stalling. I could care less about the wood of your father's desk." She smiled crookedly. "I do however care about how you're doing, and from where I stand now, you look…devastated."

"That's an astute observation." Sylvie sat down in her father's large leather chair. "A lot has changed today, and not for the better. I heard from Mom just now. They've adjusted Father's thrombolytic therapy. From what my mother could decipher, the stroke could have shut down most of the left part of his brain if we'd waited just a few minutes longer."

"But we didn't. You didn't. You took command and made sure everyone did what they were supposed to." Aeron started to round the desk, but Sylvie raised her hand to stop her. If Aeron touched her, even briefly, she'd crumble.

"What's wrong?" Aeron winced. "I mean, I know what's wrong, but right now? Between us?" She looked at Sylvie with big eyes behind her wire-frame glasses.

"Nothing's wrong. *You* haven't done anything wrong, at least. I, on the other hand, wasn't thinking straight earlier when I promised we'd see this through together." Her jaw rigid, Sylvie struggled to keep her voice even.

"I don't understand." Aeron sat down slowly in one of the leather visitors' chairs. "Please, explain it so I can grasp what's going on."

"I'm staying." The words hurt Sylvie's throat.

"What?" Frowning now, Aeron looked concerned. "What do you mean? Here in Sweden?"

"Yes. I'm the only person my parents trust to take care of Thorn Industries. If this had been only about my father, I'd have made sure he got the best care money can buy and gone back to New York. As it is now, running Thorn Industries is a matter of loyalty."

"I'm not saying you shouldn't be loyal to your parents, but so many people depend on Thorn Industries for their livelihood. I believe it's about thirty thousand people, directly speaking, and more than two hundred thousand if we count all the people who depend on Thorn Industries indirectly." Sylvie knew she sounded like she was lecturing, but perhaps her tone would expedite this meeting. If it dragged out, her heart would have time to shatter in several irreparable pieces. That couldn't happen in front of Aeron. If it did, Aeron would realize just how overwhelmed Sylvie really felt and insist on staying, thus prolonging the agony of the inevitable. "I can't be selfish about this, Aeron."

"So, you're staying indefinitely?" Aeron was pale now, her hands clenched into two small fists on her lap.

"Yes." Thankful Aeron had caught on quickly, Sylvie closed the folder again. "I've arranged for VIP service at Landvetter Airport for you when you fly home. If you want to leave straight away, it can be arranged quite easily."

"You can't wait to get rid of me, can you, Sylvie?" Aeron sounded profoundly sad. "You're not even going to ask me to stay so we can give it a try." It wasn't a question.

"I won't have time to socialize." Sylvie's chest constricted, and for several horrible moments, she thought she wouldn't be able to go through with it. She wanted to take Aeron in her arms and reassure them both they'd be together. Instead, she slammed the hatches to her soul shut and stayed on course. It was what her parents expected of her. Her duty to the company superseded everything else, no matter the personal cost.

"Socialize?" Aeron raised her voice and stood. "Here I am, offering myself in all the ways a person can put herself out there, and you talk as if we don't have time for book circles and fucking tea parties!" Getting up as well, she pressed her palms to the desk between them, not taking her eyes from Sylvie.

It dawned on Sylvie how the scene before her was like a metaphor of their situation. She was pulling back and reconciling with the destiny she'd fought so hard against, and Aeron looked like she was trying to push the massive desk out of her way, as if the desk represented Thorn Industries, Sylvie's family, and the Thorn dynasty.

"I'm sorry it can't work out the way we wanted. I had no idea my father was at risk for a stroke," Sylvie said, trying her best to hold back her sense of panic.

"Oh, don't even try," Aeron spat. "You've pulled back once before, and I, like a fool, did everything to understand and give you space. Now you have duties to your family, and I get that. I truly do, and I'm offering to stay on here, as I can work from anywhere as long as I have a laptop. You won't even let me do that. I'm not sure what's so alluring in the foxhole you keep retreating to."

"I can't ask that of you." Frustrated that Aeron didn't see how she was trying to save her from getting caught in the web of her family, Sylvie slammed her palms against the desk. "We haven't known each other long enough, and despite our legal agreement, you don't owe me anything."

❖

Aeron flinched but didn't back off. Sylvie looked at her as if she was a stranger, which brought all kinds of demons to the surface. "You just don't want me if it means making the least bit of effort or standing up to all the Thorns." Her voice hollow, she felt herself pull back and hide in the inner crannies of her soul. Another rejection. This time she could add heartbreak to the mix. Yes, they hadn't known each other very long, but she'd responded to Sylvie like they'd been soul mates for years. Unless she was delusional, Sylvie had felt the same. This had to be some sort of altruistic approach, some remnant of Sylvie's lifelong experience of never being good enough for her father. After all, the whole endeavor with Classic Swedish Inc. was yet another indication of the same desire: of showing Daniel how she could make it successfully without him.

"Nothing I can say will change your mind," Aeron said slowly, knowing in her heart she was right. "You've already locked me out." She was afraid she'd be sick. Well, if she puked all over Daniel's desk, so be it.

"I'm sorry." Sylvie looked shell-shocked where she stood, as if she were a soldier in the trenches on her side of the desk.

Aeron had to leave the room or she'd start crying. As odd as it seemed, she didn't want to add to Sylvie's burden by forcing her emotions on her. She saw Sylvie's pain beneath her austere CEO persona. Sylvie made Aeron think of a pressure cooker with all its vents sealed. Aeron couldn't wait to get on the first plane back to the Adirondacks. She needed to regroup, and she couldn't do that here with Sylvie looking at her as if she were a stranger.

"Fine." Aeron pressed her hand to her forehead, where a persistent headache had ignited with full force. "I'll grab a cab to Landvetter—"

"Don't do that. I'll have one of our drivers take you," Sylvie said quickly. If Aeron had harbored the slightest hope Sylvie would object to her leaving, it crashed and burned instantly.

"I'll take a cab. Don't worry about it. I'd rather just go on my own." Aeron left the room but stopped just outside the door and glanced back at Sylvie. She stood motionless, like a statue, her eyes locked on Aeron. Another wave of frustration washed over her as Aeron knew at that point they were both walking away from something wonderful. *Damn you, Maeve, for teaching me to expect these situations rather than to fight for what...or who I love.* She loved Sylvie. Aeron gasped and strode down the corridor toward their room. Now her tears flowed freely, and sorrow mixed with anger and resentment. How could anyone survive such raw pain?

Calling a cab and tossing her things into her suitcase took less than fifteen minutes. She didn't plan to hang around at the Thorn mansion; she'd rather wait at the airport for the first available seat on a plane home.

As the cab maneuvered through a suddenly rainy and miserable-looking Gothenburg, the people on the sidewalks hurried along under umbrellas. The parks that had been filled with people only an hour ago now lay desolate and abandoned.

Aeron curled up on the seat and pulled her hands into her sleeves. She was cold. And just like the parks in Gothenburg, she too felt desolate and abandoned.

Chapter Twenty-three

S ylvie buried herself in work. She spent twenty hours a day at the office, dealing with the board of directors, the main shareholders, and the largest daughter companies. Thomas flew over from the US, as she needed him just as many hours. Realizing he couldn't help her with the Swedish texts, she quickly hired yet another assistant, an older woman on the verge of retirement.

Now as they met in the hospital corridor, Camilla once again started asking about Aeron but stopped abruptly when Sylvie rounded on her. "Mother. Don't." The use of the word mother instead of mom was as indicative of Sylvie's agony and fury as her low growl.

"But I only—"

"I can't. I can't do that right now. Please." Her wrath turned to a plea, which she hated, but if it would keep Camilla from talking about Aeron, so be it.

"You're working yourself to a pulp. It's been two weeks, honey, and I've barely seen you. If you're not at the office, then you spend half your nights at the hospital. You're going to burn out."

"Have some faith," Sylvie said, but the halfhearted joke fell flat between them. "Mom, I need to stretch myself a bit thin in the beginning. I have to be on top of things constantly, or our stocks will go down even more. Once people realize I can do this job, that I've trained for this since I was nineteen, everything will normalize."

"Perhaps for Thorn Industries. But for you? I don't think so." Camilla shook her head sadly. "I worry."

Sylvie smiled tensely. "No need, Mom. I'll pop in to see Father for a bit, and then I'm going back to the office. How is he today?"

Camilla sighed and leaned against the wall. "Tired. He's exhausted most of the time. His speech is still slurred and he loathes it."

"What about his paralysis?"

"Still there. The nurse told me he's getting better, but I can't see it." Camilla drew a trembling breath. "He'll be glad to see you."

Sylvie wasn't so sure about that, but didn't want to further upset her mother. "Okay. I'll go in now. Why don't you call one of your friends and go out to dinner? I'll sit here until he goes to sleep."

Brightening somewhat, Camilla pushed off the wall. "Are you sure? I don't want you to—"

"Mom. Just go. You haven't seen the outside world properly in ages."

"I suppose." Camilla kissed Sylvie's cheek and hugged her. "Thank you, honey. I'll be back here before they close the main entrance for the evening."

As the sound of Camilla's four-inch heels against the corridor floor disappeared, Sylvie steeled herself and opened the door to her father's room. She hadn't seen him awake in three days. Normally she came after ten p.m. and stayed till after midnight. She spent those three or four hours studying the face of the man who epitomized strength, arrogance, and power but now looked anything but those things. While Daniel slept, his face looked slightly sunken in, his hair mussed against his pillow. That was one of the things he'd come to loathe.

Her father wasn't vain, but he was particular about the effect he had on other people—especially financial adversaries. He never left the house in anything but a three-piece suit when he was going to work. During what little free time he afforded himself, he dressed in expensive leisurewear with a nautical theme. Now, clothed in the hospital's white shirt and saggy pistachio-green sweatpants, he looked as if he were his own poor older brother.

Stepping inside, Sylvie saw Daniel was awake.

"Hello, Father." Sylvie took the seat her mother usually occupied.

"T-t-took your sch-sweet t-time getting here." Daniel's voice was low, husky, and barely understandable. One side of his mouth drooped, and a string of saliva ran down his chin.

Calmly, Sylvie took a tissue from the bedside table and wiped it away. Daniel's eyes burned with anger. Her audacious act of giving him unsolicited help clearly infuriated him but also made him vulnerable.

"Trying this again. Hi." She patted his motionless arm. "Mom says you're doing a little better."

"Fuck th-that." Daniel waved his good arm around. "Mmm-members of the—bo-board?"

"I've been in touch with all the main players, Father. I've followed your guidelines in the envelope you left for us. The stocks fell three points, but all experts estimate they'll go up again within a month. Nobody's indispensable, not even Daniel Thorn." She smiled wryly.

"You look...like...h-hell." Daniel retaliated, of course.

"I know. Nothing a little makeup won't fix." She shrugged. "Long days."

"Can't cut it...eh?" His laughter was awful, hissing and malicious. It ended with a coughing fit, and Sylvie had to help him by raising the head of the bed. Once he caught his breath and his face was no longer dark red, she calmly sat down.

"I can cut it. And I think you know it." Sylvie took her father's motionless hand. To anyone watching, this would look like a loving gesture. Sylvie knew in this instant what she probably could have figured out a long time ago, if she hadn't been so afraid of him still. Now, when she had the power and he was helpless, she could see clearly for the first time ever.

She didn't have to be afraid of this man. Just this, a mere holding of hands without fear or trepidation, merely because of compassion, proved he'd lost his grip on her. She didn't even care how this revelation had come to her when he was incapacitated.

Daniel's weakened state might as well have bound her harder to him, made her guilt-ridden and steered her back into the fold.

"You sent me to the US to fail, and when I succeeded, you never said anything positive about it. You acted as if running the US branch was like managing a tobacco store. I'm really sorry you didn't find it in your heart to give me any credit." Sylvie looked at the man in the bed with pity. "I'm not sorry for myself. Not anymore, but mainly for Mom. And yes, for you. She would have loved to see us on good terms with each other, and for her I kept trying and trying, when any sane person would have walked away a long time ago."

The feeling was so overwhelming that she squeezed his hand a little too hard.

He winced. "C-cocky."

"I'm a Thorn. It's in our DNA."

"True." A lopsided smile emphasized how his other side could move only a fraction of an inch.

"I've tried to prove myself to you for so long. It ends now. Once the company is through the worst turmoil, the doctors and you will have figured out whether you'll be able to return to the business. I'll run it for you until then, but we won't talk again."

"S-Sylvie!" Daniel jerked. "Wh-what the he-hell…"

"Listen. Once I'm done with being the provisional president of Thorn Industries, I'll go on with my own plans." Sylvie hoped she still had her own company to fall back on, but either way, she'd be gone.

"P-pathetic spa company?" Daniel laughed again, an ugly, bitter laughter. Then he began to cough. When it wouldn't let up, even while sipping some juice, Sylvie pressed the button that alerted the nurses' station. "Try to calm down, Daniel." She held him up, slightly bent forward to make it easier for him to breathe.

As the nurses entered, Sylvie stepped back and let them do their job. Whether they knew who their patient was or not, they treated him with professional courtesy, no more, no less. Sylvie saw how her father's cough lessened and his breathing improved. She stepped out of the hospital room quietly, not about to go through a drawn-out good-bye that would mean cursing on his part and defiance on hers.

She was done with this. Sylvie intended to keep in contact with her mother, no matter what, but she'd meant what she said. She refused to see or speak with her father anymore.

She was done.

❖

Maeve's Diary—April 25, 1989

I've never felt more alone in my entire life, and God knows I've had lonely moments before. I ache all over after the C-section, but having my daughter here beside me in her little cot makes all this worth it. I loathe the constant nagging from my parents demanding I tell them who her father is. And Mom's priest, Father Jeremy, going on and on about this and also how having a child out of wedlock is a threat to both of our immortal souls. I'm starting to think I have no soul at all. I'm officially numb. Only when I look at my baby do I feel anything at all. Well, perhaps the loneliness does get to me.

Her eyes are already green. The nurse said most babies start out with blue eyes, but hers have the oddest green hue I've ever seen. It hurts so much when I finally realize that she looks entirely like her father. Another thing they ask me to do is name her. How can I do that? She's not a doll. The more I think of it, the more I freak out. I wish I had someone to ask about these things. My mother's trying to explain the advantage of putting her up for adoption. I know the answer to that one. Not now, not ever. This baby is mine and mine alone. She's not something to barter for or manipulate my mother about.

I just thought of the perfect name. Aeron. This will indirectly show how much she means to me.

It's hard to remind myself he's back where he belongs, with his wife and sons. He'll never know my true identity or my age. He might come looking for me, and if he did, he might be arrested for statuary rape, as I was only sixteen when we first made love. I can't send Aeron's father to prison. He had no way of knowing I was that young. Oddly, now I feel I've aged two decades. I glanced at myself in the mirror earlier. I truly have aged.

Little Aeron will have the best money can buy. She'll attend the best schools and be respected for who she is if it kills me...

Here the ink became blotchy and the words had bled into each other. Aeron gripped the diary harder, feeling Maeve's loneliness and pain as if it were her own. Perhaps it was. She too had been rejected and abandoned by a lover. History's way of repeating itself disgusted her. Was this something akin to the sins of the fathers... or mothers, in this case? The ridiculous thought made her snort unhappily and continue reading while clutching a drenched tissue in one hand. Having been home for two weeks and trying in vain to write, she now hoped that reading this last part of the diary would put her back on track. After all, her heroine Dajala was a lot like her in a way.

I hated being sent to Austria. At least I'm back in the US, as it was important to dear Dad that his grandchild be born an American in all ways possible. The home for unwed mothers in Salzburg was a joke. I only kept sporadic notes in the diary since the matron snooped like she thought we were plotting to take over the world with our babies in our arms.

Aeron giggled and wiped at her cheeks. The last sentence was so very like her mother. The more Maeve hurt, the more she used gallows humor to distract herself from her pain.

I'm going to fight for this girl. She already holds my heart just as much as Aero does. Even if I never see him again, I'll always love him. He doesn't know about Aeron. Father unknown. That may turn out to be the biggest lie of my life.

Mom and Dad are on their way back from a dinner with some senator or other, and I'm due to feed my little angel. Honestly, I've never seen such eyes on a baby. Not that I ever was a baby-pram diver, but still. She looks at me as if she's trying to judge if I'm a good-enough mother already. I will try to be. I have yet to be good at anything, according to my parents. I'll do my best to be the best mom for Aeron.

There were a few shorter notes toward the end of Maeve's diary, but Aeron couldn't bring herself to read them. She needed to wrap her brain around the fact that her mother had once loved her. Perhaps always did, but was unable to communicate it. She'd abandoned Aeron as she'd been left by the man she loved and then her parents, albeit the latter not by choice.

Curling up on the couch in her sitting area in the cabin, she turned off the reading lamp. In the darkness she could watch the moon and the stars reflected in the still lake. The vastness of the sky emphasized her solitude, but in a way it was reassuring. This was as it always had been at some level. She'd bought this cabin from Marie Crenshaw, her boarding-school matron who'd taken Paulina's place as a mother figure. Marie had passed away only two years later, but before then she'd visited Aeron a couple of times a year. Her death had been yet another loss, and unable to deal with it head-on, Aeron had started writing about Dajala, an orphan courier in a mythical land.

She pressed Maeve's diary to her chest and remained on the couch for the rest of the night. Why move? Nobody waited for her upstairs. Nothing had turned out the way she'd allowed her mind to plan and her foolish heart to hunger for.

❖

Aeron was ready to toss her laptop through the window. Words eluded her and the plot sagged. On top of that, her main character had suddenly, two-thirds into the story, taken on several key traits that reminded her far too much of Sylvie. Groaning, Aeron looked at the blinking cursor, praying that the words that usually flowed so easily would take on the life force of Niagara Falls. She decided that another mug of coffee wouldn't hurt. Pushing herself up, she grabbed the mug still half full of cold coffee and headed for the kitchen area. Just as she put the coffee brewer on, she heard a knock on the door, a familiar two-three-one-three that meant it was Carolyn and/or Annelie.

She walked slowly toward the door, not really wanting company. These were her close friends, though, and she guessed they'd been worried about her not coming over since she got back two weeks ago. She put on a smile and opened the door. The sight of her two neighbors made her promptly burst into tears.

"Darling!" Carolyn wrapped her into a firm embrace. "Aeron."

Behind her, Annelie extended a hand and cupped Aeron's cheek. "Let's go inside," she murmured.

"Yes, we must," Aeron said, sobbing. "Your back."

"Don't be silly. My back's fine at the moment. I walked over here. I was thinking of you needing to sit down and tell us what's going on." Annelie ushered them inside and guided them to the couch. "I'll make coffee—oh, you already have a pot going. Very good. I'll just make some tea for me then."

Sitting with Carolyn's arm around her, Aeron couldn't fathom how she could be such a fool and not go see her friends right away. Having them here, fussing over her, made her finally able to breathe deeply.

"So?" Carolyn asked softly.

"Sweden didn't pan out the way I hoped. We were finding each other, even more so than before. We made love. She confided things in me that she normally never talks about. And then Daniel Thorn had a stroke."

"Oh, crap," Annelie said and pivoted. "And she had to stay in Sweden to take care of things before she could come back here?"

"Yes and no." Aeron wiped at her eyes with a paper towel. "She had to take over the running of the whole Thorn Industries worldwide. And she's never coming back. She broke our agreement. Everything."

Annelie poured two mugs of coffee and carried them over. The electric kettle roared as it brought the tea water to a boil. Aeron watched Annelie make herself some rose-hip tea, and then she joined them, taking a seat in one of the armchairs.

"Are you certain it was for good?" Annelie asked.

"Yes. She was very blunt. Bordering on...no, she was blunt in a cruel way." Aeron warmed her hands around the mug. She'd been cold ever since she got back.

"Are you sure? Not that I know her like you do, but I never pegged her as deliberately cruel." Carolyn rapped her perfect nail on her mug and then took a sip. "Could it be she spoke while still in shock at what happened to her father?"

"I thought so at first. I tried every approach I could think of. I truly did." Hiccuping, Aeron put down the mug and curled up against Carolyn. "Why do I keep crying on your shoulder?"

"Because that's what friends' shoulders are for."

"Wait, where's Piper?" Aeron needed a pause, if ever so brief.

"She's with my sister and her family in Orlando. Disney World. We were supposed to take her, but then we remembered what happened last time when I was recognized—and that was before the Maddox movies—so we thought she'd have a good time with them and their children." Carolyn patted Aeron's knee. "So she ran you out of town or, should I say, out of the country?"

"I suppose so." Aeron frowned. She hadn't thought of it that way. "She sure made it impossible for me to stick around."

"And it sounds like she did, yet again, what she did when you were here last time. Then you only knew how she regretted it because you overheard her talking to herself." Annelie leaned forward with her elbows on her knees.

"And now I'm here. If she regrets anything now, she's..." Aeron quieted. Sylvie had made damn sure Aeron had no way of finding that out. She'd struck at Aeron's insecurities, deliberately, and Aeron had tried to not let them rule her reactions but eventually fled to lick her wounds in private. Rejected again. Dismissed again.

"So you see where there can be a pattern to this?" Carolyn caressed Aeron's cheek.

"What are the two of you up to? Attempting a new career?" Making sure they knew she was joking, Aeron smiled wanly. "You're scary good at cutting to the chase."

"Trust me; we've had a lot of practice." Annelie grinned. "Our start was a bumpy one, as was Piper's ordeal. Life sure teaches you things."

"And then some," Aeron muttered. "Oh, God. I'm not sure what to think now, but I know I can't go after her again. Not now. I feel...raw. You know? Like I'm skinless and the slightest touch hurts everywhere. If Sylvie talked to me like she did last time, I don't think I could bear it. I'm barely hanging on to my sanity as it is. Besides..."

"Yes?" Carolyn said kindly.

"I haven't been able to muster any courage to read some more of Maeve's diary. It seems to just wait to drain me. I could read it together with Sylvie, but now...And I have a deadline and can't write like I normally do."

"Oh, sweetheart, that's a lot all at once." Carolyn exchanged a glance with Annelie. "Why don't you come stay with us for a while?"

"No, no. I couldn't impose!" Aeron shook her head emphatically. "You're here for some down-time—"

"Hold it." Annelie held up her hand, palm toward Aeron. "We are, but we're also very worried about you. So worried that Carolyn used her very best persuasion technique when calling your lawyer to find out where you were, as the cabin didn't even look lived in. He confirmed you were indeed here, so we guessed you'd resorted to hiding.

"And working," Aeron muttered. "Or trying to, anyway."

"Writer's block is the worst." Carolyn nodded emphatically. "A publishing house reeled me in about six months ago. They want me to write an autobiography. I said no initially, but they were very persuasive. As was Annelie. Can you believe it? Ms. I'm a Private Person."

"That train left the station a long time ago," Annelie said and made a funny face at her wife. She turned her focus to Aeron. "We can't watch you two make a mistake."

"Us two? You mean Sylvie and me?" Aeron could see how her friends were beginning to figure things out, though some of their deductions missed the mark completely, especially the way they'd reasoned around the fact that Sylvie had chosen Sweden and Thorn Industries instead of their agreement. "Too late."

"You can't know that. Don't give up on the chance to love." Carolyn pushed a strand of Aeron's hair behind her ear. "If Annelie and I could clear our hurdles, so can you and Sylvie."

"But she may not want to clear anything—hurdles or otherwise."

"As I said, you can't know."

"So what do I do?"

"Give Sylvie a little more time to find out what she wants her life to be like," Annelie said thoughtfully. "If you don't hear anything within two weeks to a month, go to Sweden and corner her."

"Wow." It was surreal to sit here in her cabin with two of the world's most famous women and know they were her loyal friends. Annelie was strong and decisive, and Carolyn, surprisingly maternal in nature. Perhaps it was Piper who had brought these traits out in them, together with their love.

"I'm so tired," Aeron said and yawned. "I'm sorry."

"Don't be. Just relax. We'll sit here and rest Annelie's back while we keep you company." Carolyn pulled Aeron closer and tugged at a blanket. Covering Aeron where she rested against Carolyn's shoulder, she kept talking quietly with her wife. For the first time in ages, Aeron felt she could relax. Carolyn and Annelie had her back, and now they were here, determined to be here for her even though she'd tried to stay away.

Images of Sylvie, naked and beautiful, floated through her mind, making her smile wistfully. Perhaps Annelie was right. She just might wait and see what happened. Aeron vowed to let the wallowing and self-pity party she'd been on cease here and now. She deserved better. Surely all that passion couldn't just evaporate?

❖

"But, Mom, you need me," Sylvie said. "Yes, I'm not going to run Thorn Industries, but I can't just move back to the US and leave you to cope with both the company and Father."

"As far as I understand, you've burned your bridges with Daniel." Camilla sounded tense, and a furtive glance confirmed that her mother looked pale and rigid.

Daniel's study at the mansion had become Sylvie's second home after his stroke as she tried to mitigate rumors and prevent the stocks from declining further. Now she leaned against the desk and looked imploringly at her mother, who in turn leaned against the door frame.

"You need to go back," Camilla said. "Run the US branch or not. Continue with Classic Swedish Inc. or not. Decide what you want to commit to. Or whom."

Gripping her folders tighter, Sylvie tried to sort the jumbled thoughts in her head. Return to the US as if nothing had happened when so much had changed for her in the past weeks? It sounded beyond impossible. Still, her heart had done a somersault when her mother tossed the words out there. "Or whom." There was only one "whom."

"Are you very angry, Mom, for what I told Father?"

Camilla closed her eyes briefly. "Angry? No. One part of me thinks it's strange you didn't come out and say those things years ago. The other part mourns."

"What do you mean?" Alarmed, Sylvie took a few steps closer to her mother, who put up her hand.

"It's all right. I mourn the end of an era when we were still a family, but I also realize this picture I have in my head is false. We never were a normal family, since Daniel dominated everything we said or did. Your breaking free is a healthy sign. You paid the price for us striving to look like a so-called normal nuclear family. I've learned in later years that there's no such thing. You need for your own life to begin, and it's way overdue. Just allow a mother a little bit of time to readjust."

"Mom, you do realize I don't hold any grudges? Not even to Father. He's a product of the Thorns who raised him, just as I'm a product of him and you. I don't think he knew any other way to conduct himself. All his life he's been the Thorn prince, the golden boy turning into a man who thought he could—and did—do just as he pleased. He had everyone dancing to his tune, but that's all over with now."

Sylvie studied her mother's body language carefully. That was Camilla's biggest tell. She sounded perfectly fine, but when Sylvie looked closely, she saw tense lips, tight fists, and a back so straight it had to hurt. Much like her own, Sylvie admitted.

"I know." Camilla nodded regally. "He's going to need me during his transition. No—not you. Me. All these years we've been married we had only one serious glitch, and I think you can guess the woman who briefly caught his eyes. We met her at your graduation."

"Marika Hjälm. One of my professors." Sylvie took her mother's hand and guided her to the leather couch by the window. "Let's sit down. Please tell me about it?"

"She was a young paralegal at another firm. She was beautiful, still is, and I believe him when he says it was a very short fling: a few weeks around May and June. I came close to divorcing him on the spot. If I hadn't had you to consider, I might have. As it were, I stayed..." Camilla pulled her legs up under her.

"Regrets?" Sylvie slid closer, caressing her mother's cheek.

"None. Well, with the exception of wishing I'd stood up for you more. I honestly thought I'd make it worse if I took your side too many times—even when it was called for. That or I took the easy route."

"Pity there had to be sides at all." Sylvie sighed and hugged her mother. "Thank you for telling me this though."

"Again, too little too late."

Hugging her mother against her, Sylvie thought of how badly she'd handled the situation with Aeron. Could she rectify it? She certainly had burned her bridges with both her father and Aeron.

Camilla began humming, a song she used to sing a lot when Sylvie was little. The ballad brought tears to Sylvie's eyes, but she merely let them fall. Tears couldn't hurt her. Her heart was already shattered, and the song, "Blackbird," by The Beatles, caressed her senses. She was a little girl again, so eager to please and never good enough, according to her father. Not even when he'd just been close to dying, and she'd been instrumental in saving him, could he give her any credit. It had never dawned on her before, because she'd been told the opposite her whole life, but Daniel Thorn was really a very, very small man.

"He's a boss and a ruler, but not a leader." She spoke into her mother's neck as something clicked into place in her mind. "I've gone a different route. My staff not only respects but also likes me. The female staff likes Father, but the male subordinates fear him. Talk about old-school. His type of running an empire is about to become obsolete. Perhaps that's why he's so adamant about clinging to his principles."

"You're right." Camilla sounded fatigued. "I've been thinking. I've decided to hire all the help he needs after he comes home from the rehabilitation clinic. He'll get every chance he needs to recuperate, but, and I'll make it an ultimatum, he's retiring. Lars-Olof, his cousin, is more than ready to take over. This will make it easier for you to follow your own path. You'll also have to promise me something?"

"Yes?" Raising her head, Sylvie gazed up at her mother.

"Don't let Aeron slip through your fingers. There's something special about that girl that I really like, a quality you won't easily find in someone else. She...she *gets* you. I can't put it any better. In her presence I saw the Sylvie I've glimpsed only when you and I are alone."

"Mom." Sylvie pulled her hands up in the sleeves of her cardigan. "I may have irreparably destroyed what we had. I...we hadn't gone very far, but as you say, sometimes you just know. And I crushed that. Deliberately. Judging by the look in her eyes, I might as well have sucker-punched her."

"If you're honest about it like you are now, she'll forgive you with time. And she's worth fighting for, right?" Camilla cupped Sylvie's cheek. "Let me deal with your father and his successor. I'm one of the largest stockholders in the entire conglomerate, as you know. They fear me too." She smiled.

"With good reason." Sylvie had to laugh even if her stomach was ready to tie itself into a neat bow. "And I'll try to gather courage. I have to."

"You'll do fine."

They sat together as the sun finally set in the middle of the night. Sylvie loved Sweden with its seasons, traditions, social welfare, and multitude of cultures. It would always be home, geographically speaking. That said, no matter how wonderful any country was, no place would feel like home unless Aeron was there. What if she couldn't make Aeron see how sorry she was for all she'd said?

It didn't matter, Sylvie decided, and vowed to arrange for airline tickets when she got hold of her laptop. Hopefully this time she was truly going home.

Chapter Twenty-four

Aeron leaned against the lawnmower and wondered how much more she would have time for before darkness fell. She'd half-finished the big lawn toward the lake. Not for the first time she debated if she should get a tractor mower like the one Annelie so proudly maneuvered. She decided to mow one more lap in the diminishing circle she moved in.

When she returned to the spot she'd started from, she saw an unknown car, maybe a rental, sitting in the driveway. She hadn't heard it arrive because of the noise from the lawnmower. Was it Lucas Hayes or someone from the publishing house paying her a surprise visit? But that didn't make sense, as she usually communicated with both via emails or phone.

She turned off the mower and pushed it to sit next to the largest of the maple trees. She'd continue tomorrow so no use putting it back in the garage. Taking off her gloves, she adjusted her ponytail and pulled off her baseball cap. She hoped she wasn't covered in grass clippings, but if so, when people appeared unexpectedly they had to take you as you came.

Aeron turned the corner and looked around for the visitor. A woman dressed in beige chinos and a blue, short-sleeved shirt stood by the front porch with a small suitcase at her feet.

Sylvie.

Aeron covered her mouth with a trembling hand. Was she slowly losing her mind, or was the Swedish mega-business tycoon here in the Adirondacks, dressed like any local person? Why wasn't she busy taking over the business world at the helm of the Thorn empire?

"Hello, Aeron," Sylvie said quietly.

"What…how can you even be here?" Aeron slowly approached Sylvie, and now when she stood closer, she saw how pale and tense she looked. Of course, she had to have jet lag if she'd arrived recently. "When did you get here? I mean to the US."

Sylvie checked her watch, the one that was the same as Aeron's. "Four hours ago."

"What?" How could that be? Aeron's mind was running in circles.

"I took a flight to Schiphol, Amsterdam, then on to Boston, and to Albany from there. I rented a car and drove straight here."

Aeron merely waved in the direction of the front door. "Let's go inside. I don't know about you, but I need some juice. I've been mowing the lawn."

"I heard. Thank you. Something to drink sounds great." Sylvie looked at her bag and then back at Aeron. "Should I bring it inside or put it back in the trunk?"

"Oh. Right." Aeron hated the idea of sending Sylvie packing without hearing her out. And what brute would reject anyone who took three flights and drove for hours to reach you? "Come in and bring the bag."

Sylvie drew a deep breath and carried it inside, setting it next to the door. Aeron poured them two glasses of apple juice and added some ice. When she turned around she saw Sylvie standing in the same spot, trembling.

"Hey, are you all right?" Aeron put the glasses on the counter and walked up to her. "You're not going to faint on me, are you?" She wasn't being facetious. Sylvie had turned slightly gray.

"I can't believe I'm here. And that you let me in. After what I did to you—to us…" Sylvie sucked her lower lip in between her teeth. "I've gone over in my mind, time and time again, what to tell you, how to explain—"

"Why don't you let me tell you what I think?" Aeron said slowly. "Come with me and sit before you do fall over." She motioned to the couches.

Sylvie slumped onto the three-seater, and Aeron brought the juice and sat in the armchair. If she was going to keep her cool, she needed some distance. She could tell Sylvie noticed this move and probably took it the wrong way.

"I think you panicked and thought you were once and for all stuck with both feet in the Thorn empire." Aeron sipped her juice. "You saw your dream of independence in the US running your own company evaporate. I don't think I'm being conceited when I think I was part of that plan. And when it began to crumble because of Daniel's illness…" Aeron stopped talking. "Oh, God, he's not dead, is he?" She covered her mouth for a second time.

"No. In a rehab clinic doing quite well, actually." Sylvie's eyes looked glazed over as she sat with her juice untouched. "How do you know all this? About what I thought?"

"Am I right?"

"More or less. And you weren't just part of my plans. You'd quickly become the biggest reason for making that plan succeed." Sylvie wiped her hands on her thighs. "I honestly thought I was doing the right thing, the unselfish thing, to let you go. To make you go, rather."

"You hurt me." Being honest was key, but Aeron hated how her words made Sylvie wince. "I was a total mess for two weeks. Then Carolyn and Annelie intervened." She wanted to move to Sylvie's side so badly, but she had to have some more information before she did. "They helped me analyze the situation and realize a few things my pain wouldn't allow me to understand."

"I'm so glad you have such friends. In my case, my mother helped me understand. Just before we talked, I'd said good-bye to my father. For good. He poisons my life, and I can't risk him getting under my skin again. Oddly enough, I had the feeling he understood my reasons. My mother was upset, of course, but she definitely understood. She ordered me, more or less, to fix my life, and first on the agenda was to tell you the truth and how I truly feel."

"Wow. That's a tall order." Aeron blinked. "And?"

"You've already told me you know the truth of my fears…and my faults." Sylvie patted the seat next to her. "I can't tell you the rest with you sitting over there. Join me, please?"

Reluctant, not because she didn't want to sit next to Sylvie, but because of how *much* she wanted it, Aeron rounded the coffee table and sat down.

❖

Sylvie could hardly breathe with Aeron so close. She looked more beautiful than ever with her hair in a ponytail and small tresses framing her face. Her eyes never left Sylvie's, and she clung to her glass of juice as if she'd forgotten she was holding it. Gently, Sylvie removed it from Aeron's hands and placed it next to her own on the coffee table.

"What my mother knew already, and of course I knew…I mean, already a few days after meeting you, I kind of knew…"

"Knew what, Sylvie?" Aeron asked quietly.

"That I love you, Aeron. I'm in love with you, and in retrospect I can see I'd already fallen for you the second time we were at the lawyer's office." Sylvie slumped sideways against the backrest, resting her head in her hand.

"You love me?" Aeron's lips parted. She looked so sweet and sexy that Sylvie had to remember to keep her hands to herself.

"Yes." Sylvie nodded, and the fatigue began to hit. Damn jet lag. And damn not having slept more than two or three hours each night for the last six weeks, ever since Daniel's stroke. "I'd have thought it obvious to you since you had everything else I felt down pat."

"I sure didn't know you love me." Aeron sounded dazed, but who could blame her?

"I know you'll find it hard to learn to trust me again, Aeron, but can I at least hope you might try? If not now, then eventually?" Sylvie wanted to grab Aeron's hands and beg, but she was simply too tired to move.

"Trust. Interesting concept. Some say trust needs to be earned."

"And you? What do you say?"

"I say trust is intimately combined with expectations. If I expect you to be truthful from now on and not withdraw—or push me away, would I be setting myself up for major disappointment or trust you to do your best?"

"I can't say I'll never screw up again. Most likely I will. But I can promise to never willfully do so or push you away because I think it's best for you. I can promise to always communicate, even if it hurts."

"One thing I feel I know about you, Sylvie Thorn, is that you keep your promises. It's your protectiveness that tends to run amok and makes you act like you did here after us kissing, and in Sweden." Aeron leaned closer and took Sylvie's hand. "Now, it's my turn."

"To do what?" Sylvie was suddenly wide-awake.

"To tell my truth." Aeron raised Sylvie's hand to her lips. "I love you." She smiled with trembling lips.

Sylvie thought she'd actually faint as small black dots swam across her field of vision. Perhaps it was tension leaving her system too fast?

"And as I'm rejection phobic," Aeron said and held on tighter to Sylvie's hand, "which is hardly a secret to you by now, I tend to overthink and also read a lot into what someone says. That's not likely to change overnight."

"You didn't read anything into what I said in Sweden—that was my fault—" Sylvie quieted as Aeron kissed her softly.

"Shh. Don't speak of faults. We both come from highly dysfunctional homes. Luckily you have your mom and I have Paulina, and one day I'll tell you all about a special lady called Mrs. Crenshaw."

"I look forward to it." Sylvie dared to finally wrap her arms around the woman she loved so much it overflowed every single one of her senses.

"And just so you know," Aeron said, "I'd just booked tickets to fly to Gothenburg two days from now. Hence my mowing the lawn like a woman possessed so it was done before I left."

"What?" Sylvie didn't think she could handle much more positive news. "You were coming to see me?"

"Yes, and no."

Frowning, Sylvie rubbed her temple. "Please. No riddles."

"Sorry. Of course I was coming to see you, but that sounds like I planned to take you out to dinner and a movie, or something. I meant to haul your ass back to the Adirondacks and then to New York."

"Now we're talking." Sylvie pulled Aeron closer and kissed her again. She took her sweet time and explored the full lips and the mouth behind them. When she raised her head, Aeron was panting and grasping for support.

"I'll say," she murmured. "I would also have come bearing gifts." She pointed to the kitchen counter.

Curious, Sylvie looked but couldn't see anything. "What gifts?"

"Actually it's one gift in many parts. Hang tight." She bounced up with a strength Sylvie envied her right now. Returning with a semi-thick envelope, she handed it to Sylvie. "I thought if I can't do anything else to make you happy, this would at least be good for your future endeavors."

Sylvie opened the envelope slowly and with a pinch of dread. "I may not be able to read it if it's legal mumbo jumbo. Tends to have long words."

"Hence the MP3 player with the short version."

Astonished, Sylvie looked into the envelope and saw a tiny media player at the bottom. She fished it out and pressed play.

Hi, Sylvie. Aeron here. I'm not sure where you'll be when I hand this over, or in what frame of mind. All I want you to know is my reason for doing this. I love you, Sylvie, and I want you to be happy. Whether it's with me or without me, here are Maeve's shares. I've signed them over to Classic Swedish Inc. And yes, it is a done deal, for which your next-in-command was most helpful. Be happy no matter how. Love, Aeron.

Sylvie gaped and stared at Aeron. "You're insane. That's so much money!"

"I know. Turns out I have tons of money. I'm going to give most of it to the Belmont Foundation." Aeron looked so happy at announcing the latter, Sylvie had to smile.

"Somehow I figured you might do something like that. Aren't you keeping anything for yourself?"

"I still have a quite healthy trust fund, and my books sell okay. I'm not starving. I did keep enough to create trust funds for any potential children." She grinned.

"Aeron, you're amazing. You realize that?" Almost pulling Aeron up onto her lap, Sylvie hugged her close. "And if you don't, I'll remind you on a daily basis."

Aeron snuggled closer. "No need. I feel pretty amazing just being in your arms. Finally. At last."

"Agreed." Sylvie was so relaxed now, she knew she might fall asleep where she sat. "I think I need a nap, darling. May I have my old room back?"

"No."

Sylvie's eyes snapped open. "No?"

Aeron caressed long strands of hair from Sylvie's face. "No. You may, however, go upstairs and have a nap in *our* bed in *our* room. And since I wore myself out mowing half the lawn, I'll join you."

Walking up the stairs hand in hand, they tumbled into bed and ended up in a close embrace in the center. Sylvie had never felt so loved and safe. As she wrapped herself around Aeron, she hoped they wouldn't nap for too long. Next on the agenda was to make love to Aeron in a way that once and for all erased any potential residual doubts.

"Stop thinking. Sleep," Aeron murmured and yawned.

Sylvie smiled against Aeron's hair and then she slept.

❖

"Did you read the last few entries?" Sylvie held up Maeve's diary.

"No. I stopped after the emotional last entry following my birth. I didn't think she wrote anything more after that." Aeron sat at her desk going through her timeline but now got up and joined Sylvie at the dining table. "What did she write?"

"For some reason I can decipher your mother's handwriting much better than printed text, but I still think it's best if you read it."

"Okay. Stay with me while I do, please?"

"Of course."

Aeron opened the diary at the page after her birth. It was blank so she flipped over two more.

New York—1992
My parents are dead. This is insane. It's beyond insane, it's crazy. How will I manage? Who will help me? There's absolutely no one! I need someone to help me with Aeron. I've never been so alone.

On another page Maeve wrote:

New York—1997
There. It's done. I should feel relieved to not have complete responsibility, but all I know is I miss Aeron so much. She's so little and so far away from home. I should go and get her from the school tomorrow. Tell them it was a mistake, that my little girl needs to be home with her mother. I'm going to—it's the only way I'll be happy again.

"Oh, my God." Aeron browsed for the next note. "And she never did. I wonder why."

New York—2001
I'm glad Aeron is away at boarding school. Nothing will ever be the same again. Two planes hit the World Trade Center and I'm home alone, glued to the TV. I hope they talk to the kids about this at her school.
Oh, those poor souls.

New York—2015

My goodness. I found this old diary and had forgotten I even used to write in it. Reading back, I was stunned at how all the old feelings came rushing back. I never did become a good mother. More of a warning example, really.

I do have hope for this year. I've been doing really well grasping the intricacies of the world of business. Sylvie, my dear, patient friend and co-owner of Classic Swedish Inc., has done this for me. She's given me hope that I might approach Aeron and show her there's more to me than partying and using drugs.

I'm glad I found this. Reading about my hopes for the future back then motivates me to do better now. It's never too late!

After crying herself empty in Sylvie's arms, Aeron blew her nose and took a deep breath. "If I'd only known." She clung to Sylvie, who held her tight again.

"How could you? She wasn't very good at sharing with the one she loved the most." Sylvie rocked her gently.

"We mustn't let that happen to us."

"We won't. Remember our promises?" Sylvie nodded toward the couch. "We promised to communicate."

"Yes. Yes, we have to." Aeron settled into the embrace. "You know, perhaps she kept this journal because she wanted me to see it eventually. And when I saw it, I'd read how she really felt and about Captain Aero."

"Are you going to try to find him?"

"Yes, I think so. If he's still married, I can be discreet. I just have so many questions."

"Then let's get the ball rolling and find a good investigator. I don't think it'll be terribly difficult, as he was in the service."

"All right." Smiling through tears, Aeron nodded. With Sylvie by her side she was ready to take on any challenge. "Let's do it." She remained in Sylvie's arms for a long while and kept her mother's diary against her heart. These last few months had been all about the three of them, one way or another. Fate had woven them together in a way that now seemed almost magical, and Aeron vowed to herself from now on to think of Maeve only as Mom.

EPILOGUE

It's here. The full report." Sylvie came up on the porch and waved a thick envelope. "Want me to give you some privacy while you read?"

Aeron sat up in her deck chair and shook her head emphatically. "No. Are you kidding me? No. You have to be here or I won't open it. After the private investigator told me my father's name or, as he put it, 'the man who with ninety percent certainty is the man who fathered you,' I've debated what I'd do once I got the dossier. Never in a million years did I ponder if you'd be here with me at this exact moment. I'm not doing this alone."

"Shh. Calm down." Sylvie sat on the wide armrest of Aeron's chair. "All right. Want to open it?"

"Okay." Aeron's fingers trembled as she ripped open the envelope and pulled out a half-inch-thick folder. She opened it and scanned the first page. "As we already knew, his name is Colonel Joshua Scott Baldwin, retired. He's sixty-one years old and lives in...now, that can't be right? That's too much. Too much." Aeron read the words out loud. "Colonel Baldwin retired six years ago, and after his wife of thirty-one years passed away he settled in his hometown of Albany. Sylvie! Albany."

"That's an amazing coincidence, darling." Sylvie wrapped her arm around Aeron and pulled her close. "Anything else?"

"Before, Joshua was married to a Lisa Iverson Baldwin, and she died in 2010. They have two sons, Joshua Scott, Jr. and James.

James is married and has a baby girl." Tears ran down Aeron's face. "I have brothers. I even have a niece. All this time, I had—I had a family. I know Maeve was protecting him, and I'm sure, herself, but still…am I selfish to wish I'd been included in that family?"

"Not at all. Actually, I'd say it's your right to be included. You were the innocent child in all this."

"So were Joshua, Jr. and James. They might have hated having a half-sister."

"You can't know that. They might have loved having a sister. Does it say their ages?"

"Let me see." Aeron ran her finger down the text. "Yes. Joshua, Jr. is thirty-two and James is…thirty." Curling into Sylvie's side, Aeron wept. "Do you think he loved my mom as much as she loved him?" Aeron accepted a tissue from Sylvie and wiped at her eyes and nose.

"I do. He must have been totally taken with her if even half of what she writes in her diary is true. He seems like a man who got caught up in a whirlwind passion with a girl who claimed she was older than she was. We know from her diary and your birth certificate that she never told him. What branch of the military was he in?"

"The marines. He flew F-14 Tomcats, it says. Stationed in Norfolk most of his career." Aeron sobbed mutedly. "And his call sign was Aero."

"Oh, darling." Sylvie pressed her lips against Aeron's. "Of course it was."

"Maeve probably knew that if she told him about the pregnancy and her true age, his career would be over. It might have been the most unselfish thing she ever did, giving him up. Not fair to you, though. And by the way, that's the first time I've heard you refer to Maeve as your mom." Sylvie kissed the top of Aeron's head.

"I did? I guess so."

"So, any thoughts what to do?" Sylvie asked gently.

"I'm going to read this through properly and then we'll see."

❖

Two days later, Sylvie sat on the couch by the fireplace, listening with one earbud tucked in to the latest report from the new CEO in Sweden. Next to her, Aeron sat shifting her cell phone back and forth between her hands. Sylvie knew Aeron needed to take her time and decide on her own how to proceed with all the new information she'd gained.

Then Aeron pressed a symbol on the smartphone and lifted it to her ear. She twirled a lock of hair between the fingers of her free hand. "Hi. I hope I have the right number. I'm looking for Colonel Joshua Scott Baldwin, who used to be stationed in the marines at Norfolk?"

The person at the other end said something. Aeron closed her eyes hard.

"Hello, Colonel Baldwin. My name is Aeron DeForest. I believe you knew my mother, Maeve DeForest, back in 1988?"

Sylvie took Aeron's hand and stopped the audio file in her laptop.

"Thank you, Josh. Please call me Aeron." Aeron kept her gaze on Sylvie's and took a deep breath. "I'm glad you remember my mother. The thing is…I was born in April 1989 and have reason to think you're my father, Josh." Curling closer to Sylvie, she looked up into her eyes. Sylvie met her gaze unwaveringly and transmitted all the love she felt for the amazing and courageous woman in her arms. Aeron listened to what the man said and didn't interrupt as he kept talking for several moments.

And then she melted into Sylvie's embrace and smiled.

About the Author

Gun Brooke resides in the countryside in Sweden with her very patient family. A retired neonatal intensive care nurse, she now writes full time, only rarely taking a break to create websites for herself or others and to do computer graphics. Gun writes both romances and sci-fi.

Website   http://www.gbrooke-fiction.com
Facebook   http://www.facebook.com/gunbach
Twitter   http://twitter.com/redheadgrrl1960
Tumblr   http://gunbrooke.tumblr.com/

Books Available from Bold Strokes Books

A Reluctant Enterprise by Gun Brooke. When two women grow up learning nothing but distrust, unworthiness, and abandonment, it's no wonder they are apprehensive and fearful when an overwhelming love just won't be denied. (978-1-62639-500-8)

Above the Law by Carsen Taite. Love is the last thing on Agent Dale Nelson's mind, but reporter Lindsey Ryan's investigation could change the way she sees everything—her career, her past, and her future. (978-1-62639-558-9)

Actual Stop by Kara A. McLeod. When Special Agent Ryan O'Connor's present collides abruptly with her past, shots are fired, and the course of her life is irrevocably altered. (978-1-62639-675-3)

Embracing the Dawn by Jeannie Levig. When ex-con Jinx Tanner and business executive E. J. Bastien awaken after a one-night stand to find their lives inextricably entangled, love has its work cut out for it. (978-1-62639-576-3)

Jane's World: The Case of the Mail Order Bride by Paige Braddock. Jane's PayBuddy account gets hacked and she inadvertently purchases a mail order bride from the Eastern Block. (978-1-62639-494-0)

Love's Redemption by Donna K. Ford. For ex-convict Rhea Daniels and ex-priest Morgan Scott, redemption lies in the thin line between right and wrong. (978-1-62639-673-9)

The Shewstone by Jane Fletcher. The prophetic Shewstone is in Eawynn's care, but unfortunately for her, Matt is coming to steal it. (978-1-62639-554-1)

A Touch of Temptation by Julie Blair. Recent law school graduate Kate Dawson's ordained path to the perfect life gets thrown off course when handsome butch top Chris Brent initiates her to sexual pleasure. (978-1-62639-488-9)

Beneath the Waves by Ali Vali. Kai Merlin and Vivien Palmer love the water and the secrets trapped in the depths, but if Kai gives in to her feelings, it might come at a cost to her entire realm. (978-1-62639-609-8)

Girls on Campus edited by Sandy Lowe and Stacia Seaman. College: four years when rules are made to be broken. This collection is required reading for anyone looking to earn an A in sex ed. (978-1-62639-733-0)

Heart of the Pack by Jenny Frame. Human Selena Miller falls for the domineering Caden Wolfgang, but will their love survive Selena learning the Wolfgangs are werewolves? (978-1-62639-566-4)

Miss Match by Fiona Riley. Matchmaker Samantha Monteiro makes the impossible possible for everyone but herself. Is mysterious dancer Lucinda Moss her own perfect match? (978-1-62639-574-9)

Paladins of the Storm Lord by Barbara Ann Wright. Lieutenant Cordelia Ross must choose between duty and honor when a man with godlike powers forces her soldiers to provoke an alien threat. (978-1-62639-604-3)

Taking a Gamble by P.J. Trebelhorn. Storage auction buyer Cassidy Holmes and postal worker Erica Jacobs want different things out of life, but taking a gamble on love might prove lucky for them both. (978-1-62639-542-8)

The Copper Egg by Catherine Friend. Archeologist Claire Adams wants to find the buried treasure in Peru. Her ex, Sochi Castillo, wants to steal it. The last thing either of them wants is to still be in love. (978-1-62639-613-5)

The Iron Phoenix by Rebecca Harwell. Seventeen-year-old Nadya must master her unusual powers to stop a killer, prevent civil war, and rescue the girl she loves, while storms ravage her island city. (978-1-62639-744-6)

A Reunion to Remember by TJ Thomas. Reunited after a decade, Jo Adams and Rhonda Black must navigate a significant age difference, family dynamics, and their own desires and fears to explore an opportunity for love. (978-1-62639-534-3)

Built to Last by Aurora Rey. When Professor Olivia Bennett hires contractor Joss Bauer to restore her dilapidated farmhouse, she learns her heart, as much as her house, is in need of a renovation. (978-1-62639-552-7)

Capsized by Julie Cannon. What happens when a woman turns your life completely upside down? (978-1-62639-479-7)

Girls With Guns by Ali Vali, Carsen Taite, and Michelle Grubb. Three stories by three talented crime writers—Carsen Taite, Ali Vali, and Michelle Grubb—each packing her own special brand of heat. (978-1-62639-585-5)

Heartscapes by MJ Williamz. Will Odette ever recover her memory or is Jesse condemned to remember their love alone? (978-1-62639-532-9)

Murder on the Rocks by Clara Nipper. Detective Jill Rogers lives with two things on her mind: sex and murder. While an ice storm cripples Tulsa, two things stand in Jill's way: her lover and the DA. (978-1-62639-600-5)

Necromantia by Sheri Lewis Wohl. When seeing dead people is more than a movie tagline. (978-1-62639-611-1)

Salvation by I. Beacham. Claire's long-term partner now hates her, for all the wrong reasons, and she sees no future until she meets Regan, who challenges her to face the truth and find love. (978-1-62639-548-0)

Trigger by Jessica Webb. Dr. Kate Morrison races to discover how to defuse human bombs while learning to trust her increasingly strong feelings for the lead investigator, Sergeant Andy Wyles. (978-1-62639-669-2)

24/7 by Yolanda Wallace. When the trip of a lifetime becomes a pitched battle between life and death, will anyone survive? (978-1-62639-619-7)

A Return to Arms by Sheree Greer. When a police shooting makes national headlines, activists Folami and Toya struggle to balance their relationship and political allegiances, a struggle intensified after a fiery young artist enters their lives. (978-1-62639-681-4)

After the Fire by Emily Smith. Paramedic Connor Haus is convinced her time for love has come and gone, but when firefighter Logan Curtis comes into town, she learns it may not be too late after all. (978-1-62639-652-4)

Dian's Ghost by Justine Saracen. The road to genocide is paved with good intentions. (978-1-62639-594-7)

Fortunate Sum by M. Ullrich. Financial advisor Catherine Carter lives a calculated life, but after a collision with spunky Imogene Harris (her latest client) and unsolicited predictions, Catherine finds herself facing an unexpected variable: Love. (978-1-62639-530-5)

Soul to Keep by Rebekah Weatherspoon. What *won't* a vampire do for love... (978-1-62639-616-6)